THE PRACTITIONER

What Reviewers Say About Ronica Black's Work

"Ronica Black's debut novel *In Too Deep* has everything from nonstop action and intriguing well-developed characters to steamy erotic love scenes. From the opening scenes where Black plunges the reader headfirst into the story to the explosive unexpected ending, *In Too Deep* has what it takes to rise to the top. Black has a winner with *In Too Deep*, one that will keep the reader turning the pages until the very last one."—*Independent Gay Writer*

"...an exciting, page turning read, full of mystery, sex, and suspense."—*MegaScene*

"...a challenging murder mystery—sections of this mixed-genre novel are hot, hot, hot. Black juggles the assorted elements of her first book with assured pacing and estimable panache."—*Q Syndicate*

"Black's characterization is skillful, and the sexual chemistry surrounding the three major characters is palpable and definitely hot-hot-hot...if you're looking for a solid read with ample amounts of eroticism and a red herring or two you're sure to find *In Too Deep* a satisfying read."—*L Word Literature*

"Black is a master at teasing the reader with her use of domination and desire. Black's first novel, *In Too Deep*, was a finalist for a 2005 Lammy. ...With *Wild Abandon*, the author continues her winning ways, writing like a seasoned pro. This is one romance I will not soon forget."—*Just About Write*

"The sophomore novel by Ronica Black is hot, hot, hot."—*Books to Watch Out For*

By the Author

In Too Deep

Wild Abandon

Deeper

Hearts Aflame

The Seeker

Flesh and Bone

Chasing Love

Conquest

Wholehearted

The Midnight Room

Snow Angel

The Practitioner

THE PRACTITIONER

by

Ronica Black

2017

THE PRACTITIONER

ISBN 13: 978-1-62639-948-8

THIS TRADE PAPERBACK ORIGINAL IS PUBLISHED BY
BOLD STROKES BOOKS, INC.
P.O. BOX 249
VALLEY FALLS, NY 12185

FIRST EDITION: JUNE 2017

CREDITS
EDITOR: CINDY CRESAP
PRODUCTION DESIGN: SUSAN RAMUNDO
COVER DESIGN BY SHERI (GRAPHICARTIST2020@HOTMAIL.COM)

Acknowledgments

I have many to thank for this book. First and foremost, my best friend and love, Cait. Your never-ending encouragement always gets me going. Thank you.

To my publisher, Len Barot, who always comes through for me when I need her most. Thank you for continuing to give me a wonderful, thriving place in which to write. Your continued belief in me keeps me going even on the dreariest of days. Thank you.

To my editor, Cindy Cresap, who wrote me the sweetest, most amazing note about this book. You made me cry. You've taught me so much. I'm forever indebted. Thank you.

To Sheri, for a wonderful cover. Thank you!

To all those behind the scenes at Bold Strokes Books. Sandy, thank you for always answering my crazy emails! Ruth, thanks for teaching me how to better work Gmail! To everyone else, your hard work and efforts to make my book the best it can be are very much appreciated. Thank you all!

And finally, for those of you who struggle with anxiety on a daily basis. Please know that you are not alone. There are people in every nook and cranny of the world who feel the same, who understand. It's just a matter of finding a kindred spirit. Please don't ever give up. You are stronger than you know.

Dedication

For my one and only, for making me laugh, making my
heart sing, and for making me keep writing
despite my artistic woes. I love you.

For my mother, Ramona.
For your love, support, and unwavering devotion
to make sure I'm okay. It hasn't been an easy year,
but I know things will get better. Why?
Because I've got you on my side. I love you.

PROLOGUE

The beer mug was foggy with chill, the head of the dark beer frothy and thick. Johnnie slid her fingers around the glass and inhaled. She loved the smell of a good beer almost as much as the taste. She took a long, slow sip and tried to relax. Then she closed her eyes and prayed. *Please let it come today. Please.* She opened her eyes and stared at the sign hanging behind the bar. *Keep Calm and Ain't it Grand.* An Irish flag was next to it, along with several beer ads. Guinness, Harp, Smithwick's. She loved them all. But for her ritual it was Guinness. The frothy head, the deep, dark, rich flavor. The way it slid down her throat and warmed her from toes to tip-top. Yes, Guinness was the one. The magic maker.

"Any luck yet, Johnnie?" Sean asked, pushing a basket of fresh soda bread her way.

She shook her head and stared into her pint. "Nothing."

"Today will be the day. Don't you worry now."

He moved off to another customer and she sat in silence, hoping he was right. That was the thing about Sean. He always saw the bright side, and yet he knew to leave her to herself. Artist's brooding was what he called it. She was glad she found the place and lucky to have him instead of a chatty bartender talking her up. She'd gone through several of those. But finally, yes finally, she'd found this place. A small Irish owned pub in the back of a deserted shopping plaza. It was the perfect hole-in-the-wall. One so dark her arm shot up automatically to protect her eyes when the door opened. And the smell of it. The smell of it was perfection. Spilled beer, warm bread, wet shoes from the street, and must. If it had smelled clean, she would've split because a real true hole-in-the-wall didn't smell like roses and lavender and cleaners with bleach. And what she needed was real.

She took another sip and turned to make her way to the back booth. She chewed on a piece of bread but left the basket on the bar. She needed to feel the Guinness, and the bread would hinder that. She sank into a well-worn booth and opened her sketch pad to a blank page. She readied her charcoal pencil and sat back to wait. She noted only a few other people, most of them sitting alone like her, lost in their drink. Coming in the early afternoon had its advantages. Lunch goers were gone and happy hour hadn't started yet. She had about two hours to sit and drink and think before that lot came in. She ran her fingertip along the etched names in the tabletop. Warmth from the beer began to spread through her, and she wanted to dissolve into the old seat.

The drinking was new to her. She'd always liked beer, but she never had been a big drinker. Hard liquor was out of the question; she couldn't get past the taste, no matter how many ways they tried to hide it. So she stuck to beer. A sip here and there to savor it. Not to get fucked up. No, normally, she would come in, order a pint, and sit and sip and draw. She'd barely finish one, and she'd never order a second. Inspiration had just been there, sitting right across the booth, grinning at her, giving her all she needed. But lately… inspiration was nowhere to be found. She had no ideas, no images, no dreams. Just a tree.

She took another large sip and sighed. She flipped to the previous pages in her pad. Tree after tree after tree. One lonely tree on every page. Nothing else. Every day it had been the same.

Why was she only seeing a tree?

She'd had weird images come to her before, but they usually evolved. This one did not.

"Damn it."

She tossed her pencil and pushed away the pad. For now, she would sit and drink just as she'd done the previous two weeks. At least the beer was good. Beer number four would be even better. She took another sip.

The door opened in the distance, and she recoiled at the bright desert light. Spots remained in her vision even after it closed, blocking her view of who entered. She heard Sean speak. Heard the reply that was unmistakable.

Fuck.

She'd been found.

"Finally," Eddie said as he approached. "You know how many of these dumps I've been to?" He wiped at the seat as if were covered in filth and settled in across from her. He hesitated to put his elbows on the worn table. He decided to keep his arms at his side.

She blinked at him and did her best to focus. He had shaved his shadow and cut his hair. The earring was gone too. Good-bye, bad boy; hello, good boy. He was so fresh and crisp, what the hell was he doing hopping bars looking for her? "What do you want?"

"Well, nice to see you too, sunshine."

"Aww, don't start with the guilt trip. Please, Eddie? I don't need that right now." She knew she should've called. Should've clued him in.

He stared at her then eyed the beer. "Are you drinking that?"

She gave a shrug. "Yeah."

"Since when?"

"Since now."

He rubbed his face in obvious frustration. "I take it you still haven't been able to paint?"

"Does it look like it?" Again, she shoved the pad away and took another sip. A big one.

"You think that will help?"

"Lots of artists drink."

"Yeah, well, you don't. And you shouldn't start. What happened to just ordering one and staring off into space?"

"It's not working." She looked beyond him, unable to hold his gaze for very long. He looked concerned and a little upset. She knew she'd been a right shit lately, and she deserved it. But still, she didn't want to deal with it.

"Let's get out of here," he said, trying to brighten the mood. "Let me buy you dinner."

She squeezed her beer and shook her head slowly. "I don't want your charity." True, she was headed for financial disaster, but she didn't need handouts. Not yet.

"Charity? Fuck you, Johnnie. It's dinner. You're my best friend."

"Still…I'm not in the mood."

He sighed. "You look like a meth addict. You should eat."

She laughed. He was always so dramatic.

"A few months ago I was too heavy."

"Yeah, you were. Now you're scary. Stop it."

"You know my weight fluctuates. I'm fine."

He rolled his eyes and they sat in silence for a while. He was like a brother to her, and they often squabbled and pissed each other off. But they looked out for each other. There was no denying that. After another long moment, he straightened and placed his palms on the table.

"What if I told you I had something that might help?"

She looked up at him. His eyes sparkled. He had the flame of life in him. Eternally.

Her flame often burned low, so low it was hard to see, to feel. It caused him to worry.

"Eddie, I don't think you can help. There's just nothing there."

His fingertips drummed the table. "I think I can."

He stared at her with a mischievous grin. Eventually, she rolled her eyes and asked, "What?"

He dug in his back pocket and slapped a business card on the table. When she didn't speak, he pushed it forward.

"This."

She took it, looked at it, and then looked back at him. "There's just a number."

"Right."

"I don't get it."

He reached for her hand and held it warmly in his own. "Remember Pedro?"

She searched her mind. Pedro. Pedro. Pedro. Ah, yes. Pedro.

"The guy you raved about for six months nonstop? How could I forget?"

"Remember how I said he helped me through so much?"

"Your emotional baggage and your incessant need to be with somebody, anybody?"

"Yes!"

She looked at the card. "I don't need a shrink, Eddie. I need inspiration."

"He wasn't a shrink. He was…inspiration."

She felt her eyebrow raise.

"Just call."

"Eddie, Pedro can do little to inspire me. Trust me on that."

"No, silly." He paused, then glanced around as if nervous. "You wouldn't get Pedro."

"I'm not following." She searched his eyes and saw the blush. "Eddie, what the fuck are we talking about here?"

"Just call."

"No."

"Please. It will help. Promise me you will."

She refocused on her beer. "I just want to sit here."

"And drink."

"That's the idea."

He gave her hand a squeeze. "Johnnie, you need to paint." He held up a palm. "I know you don't need pressure, and I'm not trying to add any. I'm just simply saying that there is inspiration out there. Sometimes you just have to know where to look." He watched her closely to see if he'd gotten in. "How much money do you have?"

"Enough."

"Enough for a few sessions with someone special?"

She eyed him. "A few sessions of what exactly?"

He looked sheepish. "A little creative inspiration. A much needed match to light your flame."

"Are you talking about sex?"

He blushed again.

"Eddie, you want me to pay to have sex with someone?"

"No, it's not like that. It's…"

She stared at him, searching for answers. He gave away nothing. "Just call. Please." He stood and pushed the card toward her. "Tell them you were referred by Pedro's client."

He squeezed her shoulder. "You've got nothing to lose."

She touched his hand. "Thanks. For caring I mean."

"You know I do." He leaned down and kissed her cheek. "Call me," he said as he walked away.

He pushed out into the light, and this time she didn't recoil. She let it burn.

CHAPTER ONE

"Mm, when's it gonna be my turn?" the young woman asked, her voice scratchy from a long orgasm. She looked up at Elaine with liquid eyes, long lashes flashing.

Elaine pushed away, slung her legs over the bed, and slid into the thick hotel robe.

"Where you going? Don't you want to snuggle?"

Elaine tightened the belt and left the bed.

"Are you coming back?"

She disappeared into the bathroom and locked the door behind her, ears straining to hear if the woman was following her. Quickly, she turned on the water to drown out any other annoying questions from her guest. She leaned on the counter and stared at her mussed hair and smeared lipstick. Her eyeliner had smudged with sweat and exertion. Unable to stand the image, she scrubbed her face with the hotel bar soap. She turned off the water and pressed a towel to her skin. Then she pulled back her hair and turned on the shower. A knock came from the door. She sighed.

"Are you coming back? I miss you. Hello?"

"Yes?" She pulled open the door and breezed into the room. The woman was standing and smiling like they were both in on a secret. The bedding was draped around her nude body.

"Can I shower with you?"

Elaine grabbed her phone and her clothes. "No."

"Why not?"

Elaine felt herself grimace. This one was particularly clingy. And pouty. Question after question. Call after call. No more.

"I want to be alone."

"But why? I thought we had a good time. We always have a good time."

"We've been together twice."

"Right." She smiled, oblivious to the point. "And we've talked, a lot."

"You call, ask personal questions." She carried her bundle into the bathroom and set it on the counter. "Questions I'm not going to answer. Questions I told you I'm not going to answer."

"But I want to know you. Don't you want to know me?"

Elaine returned to the room to get her shoes.

"Did I ever ask you any questions?"

The woman seemed to think for a moment.

"No. Why didn't you?"

"Because if I had you would've ran with it, thinking I was interested."

Her face fell. "Oh."

She retrieved her heels and tossed them in the now steamy bathroom. "I told you, I have nothing to offer you. Nothing. I don't want a relationship."

"I said we could take it slow. Slow is okay."

"I don't want slow. I want nothing. Why can't you hear me?"

"But we've talked, we've—"

"It's sex. That's all. And talking on the phone does not constitute a relationship. One that I don't want. That I've been very clear about."

The woman let the bedding drop. "Fine, I'll just go. You'll never hear from me again."

Elaine watched her dress, knowing her words meant nothing. She would pout and not call for a while. And then in a month or so she'd call and apologize. But the next time, Elaine wasn't going to bother to bite. No matter how cold her bed was.

The woman turned at the door, knob in her hand. "Good-bye." She clenched her jaw and steadied herself as if waiting for Elaine to say *Wait, don't go.* Elaine didn't speak, just walked toward her. She removed her hand from the knob and replaced it with her own. She tugged the door open and swept her arm, motioning for her to go.

"Bitch." The woman glared at her and walked out.

She closed the door, engaged the lock, and leaned against it.

If the shoe fits, I'll wear it.

She felt drained, and her mind was spent from dealing with someone who refused to hear her. She slowly crossed to the bathroom and let her robe fall outside the shower door. She entered and melted beneath the hot spray. She did her best to wash the woman away, lathering up and rinsing a few times. If she scrubbed, she could dissolve the evening away, watch it slip down the drain, never to return. But she knew it wasn't as simple as that. Women, no matter how casual she tried to keep things, were complicated. And as for herself, she knew she wasn't exactly the nice guy.

She killed the water and stood leaning against the wall while allowing the steam to come off her body. She thought about just collapsing into the sheets and spending the night, but the sheets were tainted and she needed to get home. Thankfully, she never met anyone at her home. She couldn't imagine the trouble that would cause. So she used a pay as you go phone and always kept it at hotels.

She stepped from the shower and pressed herself dry. Then she slid into her clothes and stepped into her heels. She never carried a wallet in with her, only her phone. She pulled it out of her pocket and saw that she had a message. She dialed her voice mail and entered her code.

"Yeah, Elaine, it's Michael. Sorry to call you on the booty call phone, but I have a client for you. Call me."

She hung up and dialed her partner's number. She hadn't had an intriguing client in months, but right now she'd settle for anyone new. Anyone to change up the game a little. Her numerous male clients were so caught up in power struggles and sexual attraction, it was growing tedious. She could use some good old-fashioned work on a willing client.

"Michael, it's me." She sat on the edge of the bed and slipped in her earrings. "Please tell me it's someone interesting."

He laughed. "I bet you would pay for an intriguing client at this point."

"I would. But don't tell them that. Tell me all about him."

"Actually, it's a woman."

She straightened. "Oh?"

"She's thirty, single. Looking for creative inspiration. Those are her words."

"I see." Her heart sped up a little at the thought of a woman. But she calmed herself, knowing that clients were never what she dreamt them to be. She'd lost that fantasy long ago. Besides, a client was a client, nothing else. No matter how badly they wanted it to be more.

"Did she check out?"

"Yep. No criminal history, no craziness. Just an average woman. And I won't tell you anymore because I know you don't like that."

"No, I don't." She preferred to read the client herself.

"Anyway, Julia has set up the appointment for tomorrow afternoon. All right by you?"

"Sure."

"Okay, then. See you at the office."

"Hey, Michael? Did she say…why she wanted a woman?"

"I'm not going to tell you."

She closed her eyes. "Fine. See you tomorrow."

She ended the call and rose to look out the window. For the first time in a long time, she looked forward to tomorrow.

CHAPTER TWO

The desert was never ready for rain, nor were Phoenicians for that matter. Johnnie was no exception, and the constant smattering of the drops made her all the more agitated and depressed. Truth be told, she was anxious, and when she was anxious she grew cranky. Her windshield wipers whined as if to drive the feelings home, one of the rubber pieces hanging from the blade like a limp snake as it moved across the glass. The relentless desert sun had rotted it in the scorching heat, making it useless when the time came to actually use it. The sun was merciless that way, and it would eat at you down to the bone if you weren't careful. But sun she was used to. She liked sitting in her hot car after being inside a cold building. She'd become reptilian that way, craving the heat and sunlight, needing it to feel alive.

She wished for that sun today, but wishes were just that, and she knew she was in for more rain the rest of the week. The winter had been cold and wet. She might as well give in and get an umbrella. She might as well give in and get new wipers.

"Fuck that." She eased down her window and took in a palm full of droplets. The cold water did nothing for her. She sighed and powered the window back up, then muted the radio. The door in front of her loomed and the wipers whined. She wrung her hands along her steering wheel.

She should put the truck in reverse and get the hell out of there. Fucking tell Eddie it wasn't for her, that she didn't really need it after all. She was fine, just a little off her mark. Nothing a trip to

Sedona couldn't fix. Sit in the sweathouse and ooze it all out, then emerge and put it all back in, this time better, purified. But Sedona wasn't beckoning, and the truck was only a year old, and she'd updated to a high loft in prominent downtown, along with a larger studio as well. Bottom line, she had shit to pay for and she wasn't producing.

She slammed the heels of her hands against the wheel. She had to do this. She had everything to lose if she didn't. She killed the engine and opened the door. Then she shut it. Then she cussed and opened it again. She cowered from the rain like a lizard worried about its scales, like a Phoenician, and hurried up to the door. She didn't give herself time to think as she turned the knob. She just walked right in and stood, chime sounding, welcoming her, the door closing behind her. The waiting room was small but empty. Relief washed over her a little at not having to see anyone, but it didn't last.

"Are you my three o' clock?" The voice came from behind a wall of glass. Johnnie's shoes squeaked as she approached the check-in counter. The woman was young, maybe twenty-two tops. She was made up nicely and had a very bright smile against tanned skin. She looked like she worked at a spa.

Johnnie couldn't think of what to say. She was disappointed and hoped like hell she didn't have to pay. This was not what she had hoped for and not what she'd requested.

"Riot?"

Johnnie looked away with embarrassment. The pseudonym was ridiculous, but then again so was what she was about to do. The woman apparently took her shame as a yes and nodded as if trying to comfort her.

"Great. I'm glad you showed. First time jitters and all."

"I've been in my truck," Johnnie found herself saying. "Outside." She hitched her thumb back at the parking lot like an idiot.

"Right." The woman dug a nail file out of a drawer full of Post-it Notes. "We get nervous. Nervous we understand." She analyzed her well-manicured pinky and went to town on it. "No-shows we don't understand. So don't ever do that."

Johnnie lowered her hand, trying to look casual but failing desperately.

The woman looked bored, like she'd seen it all before and then some. "You can go ahead and have a seat. I'll be with you in a moment."

Johnnie took a step back and then stopped. The woman looked up at her, questioning her with her lifted eyebrow.

"It's just that...I requested...someone older."

The woman stopped filing, and the corner of her mouth rose. She was amused, and Johnnie wanted to die.

"Your appointment's not with me, sweetie."

Johnnie heated, and if spontaneous combustion were real, she'd be able to prove it at any given second.

"Have a seat." The woman continued to smirk as she went back to her nails, completely ignoring Johnnie.

Johnnie sank her hands into her back pockets and then changed her mind and wiped her palms on her jeans. Anne Murray was playing through the speakers overhead which took her back in time and made her feel all the stranger.

She felt like she was in the wrong place. The professional decor, the music, the receptionist, it all seemed a little too bizarre. As if she were waiting for a business meeting or waiting to see a podiatrist. What the hell was this place?

The receptionist tapped the glass and slid a clipboard with papers through the slot. "We need you to fill this out. And just as a reminder, we're cash only. Do you have your funds for your visit today?"

Anne Murray kept on. Her cheeks burned. "Yes."

"I'll need that now."

Johnnie dug into her worn, paint splattered jeans, found the fold of hundreds, and placed them on the counter. "Don't I pay... after?"

"Oh, no. We take it up front. No pay, no play."

Johnnie couldn't hold her gaze as the words settled in. "But what if I—"

"That contract explains it all. Read it, sign it, go in. Or don't. It's up to you. We don't make you do anything here."

Johnnie took the clipboard and sat. It was still up to her. She could still back out. Her foot began to move on its own accord as she read, and she knew it showed her nerves. But each time she stopped, it started up again when she wasn't paying attention. Nail biting was out of the question because she didn't have any long enough to bite, and she didn't want to say or do anything more to show how freaked out she really was.

Are you currently or planning to become pregnant?

What the fuck? She thumbed through the questions.

Have you ever been suicidal?

Do you have any major health concerns?

Practitioner has the right to refuse service at any time.

Only validated appointments will be allowed into the waiting area.

Do not loiter in the parking lot.

Johnnie read them all and her mind shot up red flag after red flag. Still, she checked the boxes, like a drone, a drone paranoid and about to go haywire. She rose to turn it in, but she knew she couldn't do it. She'd turn it in and leave. This was crazy. Too fucking crazy, even for her.

But to her surprise, the receptionist pressed a button, and the door to Johnnie's left clicked as it unlocked.

"Go on back."

"But—" She held up the paperwork. She hadn't signed yet. Didn't she have to sign? Couldn't she still go?

"First door on the right. Your practitioner will be right with you."

Practitioner. Is that what they are calling it these days?

Johnnie hesitated. Her insides screamed at her to run. Her legs, however, remained grounded.

The receptionist cocked her head. "It's okay to be nervous. Everyone is."

Johnnie glanced back at the door. It looked like an average door. But she knew anything but average remained beyond it.

"You've already paid; you might as well go in and talk." She smiled, sincere like. Johnnie bought it and grasped desperately to it.

"Talk. Yeah, I can just talk."

CHAPTER THREE

Johnnie's heart jumped to her throat. She opened the door and stepped into a hallway with several doors. Her senses keyed in, and she was poised for noises. But there was only silence. She took a step and focused on the first door to the right. It was open. Warm light seeped into the harsh fluorescent hallway, lulling her forward. The sharp, spicy scent of cinnamon hit her before she stepped into the doorframe.

"Did you sign the bottom?" a throaty voice asked from inside.

Johnnie stopped and stared into the room. A large, deep red sofa sat off to the right, bookshelves lined with dozens of books sat straight ahead, and what appeared to be a well-polished desk to the left, just behind the door, hiding the voice.

"You can't come in unless you sign."

Johnnie inhaled the cinnamon, stared into the lit candles, and eyed the luring sofa.

"Come inside, Riot. We have a lot to talk about."

With a slight tremble to her hand, Johnnie signed the last page and took a step inward.

"Good. Now come in farther and close the door."

Johnnie licked dry lips and stepped in farther with the clip-board, nervously tapping her outer thigh. She closed the door but still could not bring herself to face the voice. She hoped to get lost in the flicker of candlelight. To somehow ooze into the dancing shadows of the wall.

"You don't want to look at me?"

Johnnie pushed out a breath that shook. "I can't."

"Why not?"

Johnnie struggled for the right words but found none. "I'm nervous."

"Because of me?"

"Because of this."

Johnnie heard movement from behind the desk. The thrumming of her heartbeat muffled out the rest.

"I won't bite."

Johnnie let out a laugh before she could stop it.

"Glad to see you have a sense of humor. It makes my job less tedious."

"Tedious?"

"Did that also amuse you?"

"I just can't imagine this being tedious."

The voice was silent. "What exactly is this, Riot? Do you know?"

Johnnie flushed and searched the wall of books. There were numerous books on psychology, philosophy, and then she noticed the books on sexuality, the *Kama Sutra*, and several more. She had no idea what to say in regard to her question or what to think in regards to her books. "You know—what it is you do."

"And what is that?"

Johnnie closed her eyes and tried to slow her breathing. "I don't know."

"Yes, you do. You're just afraid to say it out loud."

Johnnie stood very still. Had she insulted her?

"Tell me what you think this is."

"I-I'm not sure exactly what this is," Johnnie said softly.

More silence. More movement behind the desk.

"You don't have to look at me. Not if you don't want to."

"I don't." It came out before she could stop it. If she looked she'd panic. The woman sounded like sex on a stick. If she was, it would be too much, and she would either run or pass out right there on the expensive looking rug.

"I do, however, want to look at you, Riot."

"Why?"

"Because, unlike you, I cannot help myself. I'm curious. And intrigued."

"I feel underdressed," Johnnie stammered, suddenly worried about it.

The woman laughed. "I'm not worried about your clothes. They are the least of my concerns. What I want to see is…you."

Johnnie felt herself tremble. She could feel the weight of her words, her stare.

"Close your eyes, Riot."

Johnnie closed her eyes.

"Now, turn and face me."

Heart hammering, Johnnie turned. She struggled to breathe and nearly dropped the clipboard as she allowed herself to be analyzed.

"Can you feel me looking at you?"

"Yes."

"Do you sense my gaze traveling up and down your body?"

"Yes."

"What does it feel like?"

"Warm. Heavy."

"Electric?"

"Yes."

"Almost as if I were touching you."

"Yes."

"Very nice. You can turn and face the couch now."

Johnnie turned and opened her eyes. She felt dizzy and stirred.

"We will do things your way today." More movement and the sound of a chair wheeling. She knew the woman had stood.

"I'm behind you now, coming up very slowly. I'm pushing my chair. Can you hear it?"

"Yes."

"Good. I'm behind you now. You can sit."

Johnnie sat very slowly, very carefully, as if she didn't trust her own legs. She could feel the woman behind her. Her presence infiltrating hers. Warming it, caressing it, welcoming it.

"Hand me the clipboard and pen."

Johnnie did as requested and realized that the tendons in her hands and fingers were sore from her tight grip.

She heard the woman flip through the pages.

"You're an artist."

"Yes." Johnnie's brow furrowed. "I didn't put that in there."

"Your jeans and your hands give you away I'm afraid."

"They're clean," Johnnie said quickly. "Just the paint is hard to get off..."

The woman laughed, rich and deep. "I'm not complaining."

Johnnie burned.

"You're a worrier," the woman said and tossed the clipboard back onto the desk, causing Johnnie to jerk with surprise.

"No, I mean, not really."

"You're a worrier," the woman said again, this time leaning down near her ear. Johnnie could feel her breath, and gooseflesh erupted along her skin as if she'd just licked the length of her spine.

Johnnie straightened and cleared her closing throat.

"No need to answer, my dear. I already know."

A touch came, light and singular and ran around the rim of her collar. "You're depressed. Very sad." The touch halted. The woman leaned in again, this time breathing upon her other ear. "And very lonely."

Johnnie felt her skin erupt again, and she gripped the armrests for some sort of control.

"You don't have to answer. You don't have to look. You just have to listen. And feel."

CHAPTER FOUR

Fingers, nimble and warm, crawled up into Johnnie's scalp. The sensation was so sudden and so erotic, a strange noise escaped her throat.

The fingers tightened and gripped her, holding her still. The sensation caused her clit to pulse and engorge. "You haven't been touched in so long, Riot. How long has it been? Years?"

"Ye-yes."

"How many?"

"Four."

"You could come right now couldn't you? Just to the sound and feel of my voice in your ear and my fingers in your hair."

Johnnie made another small noise as the fingers massaged and then tightened again.

"You're so starved for it you're like an exposed nerve ending. The slightest little thing will send you over. That's why you won't look at me. That's why my touch is electrifying you in that chair."

Johnnie was busy struggling for words when the woman suddenly released her and Johnnie nearly fell limp like a ragdoll in the chair. She straightened quickly and tried to believe that her bones weren't melting.

"Turn to your right. I'm going to sit on the couch."

Johnnie turned and faced the door. She was so frazzled and so stirred, she wasn't sure what she should do. Should she stay? Run out the door? Despite her whirling mind, her body was thrumming, and she was so wet she was afraid to move.

She heard the woman cross to the couch, and she heard the shushing of the cushions and pillows as she made herself comfortable.

"I'm crossing my legs," she said, somehow knowing it would stroke Johnnie deep inside.

"Can you see me in your mind's eye?"

"Yes."

"You're going to answer again now?"

"If I'm able."

"So you are willing…just not always able. Interesting. You feel things very deeply don't you?"

"Yes."

"Things that don't affect most others."

"I guess."

"Oh, please don't guess. I want you to know for sure before you admit something like that."

Johnnie cleared her throat. "I do, yes."

"Much better, thank you. Be strong with your words. Even if you can't be strong emotionally. I want you to know who you are. Own it. We can't get anywhere until you know yourself."

Johnnie stared through the door and listened. She could see the woman uncross her legs and then cross the other over.

"Do you want to know what I'm wearing?"

Johnnie grew brave. "I know what you're wearing."

"You do?"

"You're wearing what I requested."

"How do you know?"

"Because you're good. You're really fucking good at this, and you wouldn't want to disappoint."

"Clever girl."

Johnnie could see the outline of her in her peripheral vision. She had dark, raven-like hair. The kind that reflected the candlelight. She was wearing an off-white silk blouse, a short black skirt, and black heels. Johnnie couldn't tell, but she knew she had on the thigh highs as well.

Exactly what she'd asked for.

"I aim to please," she said. "Do you find the room comfortable?"

Johnnie loved the scent, the lighting, and the cozy feel. "Yes."

"As you grow, we will move."

"We will?"

"Oh, yes."

"What if I don't grow?"

"There's that worry again."

"Sorry."

"Don't apologize."

Johnnie could hear scratches on a paper. She was writing.

"You're taking notes?"

She didn't bother to stop. "Does this bother you?"

"It surprises me."

"Why is that?"

"Because this is just...you know."

"Just what?"

"Sex."

The woman stopped. "I know you don't really think that."

"I'm not sure what to think."

"Would you like me to tell you what to expect? Or would you prefer to...wait and see?"

Johnnie shifted. The choice was once again hers, yet she still felt completely out of control.

She couldn't bear to know. She couldn't handle it. It would excite her to no end.

"I will wait."

"Daring. I like it. Tell me, how do you feel right now?"

Johnnie shifted, uncomfortable with the question. "I'm not sure."

"Tell the truth. Nothing more, nothing less. There are no right or wrong answers."

"I'm nervous. Excited. Terrified."

"Turned on?"

Johnnie swallowed. "Yes." Then she struggled to change the subject, too moved by what she had just admitted, too moved by what she was feeling. "What if I don't grow?"

"You already have. You're here aren't you? Sitting with me... talking...experiencing."

Johnnie closed her eyes. She had no control. Her body was reacting and her mind reigniting like a pilot light that had long been out.

"How do you know?"

"It isn't difficult to know."

Johnnie knew it was true. She was electrified and it had taken so little. She opened her eyes and focused on the door. It wasn't locked. Anyone could walk in. What if someone did? What if someone saw her?

"You're worrying again," the woman said.

Johnnie nearly turned to argue. But she stilled and swallowed the observation, owning it.

"You find it very hard to relax don't you? Intensity buzzing through you night and day. I bet you dream. Vividly. And the night-mares…" She took a breath, and Johnnie sat with her heart racing and her head cracked open, oozing out all of her secrets.

"Your art is your outlet. Without it you are…lost."

The last comment hit a nerve, and Johnnie grew angry at feeling so exposed. "How do you know so goddamned much about me?"

The woman shifted and laughed a little. "It makes you uncomfortable."

"A little."

"How can I help you if I don't know you?"

Johnnie shrugged. "I don't know. I thought sex was sex."

"I know you don't believe that."

"Maybe I do."

"You don't."

"And why don't I?"

"Because it's written all over you. You're an artist, a creator, a sensitive soul. You feel and sense what others cannot or refuse to feel and see. You take everything in and digest it whether it's good for you or not. You feel. It's what you do. It's what makes you who you are. It's what makes you such a good artist."

Johnnie clenched her jaw against the rapid thumping of her heart. "I just want sex. I need sex."

"No."

"I'm paying you, right?"

"You are, but you don't have to. You can leave at any time."

"You'll give me my money back and I can just walk right out the door?"

"Yes."

Johnnie stared at the doorknob. She wanted to stand and reach out for the motherfucker, but she sat nailed to the chair. The woman had her wide open, and she was verbally teasing her with long strokes of a feather. It was killing her, but she wanted more.

"You're sadistic. You're going to get off on teasing me."

More soft laughter. "Such harsh words. I know you don't mean them."

"You're going to hurt me."

"Never."

"I didn't mean physically. I meant—"

"I know what you meant, and the answer remains the same. I will not hurt you."

"This is hurting me."

"No, it isn't. It's me reading you, and you're reacting because no one has ever truly done it before."

"I can't do this."

"Yes, you can."

"I don't want to do it."

"Yes, you do."

"How do you know?"

"Because you haven't moved. You're still sitting there."

CHAPTER FIVE

Johnnie turned quickly to yell at her, but the sight of her took her breath away. Fiery green eyes, dark hair, cheekbones the wet dream of a sculptor, she sat there with a wicked grin, devouring everything Johnnie did and said. Johnnie turned back, breathless, chest heaving.

"Did you like what you saw?"

Johnnie clenched the armrests and pushed back against the chair. Why couldn't she just fucking stand?

"I'll take that as a yes."

"Christ, this is maddening. I just want to fucking stand."

"Then stand."

"I can't."

"Why not?"

"Because you haven't told me to move."

"Why do you care if I give permission?"

"Because I want you to fucking touch me again."

Johnnie was sweating now, and she could feel it along her spine and near her ears. Her muscles were taut and she was still holding on to the chair for dear life.

"You want it that badly?"

Johnnie couldn't answer.

"Turn and face me."

Johnnie trembled. She was unsure if she could.

"Turn and face me. I want you to look at me."

Johnnie turned, and her eyes traveled up the long legs to the blouse to the face, to the fiery eyes.

"No, don't look away."

Johnnie held her gaze and trembled as her eyes flashed in the candlelight.

"I'm going to tell you something, Riot. It doesn't happen often, but I very much like the look of you. I like the paint on your jeans, the strength in your arms and hands. I like your face, your captivating eyes and the way your upper lip trembles when you feel excited. I'd very much like to touch you again, but like I said before, this isn't just about sex. It's about you."

She eased back further into the couch.

"Tell me something, Riot. Where do you want me to touch you?"

"Anywhere."

She leaned forward and uncrossed her legs.

"Come closer."

Johnnie eased her chair forward. The woman tugged on the armrests and pulled her in. Johnnie saw her face soften and her eyes warm. It caused her heart to nearly beat out of her chest.

"Can I touch your face?"

Johnnie got lost in the depths of her eyes. "Ye-es." Her entire body shook with anticipation.

Her warm hand cupped her jaw, and her thumb lightly stroked her skin. Johnnie heated beneath her.

"So beautiful." She stared at Johnnie's mouth and moved in as if to kiss her.

She took Johnnie's hand in her own. "Close your eyes," she said softly.

Johnnie did so with her whole body on fire from her touch.

"Tell me what you've been feeling these past few weeks. Tell me how you feel lost and alone and sad."

"I do. I am."

She turned her hand palm up and began lightly tracing her fingertips along her hand.

Johnnie struggled to breathe, struggled to sit still.

"Tell me how it would feel if I came into your home and touched you like this when you were feeling so low."

"If you just showed up at my door?" Johnnie couldn't imagine. The thought alone was almost too much to bear.

"Yes. What if on this very rainy evening I rang your doorbell. Would you let me in?"

Her fingers continued to tickle Johnnie's hand.

"Yes."

"Would you sit like this and allow me to touch you?"

Johnnie opened her eyes. The woman was looking at her with such a soft expression. The predatory look gone. Johnnie blinked at her, moved.

"Yes," Johnnie breathed.

"Would you be able to sit still?"

"I would try."

"Even if I did this?" She traced her fingers up the inside of her forearm.

Johnnie inhaled sharply at the sensation. "If you wanted me to, I would sit still."

"You're doing very well, Riot. Sitting still, feeling, even though the sensation of it is awakening you, overwhelming you. You're doing very well." She was breathing quickly and it nearly matched Johnnie.

"I feel like I'm going to faint," Johnnie said.

The woman smiled. "You're wound so tight, that doesn't surprise me."

She took her hand and lifted it to her mouth. She placed it along her cheek and then kissed her palm. Johnnie moaned, and the woman inhaled deeply and then released her. When she looked at her again, the look of desire was gone.

"Tonight, you go home. You go home and feel."

"Please…" Johnnie wanted the look again. Needed the look.

"You're getting all that you need right now." She straightened, as if regaining control of herself.

"But I—"

She wouldn't look at her. "Make an appointment for next week."

Johnnie watched helplessly as she rose, grazed a finger along Johnnie's jaw, and returned to her desk.

"That's it?" Johnnie was still breathless and thrumming, a live wire.

"For today, yes." She pressed a button on the phone and spoke. "Yes, schedule Riot again for next week will you?"

She ended the call and returned slowly to Johnnie. Her eyes were dancing in the candlelight. They were predatory, but distant. She leaned in to whisper in her ear. "We have much more work to do."

Johnnie blinked. "Work?"

"Yes."

"But I'm—"

"What? Feeling alive? On fire? For the first time in how long?" She sounded irritated and edgy.

Johnnie couldn't answer.

"Go home, Riot. Go home and feel all these feelings."

Johnnie forced herself out of the chair. Her legs felt weak, and for a moment, she wondered if she could walk. The woman opened the door. She stood eye-to-eye with Johnnie, with a flush of her own coloring her cheekbones.

"Good night."

"Night."

Johnnie walked out. The door closed behind her before she had a chance to look back.

CHAPTER SIX

Elaine locked the door to her office, rounded her desk, and pulled out the bottle of expensive scotch she had hidden in her drawer. She kicked off her heels, poured a glass, and crossed to collapse on the couch.

"What the hell just happened?" She sipped the scotch and massaged her temple. She'd never lost control in a session before. Then again, she'd never had personal feelings for a client before. She'd been attracted to some, yes, but never moved. Not like this. She sipped more alcohol and willed it to sort some sense into the mess of her mind. She'd have to end it. Here and now. She couldn't see her anymore. Michael would understand. It had happened to him.

She groaned at the realization. Michael had ended the sessions, yes. But then he'd married him. They were going on ten years.

"This can't be happening." Who was this Riot? Why did she have to be so...everything? Sensitive, artistic, beautiful, intelligent. Why couldn't she be like her other clients? Boring, mundane, complaining about their wives, money, sex, and a receding hairline. Those guys were easy to help. Show 'em a little leg, boss them around, teach them how to treat women, and bam, off they go, well trained and better for it. They feel better about themselves, their sex lives improve, and they are happy. But Riot, this woman. She was different. She had looked at her with such soul, such heart. And the way she'd reacted to her touch. It had stirred something she'd thought she'd buried deep long ago. How could it be that it had drifted so close to the surface again and she not know?

She drank more as her mind spun. She thought of Riot's fierceness. The way she fought losing control. Squeezing the chair, pushing back against it. The internal battle she'd fought had been obvious, spellbinding. Elaine had been captivated by her. She had been fighting her feelings, fighting what they both felt, and Elaine had been right there with her, battling inside herself.

But she'd messed up. She'd let it out and let her true feelings surface. She was sure Riot had seen it. It was too late now to fix it.

CHAPTER SEVEN

A knock came from Elaine's office door. She rose, felt the tingling of a buzz, and opened the door.

"How did it go?" Michael, her partner for over ten years, entered with a smile.

She collapsed again on the couch and nearly spilled her drink. "Michael, what the fuck did you do to me?"

He laughed softly and closed the door behind him. "So you liked her?"

'You're evil," she said. "The devil himself in pressed chinos and a polo shirt."

"I thought you might find her…interesting."

"She's gay."

"Yes."

"She's gorgeous."

"I wouldn't know."

"Somehow you knew. Don't be smug."

"She was into you?"

She sat up and tucked her legs in under her. "You knew she would be. Did you know she requested this outfit?"

He sat next her and rested his cheek on his fist. "Maybe. It's something you would've worn anyway."

"That's not the point."

"What is the point? I asked her what she found the most appealing, and what she described was you."

"Not Nancy?" Nancy was younger, sporty, sparky. Lesbians loved her.

"No, not Nancy."

"What about Claire? She's around my age."

"Claire isn't you. Claire would bore her. You are what she needs."

"Michael, I can't do this. You know I can't do this." She closed her eyes.

"Can't do what? Feel?"

"Don't fuck with me."

"I wouldn't dare."

She opened her eyes. They stared at each other for a long moment.

"You like her don't you?"

She didn't answer. Couldn't answer. She sipped her drink, wishing it could make her disappear.

"It's okay to like her," he said softly. "I thought you'd be thrilled at having a woman for a change. A gay woman to boot."

"I'm not ready," she said.

Michael sighed. "Elaine, it's been five years."

"Michael, don't." Her throat tightened. "Please."

"Okay."

"I have to end it."

"Because you like her."

"Because—because she likes me."

"The men like you. What's the difference? You help them."

She shook her head with frustration. "It's not the same."

"Why not?"

She didn't answer.

"Can you help her?"

She looked at him. Met his deep brown eyes. He was such a good guy. Had such a good heart. Why was he doing this to her?

She finished her drink and rose to get another.

"Elaine?"

She poured herself another glass. Took a long sip before she answered. "I don't know."

"I think you do."

"Stop using my words against me."

"Be certain when you speak. Even if you don't feel it."

She rolled her eyes.

"Tell me."

"Yes, I think I can help her."

"Then you must."

She sank into her desk chair. "It's not a good idea."

"Then end it and date her."

She balked, struck at his forwardness.

"I'm serious. Either suck it up and help her, like you do all your clients. Or end it and ask her out."

He stood and approached the door.

"How about I just end it?" she said, holding up her glass to him.

He pressed his lips together in disappointment. "That would be running. And you've done enough of that for many lifetimes." He opened the door and walked out, leaving her alone with her scotch and swirling thoughts.

"Fuck."

She stared after him, half wanting to throw the glass at the door, half wanting to down it quickly. Instead she did neither, and placed it on her desk. The candles still burned, causing shadows to dance along the walls. She pictured Riot standing before her with her eyes closed. She remembered allowing her gaze to linger as it moved up and down her body. Her T-shirt had been tight, showing off a flat stomach and ample breasts. The jeans were loose, hanging off her hips, showing just a peak of her underwear when she breathed deeply.

She felt her skin flush with desire again, burning hotter this time, fueled by alcohol. She thought of Michael's words. *End it and date her. End it and date her.*

She couldn't do that.

She wasn't ready. Probably never would be. The idea brought on anxiousness and a need to flee. Michael was right; she was a runner. But there was no use changing her ways now. She needed to get out of there. Get her mind right again. She grabbed her phone and opened her dating app. She scrolled through her possibilities. *No. Not her. Not her. I need younger, no a bit older. Blonde. Yes.*

She sent a message.

The woman didn't look exactly like Riot, but she was close enough. She knew what she was doing and what it meant, but she didn't care. She had to do it to make the madness stop. She never claimed to be the healthiest person around, Michael knew that. She had her issues just like anyone else. But what Michael didn't like was how she handled hers.

She left the scotch and rose to sling her purse over her shoulder. She crossed the room and blew out the candles, then locked her office door behind her. She walked down the hall and exited the building through the rear. Rain knocked on her umbrella as she hurried to her car. By the time she crawled inside and lowered her umbrella, her phone had dinged with a new message. She closed the door, called the service, and listened.

"Yeah, I'm Kyle, twenty-seven, five foot seven, short blond hair, brown eyes. I'm up for anything and everything. Looking for older women, fit and fine. Bi-curious okay with me. First time with a woman? Let me be the one. Call me at 602-555-1437."

Elaine sat for a moment and watched the rain run down her windshield. She shouldn't have drunk; that was a no-no. And the excitement of the session had been more than she was used to. And though she fought it, she could feel the desire coming on. The wise thing to do would be to go home. But home was the worst. Pain lived there. Festered there. It was often suffocating. She placed her palm on her heart and willed the fluttering to stop. After a few minutes of deep breathing, she felt a little better. With a new determination, she dialed the number and put the phone to her ear.

CHAPTER EIGHT

Johnnie hurriedly entered her loft and closed the door behind her. Breathless, she leaned against it and tried to get her bearings. She'd driven straight from the woman's office on autopilot and could not recall the drive home. The woman's voice thrummed through her and her skin still burned from her steady gaze and heated touch. She opened and closed her hands. They were sore from gripping the steering wheel. She'd almost had to tear them off once she'd pulled into her parking space.

What the fuck is happening to me?

She took in her spacious loft and inhaled the clove smell of her scented candles, which lingered long after they were blown out. She thought about sinking down onto the couch to relax in the scent, to try to rid her of the spicy cinnamon smell of the woman's office. But she knew she wouldn't be able to sit still or be able to concentrate on a movie. So instead she glanced at the bed with the sheets messy and strewn. It called to her, but she knew she wouldn't be able to sleep.

She rubbed her temple and crossed, zombie like, to the fridge and opened a cold bottle of water. Once she swallowed, she could hardly bring herself to stop, a raging thirst overtaking her. She hardly stopped long enough to breathe before she was twisting open another. The cold felt good coating her windpipe, but it did little to cool the fire still burning inside her. She emptied half the second bottle and tossed her cell phone onto the kitchen counter. There were texts and messages, but she couldn't deal with them right now.

Instead she walked to her bed where she placed the water on her nightstand, and sat to remove her shoes. She noticed the tremble still remained in her hands as she fumbled with the laces. Her T-shirt was clinging to her back, and her heart still raced beneath her chest. If she closed her eyes she could still feel the woman's touch, feel her palming her jaw, so delicately, as if she were cupping a baby bird. As if Johnnie were fragile and would crumble right before her.

No one had ever touched her like that before, so gentle and caring, looking at her like she was something precious, something that would vanish into thin air if not treated with great care. She ran her hands through her hair and realized she didn't even know the woman's name. She didn't know anything about her. Only that she had moved her in ways no one else had ever done and she'd done it all in under an hour.

Go home and feel all these feelings.

What did that mean? What was she supposed to do?

She couldn't even control the shaking of her hands, much less anything else. Unable to sit still, she rose and walked into her living area. Somehow, she had to slow herself down and get control. She had to do something. She eyed the large canvas against the wall. It was behind several others that were smaller in size. She moved those aside and brought out the big one. She placed it on her easel and ran her hand across the surface as she imagined what she would paint. She loved the rough feel of the canvas and the way it sounded as she moved her hand along its surface. Sometimes she could sit for an hour, running her hand over the canvas trying to dream up an image to paint. It usually soothed her, but tonight it only fed her growing fire. She closed her eyes and breathed deeply. The woman would not leave her mind. She opened her eyes.

Yes, the woman was perfect. The woman would do.

She tore off her T-shirt and got to work with her mind focused. She had to get her on canvas. To capture that look, the one of desire. She had to bring her eyes to life, and paint her skin as it glowed in the candlelight. Her hand didn't shake as she began to sketch. Her heart rate slowed a bit but still beat heavily, which only fueled her mission. When she painted, nothing else mattered. Nothing could infiltrate her focus. Though inwardly she wanted to celebrate at having the urge to paint, she kept her focus on her work, too determined to take the time to smile.

Somewhere in a far-off land, her phone rang. Light years later, someone yelled at someone outside her door. She only moved from her stool when the sun fully set. She turned on her standing lights, angled them at the canvas, and continued. When she grew thirsty again she ignored it. Hunger long ago had faded. When she looked at the clock for the first time, it said nine fifteen. When she looked again, it was after eleven. When she finished, it was after one.

She didn't bother to stare at the painting; she had the image burned in her mind. She killed the bright lights and sank into the couch with her paint splattered hands in her lap. Her arm and shoulder singed with pain, but she didn't care. She felt pleasantly spent, as if she'd just ran a marathon.

When her eyes threatened to close, she cleaned up. When her step grew heavy, she stripped, and stepped into the shower. She wanted the water hot, and she stood still under its assault, letting it beat up her skin and taut muscles. She let it wash away the day and the dry paint but it could not wash away her mind. She could not lather the woman away, rinse her off, and then repeat. The most she could do was dry off, stumble into bed, and pray for sleep. But the high ceiling loomed and the fan she kept on for sleep taunted her. Her mind began to slow and melt, and it jumped from the woman to her friend Jolene, to a time when they walked the hot streets, searching for a purpose, a life, a home.

A tear slipped down her cheek and her mind fell into another file, this one from her childhood. And an image of Ashley came. Her best friend. They were twelve years old and growing closer. Too close. They'd lay in bed at Ashley's father's house, giggling into the night, talking about the boys at school. But then Ashley had grown quiet and Johnnie had turned to look at her, to make sure she was okay. To her surprise, Ashley had kissed her. The move had startled her and she'd stared, confused. Ashely turned and leaned down and kissed her again, this time, reaching down to touch her between the legs. Johnnie had made a noise of surprise and pleasure.

She kissed her back and stared up at her as she touched her through her pajamas. A light came on and it pierced her eyes. Ashley was torn from her and drug from the room, crying. Johnnie had sat up and watched with horror as her father ushered her away. And there, at the doorway, stood Ashley's mother with her arms crossed.

"I'm calling your mother. You're no longer welcome here."

Johnnie blinked heavy eyelids. More images came. Short and blurred. Voices, some clear, some muffled, calling from the past. This was how it was every night. The past coming back to haunt her and torture her. She would lie there and feel it all again. Shame, embarrassment, sorrow. None of the memories that came were good.

She blinked again and this time held the image. It was the woman and she was smiling at her and reaching out for her. Johnnie stared and warmed as she reached for her in return. When their hands touched, she fell into the woman and then fell into sleep, with all the rest dissipating from her mind.

CHAPTER NINE

Elaine found Kyle quickly at the small coffee shop. She was sitting in the back corner, sipping a coffee while staring out the window. Her taut muscles showed through her tight T-shirt. Her hair was longer than Riot's, but her jaw was nicely angled and set, as if she were on a mission of great importance. Elaine refocused and ordered an iced chai latte. When it was ready, she walked slowly to the table and extended her hand.

"I'm Elaine."

"Kyle." She seemed pleased as she gave a firm handshake. She motioned for her to sit and Elaine did.

"I have to admit, I'm not usually into the whole meet for coffee thing," she said with a coy smile.

"I'm not either," Elaine confessed. But for some reason she needed to meet this woman first. Was it because of Riot? Or was it because of her latest fiasco with a woman? Both were at the forefront of her mind. But with a long sip of her chai latte, she pushed them both firmly away.

"So how do we do this?" Kyle asked.

"I don't know. I think we're supposed to talk."

Kyle sat back. "Is this your first time?"

Elaine laughed, amused. "What do you think?"

"I don't know. You seem a little nervous."

"Do I?"

"Yes, a little uneasy."

Elaine took in a deep breath and sat back to cross her legs. "It's been an unusual day."

Kyle leaned forward. "Instead of asking about it, how about I just make it go away?" She reached for her hand. Elaine allowed her to cover hers. The touch did nothing for her. Her skin felt warm but unremarkable. Not like Riot's.

Elaine stared at their hands and then stared into her face. Kyle was young, confident, strong.

"You don't want to know all about me?" Elaine asked.

Kyle smiled. "Only what you want to tell me."

"That makes this very easy then."

"Good."

Elaine removed her hand. Her heart fluttered and she felt a little lightheaded. She wouldn't be able to push things tonight. "I'll tell you what I like, and you tell me if you're interested."

Kyle drew closer and pushed her coffee away.

Elaine whispered, "I like to watch."

"To watch."

"Yes."

"Me?"

"Yes, you. I want to watch you do things to yourself."

Kyle looked out the window and mulled it over for a bit. "Alone?"

"Yes."

"Do I get to touch you?"

"No."

"Will you ever touch me?"

"No. Not tonight."

Kyle sat back as if in deep thought.

Elaine sipped her latte. "I will, however, tell you exactly what to do."

Kyle raised an eyebrow. "Really?"

"Oh, yes."

She smiled. "That sounds interesting."

"I think so." She pushed back from the table to stand.

Kyle stood with concern marking her face. "You okay?"

Elaine waved her away and took a deep breath. "Yes, I'm fine."

"You sure you're up for this?" Kyle asked.

Elaine closed her eyes and immediately saw Riot. "Yes, definitely."

"Okay, where are we going?"

Elaine steadied herself and then straightened with confidence. "Follow me." She knew she shouldn't do this. She was breaking all the rules. But the way she was feeling, she couldn't imagine another hotel. "We can go to my house."

CHAPTER TEN

Johnnie awoke to banging. It startled her at first, and then it pissed her off. She yelled at whoever it was then flung on a flimsy robe, and yanked open the large door.

"Eddie, what the fuck?" She collapsed against the doorframe, relieved it was him but still pissed off nonetheless.

"Good morning, sunshine. Or should I say afternoon?" He breezed past her and headed for the kitchen with his hands full of bags and drinks. "I brought you a smoothie and some bagels. And some vitamins because you look like I said…meth addict."

"Great, thanks." She closed the door and crossed to deposit herself on a bar stool.

"No, it's not great. You look God-awful."

He slid her smoothie across the counter. She tipped it. "Cheers, mate."

He ignored her as he spread smear onto a bagel and then slid that across to her as well.

"You haven't been answering your phone so I knew you were either working or getting laid. I assumed it was the first rather than the latter."

"You assumed correctly." She took a bite of her bagel and then motioned for more cream cheese.

Eddie sipped his drink, and she watched as his cheeks caved.

"You look fresh," she said. "Well moisturized."

He smiled. "I like it. And so does a certain someone."

"Gary?" He'd long had a crush but had been too shy to do anything about it.

"Maybe." He grinned again and started in on his bagel. "So when can I see your latest? Or is it top secret?"

She swallowed more smoothie, so thankful he got the berry blend. "It's in the living room."

"No shit?"

She motioned toward the living room. Eddie rounded the counter and whistled as he walked up to the painting.

"Oh my goodness, girl. Who is this fine woman?"

"You mean you don't recognize her?" She had thought he might.

He gave her a confused look. "Should I?"

"She's the woman I met with yesterday." When he still didn't show signs of understanding, she told him more. "You know, at the place?"

"Place?"

She sighed in frustration. "She's my…practitioner."

Eddie's eyebrows rose. "Oh, the place. Holy shit, you went? I didn't think you would do it. Oh, my God." He looked back to the painting. "Oh my God, that's why you were able to work. It's working already."

Johnnie stared at the painting and realized he was right. The session had helped her work, even if she'd been too caught up in her own intensity to notice.

"Oh my God, Pedro worked miracles for me. Miracles."

He had gone on and on about Pedro and how he had helped him through so much emotional baggage and self-sabotaging. So much so that she had begun to think Pedro was some sort of guardian angel rather than a real human being.

Eddie returned to his bagel and smoothie. He batted his lashes at her. "So, tell me all about her."

Johnnie shrugged. "I know absolutely nothing about her. Not even her name."

"She's coy, this one. Pedro was kind of like that at first. But he came off as more the nurturing type."

"What do you know about Pedro? I mean, who are these people?"

"I don't know. I just know they are very, very good at what they do."

"Is Pedro even his real name?"

He sucked on his drink. "Do I even care? No. All I care about is the fact that he helped me."

"Did you, you know...have sex with him?"

He rolled his eyes. "As if I'd tell you. Those sessions were private for a reason."

"I just don't know what to expect."

He smiled. "That's good. She probably doesn't want you to."

"I don't know; I feel so weird about the whole thing. It feels... strange and exciting and somehow forbidden."

"Which sounds like it's exactly right up your alley."

"I don't know." She still couldn't get past the fact that the woman was a stranger.

"Just relax and go with it. Anything to get you working, right? I mean you did send up the SOS did you not?"

"Yes."

"Then what's the problem? Go, have fun. Let her help."

"I just have so many questions."

He chewed on a bite of bagel as he leaned against the bar. "So ask her."

"It's like she stepped right out of my dreams."

"Mm, they are good that way."

He looked over at the painting and cocked his head. "So that's your dream girl...not bad. Dark, mysterious."

"Intelligent."

"You're never going to let me live that down are you?"

"Never."

"It was a blind date, and I didn't know she was—"

"She didn't know who Winston Churchill was."

"So she's not good at history."

"She was English, Eddie."

"Okay, okay. You're so picky."

"If that's what you want to call it."

"Seriously, when are you going to give up the ghost on the whole picky thing?"

She shrugged. She had to admit, she was particular. In fact, there had only been one person who'd grabbed hold of her spine and wouldn't let go, despite her bad behavior. Her ex, Gail.

Eddie continued. "I can't come around and check on you forever you know. Eventually, I too, will settle down and get a life."

"You'll still care."

He sighed. "God, I know. I won't ever stop."

"I'm fine, Eddie. Really. I'm happy being alone."

"You look really awful. Like you're going to blow away in the wind." He took both their plates and threw them away. Then he leaned on his elbows and looked her dead in the eye. She confessed and knew he'd accept nothing less.

"I'm stressed. Who wouldn't be, given my situation?"

"I'll give you that. But, sweetie, you lock yourself away in here or in the studio. Don't come out for days. You're a recluse."

"I could be worse."

"Seriously, come out with me. Hang with the gang. Just to breathe fresh air."

"Maybe."

He groaned. "I'm going to stop asking."

"I'll think about it."

He pushed off from the bar in frustration. "Will you at least get some plants in here? Can you keep them alive?"

"I'll try." She finished her smoothie and looked at the painting. The woman sat looking at her with her long legs crossed, firelight caressing her skin and reflecting in her hair. Her red lips were open, just a bit, as if she were about to speak about the desire in her eyes. Johnnie couldn't tear her gaze away. "She looked at me like that," she said softly, more to herself.

Eddie followed her gaze. "Really? Damn."

"I know."

"Are you seeing her again?"

"Next week."

"Are you excited?"

"I don't know. I think I'm still scared shitless."

"Of her?"

"Of how she made me feel." She pushed away her half-eaten bagel, rested her elbow on the counter, and leaned into her hand. She felt exhausted, like she hadn't slept at all.

"I thought she made you feel wonderful."

"Alive," Johnnie said.

"What's wrong with that?"

"I can't fall for this woman, Eddie."

"Why not?"

"I thought it was going to be about sex."

He held up his hands. "I never said that."

"Well, you didn't not say it. So I went in there expecting something sexual. I don't know." It sounded crazy now. "I just—I had the wrong idea."

He sighed and rested his face in his hand at her eye level. "It is yet it isn't."

"You sound like her."

"It's about you. What you need, what you desire."

"I wanted her. And trust me I haven't wanted anyone in a very long time."

He looked at her like she was crazy. "Um, yeah, I know."

"It's just so much more involved. I mean she cracked me open and read me. The real me."

"And that terrified you."

She nodded. "I don't want it to be about me. I can't do that."

"Sweetie, that's just it. It's never about you. It's always about someone else. First it was your mother, then your first lover, and then Gail, and my God, what more could you have given her? I've never seen someone try so hard to make a relationship work. It's time to focus on you. Work on you. Do something for you."

"I don't want to."

"You're scared."

"Yes."

He reached for her hand. "I know how hard it must be for you to let someone in. Because when you have, they've hurt you. But those people, your mother included, were selfish. They loved themselves; they didn't love you."

Tears stung her eyes. She pulled away from him and turned away, forcing them down.

He was silent for a while, allowing her to get control. "I think it would be really good for you to do this."

"I don't." She turned to face him.

"She's gorgeous. She already helped you paint—"

"She wrecked me, Eddie. I mean she really reached in and grabbed me. How do you handle that? How do you recover from that?"

"Who says you have to?"

"I do."

He shook his head. "No, Johnnie. What you do is you go with it. You walk right back in there and you go with it. She's doing what she's doing to reach you. To show you yourself."

"I don't want her to see me."

"Why not? What is so wrong with you?" He walked over to the painting. "See this look? This is a woman who wants to see you. She wants to see you, Johnnie. She's already seen a little and look at her. She wants more."

Johnnie looked at the painting and stared into her eyes. She'd give anything to see that look again. Even if for just a second.

Eddie read her face. He smiled. "Good. Now go to that appointment." He looked around and waved his arm. "And get some plants for God's sake!"

She laughed and he left without saying good-bye as he often did. Slowly, she rose and approached the painting. She reached out for it but didn't touch it.

Who was this woman?

And why, oh why, did she move her so?

CHAPTER ELEVEN

Elaine could feel the morning light shining on her face. She opened her eyes and squinted against the sun pushing in through her blinds. At first, she was unsure of her surroundings. But soon, familiar objects put her at ease. She was in her living room, curled up on the couch. The ceiling fan was on and she was cold. Her throw blanket was nowhere to be found. She pushed herself up and soon regretted it. Her head was splitting, and her body felt limp with fatigue. She rubbed her right arm and noticed a picture frame pressed into the couch where she'd been sleeping. She didn't bother to turn it over. The image was often too much to bear. She forced it from her mind.

What time is it? Her wrist was bare so she stood and walked into the kitchen. She smelled the coffee before she saw it. She thanked the universe for the time setting on it. As she reached for a mug, she saw that it was after eight, and she panicked a little until she remembered her first appointment wasn't until eleven. Relaxing, she poured her coffee and sat down to go over her appointments for the day. She dug in her leather satchel and removed her notes. She had two new clients, both of them men. One was having trouble meeting quotas at work and the other was having problems writing. The two remaining clients had been seeing her for a while, and their progress was slowly coming along. Most needed self-confidence and reassurance. She found it easy to give, mainly because all of her clients were talented in one way or another. Some just needed redirection.

She sipped her coffee and made some notes on her well-known clients. Then she flipped ahead to check her schedule for the next few weeks. The name Riot caught her eye, and a wave of heat came over her. She sat back and stared, recalling everything from the previous day.

A noise came from her left, from down the hallway. A woman was walking toward her with her large round breasts showing as she tugged on a tight T-shirt.

"Oh, fuck." Her heart raced. "Oh fuck, what did I do?" She must've been staring with her mouth wide open because the woman, whose name she could not remember, looked at her funny.

"What's up? Did you not remember I was here?" She scratched her mussed hair.

Elaine blinked rapidly and began organizing the table. "No, yes. Of course I knew you were here."

The woman pointed at the coffee. "Mug?"

"Just above the microwave."

She helped herself to a mug, poured the coffee, and then sat next to her. Elaine couldn't stop staring at her. How had she let this happen? What exactly had happened?

"Your bed's really nice. I slept like a bear." She blew on the coffee before she drank. "Why'd you leave? Was I bothering you?"

"What?" Elaine had no idea what she was talking about.

"You got up and left at some point."

"Oh."

The woman stared at her for a while. "Are you okay?"

Elaine forced a smile. "Fine. Everything is fine."

"Well, at least you look a little better. You kind of scared me last night."

"I did?"

"Don't you remember?"

Elaine looked away and tried to sip her coffee casually. But the woman didn't buy it.

"Do you remember anything?" They sat in silence. "You don't do you?"

Elaine rubbed her neck with nerves. "Honestly, I don't remember much at all."

The woman laughed. "Well, you did have more than a bit of wine."

"What?" She searched her mind, and memories began to surface. The wine, the candles, the woman on the bed, stroking herself at her direction. She flushed, not with shame, but with desire. The woman had done whatever she'd requested, including straddling the corner of the bed, phallus deep inside her, pinching her own nipples. She'd climaxed several times, and Elaine had watched it all, directed it all. Imagining all of it was Riot.

"It got pretty hot. You were definitely turned on. And let me just say…you have one hell of an imagination. Pouring the candle wax down my chest while I was coming…that was…Jesus."

Elaine glanced down at her satin robe. She tightened her belt, feeling that she was nude beneath. The memory was hot, and she recalled the red wax streaming down the woman's full breasts as her chest heaved in orgasm. As hot as it had been, she found herself feeling exposed and uneasy.

"Do you remember now?"

"Yes."

The woman studied her closely. "Are you regretting it?"

Elaine looked at her. "No. I just don't usually have people come here."

"Oh."

She sipped her coffee and Elaine did the same.

"Don't worry. You didn't do anything you didn't want to do. Eventually, your eyes began to drift closed and I helped you to the bed. You were very tired, just limp in my arms. I would've left, but I was a bit concerned about you."

"Did…anything else happen?"

"Nope. I fell asleep with you, woke up after midnight, and you were gone. I found you on the couch clutching a photo. I didn't want to wake you. So I went back to bed."

"Mm." She turned her coffee mug around and around in her hands. "Thanks for that," she said, unsure what else to say. She was lucky. Damn lucky. "You could've robbed me blind, but you didn't."

"Yeah, well, that's not me. Are you sure you're okay?"

Elaine tried to smile again. "Of course. I just drank too much is all."

The woman took one last sip of her coffee and stood. "Okay then. I'm going to take off." She fished her keys out of her pocket. "You think you might want to give this another shot sometime?"

Elaine looked into her coffee. "I honestly have no idea."

"If you do, you know where to find me."

Elaine nodded and gave her a polite smile.

She turned and left, and Elaine heard the front door close behind her.

Elaine sat for a long while, thinking, chastising herself for her letting a stranger into her home. It was careless and dangerous. And so unlike her.

She rose and headed toward her bedroom for a shower. She felt somewhat better physically, but some fatigue and weakness still lingered. She needed to take it easy, and she needed to quit putting off that doctor's appointment.

She turned on the faucet and changed her mind about the shower. She turned it off and instead walked to her large tub where she let the hot water tumble in. It hypnotized her as it cascaded, and by the time she stepped in and melted into it, she was ready to let everything on her mind go. But as she lathered with the wonderful smelling sliced soap, there was one thing she couldn't let go.

Riot.

CHAPTER TWELVE

The constant smattering of rain had slowed to a spitting drizzle. Johnnie drove with her useless wipers off but her stereo loud. Alabama Shakes was setting her mood, and she tapped her thumbs along her steering wheel as she drove. Traffic wasn't that heavy, but everyone was being overly cautious in the rain. Large puddles along the sides of the road were slowing traffic even more, and she braked to ease through one. Ahead of her and off to the side, a small car had stalled. The large puddle had been too deep.

Johnnie changed lanes when she could and breezed by the other vehicles. The day was overcast but mild. Phoenix was drenched, and all the rain had been the big news. She'd avoided most of it by staying in her loft or venturing out to work in her studio. But truth be told her nerves were frayed and firing off inside her like live wires. She felt more alive than she'd felt in a while, and it made it difficult to settle and work. But somehow she had, painting one subject only. She was also anxious about her upcoming visit with the woman. She was still quietly debating the whole thing, going over and over the possibilities, the exposure. Did she really want someone to see that far inside her? A woman like her? So beautiful and confident and sexual?

An answer wasn't simple, and ideas weren't forthcoming as to what to do. Her one day of painting had produced another image of the woman. This time lounging on the couch, with her long bare legs leading up to a tease of a garter before the skirt. Desire had thrummed through her as she had painted so quiet and intense, as if the woman could really feel Johnnie touching her skin with her brush. Johnnie had worked for hours nonstop, so much so that her legs, back, and shoulders ached when she finally finished and crashed on the twin bed in the corner. She'd spent the night there in her studio, dreaming of her, hearing her voice as if she were there, and whispering in her ear. When she awakened she studied the painting closely and wished the image were real. But what would she do if it were? Would she have the courage to let her in? Would she have the courage to touch her? She knew if she did all would be lost. And she'd worked too hard for this life, for this castle of safety. She would be crazy to let it all come crashing down.

She'd been considering that when she went digging for a canvas along the back wall of the studio. Old paintings she'd kept for nostalgia lived quietly there, and sometimes she dug them out to remember. She found the large sketch board with all her charcoal drawings clipped to it. She kept every sketch of every painting she'd thought of. And some of the sketches were of life itself or people she knew. She had been flipping through them when she came across the one of Jolene. Her heart had warmed instantly, and she'd carefully removed it and lightly touched it. It was a portrait she had done years ago. They'd been at the park, sitting on the grass under a tree. The bright sunlight had caused Jolene to squint, which showed off the deep grooves in her sun weathered skin. Johnnie had found her beautiful and soulful, and she'd had to sketch her.

Studying the drawing brought back a flood of memories, and suddenly, Johnnie had needed to see her. After placing the sketch in a folder to protect it from the rain, Johnnie had laced up her boots and locked the studio behind her.

Now she was speeding in the sporadic rain, anxious to get there. Jolene lived outside of Phoenix, on the far west side. Johnnie always liked the drive. It went from three lanes of packed cars to one, by-passing old farms and empty fields. Once you were past those it was mostly desert, save for the mountain range directly ahead. Jolene liked the mountains. She preferred them over people. They were her guardians, her fortress.

As she approached Jolene's turnoff, she slowed and crunched into the dirt and gravel. Jolene lived on land that had yet to be snatched up by developers. She'd inherited the five acres from an uncle, which had given her a refuge from the streets she and Johnnie had lived on. Johnnie had even lived with her for a while, and she'd learned to love the desert and its wildlife. It's where she'd started to paint.

Johnnie crawled toward the small house and smiled at the plethora of wind chimes. She pulled up and parked in front of the house where she could be seen, killed the engine, and then sat and waited. Jolene had yet to see her new truck, so she knew the visit might make her nervous. She gave a wave out the window and waited some more. It was rude to walk up to the house uninvited. You must wait to be welcomed. Johnnie smiled when the front door opened and Jolene's curious face poked out. Johnnie waved again, but Jolene wasn't convinced. She stepped out on her porch and bent down to see if she could see through the windshield. Johnnie reached up and tapped the dream catcher Jolene had made for her. It swayed from her rearview mirror. Jolene saw and walked slowly across the desert landscape to the truck. She shaded her brow though there was no sun. Her skirt was long and cool looking and ended at her bare feet. Her belt was thick and made of turquoise that showed off her loose fitting blouse as it billowed in the breeze. She approached the driver's side cautiously and then lit up with a smile when she saw Johnnie.

"What are you doing here, white girl?"

Johnnie laughed and crawled from the truck. She embraced her in a tight hug. Jolene smelled of wood smoke and fragrant herbs. Johnnie could inhale her for ages.

"You look…" They pulled apart and Jolene scrutinized her. "Skinny." She squeezed her arms and touched her cheeks. "I don't like it." She turned and waved her hand toward the outlying desert. "My coyotes look better fed than you."

"I know, I know."

Jolene led the way toward the house. "If you know, why don't you eat?"

Johnnie reached in and grabbed the folder and the drink from her console. "I brought you your favorite."

Jolene turned and her eyebrows rose with amusement. "Oh, you did didn't, you."

Johnnie handed her the horchata and watched her suck on the straw. She gave a long sigh, smiled, and then stepped onto the porch and sat in a lawn chair. Johnnie joined her, and soon they were staring out at the wet desert.

"I brought you something else," Johnnie said, handing over the folder.

Jolene opened it and carefully removed the drawing. She studied it closely, and her hand trembled.

Johnnie looked away as emotion overcame her too. "Remember the day I drew that?"

Jolene, too, looked away from it to stare out at the desert. "We were living off a loaf of stale bread. You looked skinny. Like now. I didn't like it then and I don't like it now."

Johnnie understood that seeing her so thin reminded her of bad times. Times they'd both like to forget.

"Why did you bring me this?" Jolene asked, lightly touching the drawing.

"Because it's beautiful. You are beautiful."

Jolene scoffed a little and then laughed.

"I think you should have it," Johnnie said. "It makes me smile to see your face."

"Even then?"

"Especially then."

Jolene tucked it back into the folder.

"We've come a long way," Johnnie said. "It should feel good."

"It doesn't."

Johnnie watched a young jackrabbit run around a bush. "I know."

"Tomorrow it could change."

Johnnie knew she was right. And it had been on her mind a lot lately. "Yes."

"You still dream," Jolene said.

Johnnie nodded.

"Me too."

Johnnie sat back and crossed her feet. "Remember that man who kept giving us six-packs?"

Jolene laughed. "Made me love beer. Hot beer."

"Yep."

"I won't drink it now."

Johnnie was silent. She didn't used to either. But times were hard again.

They stared out into the increasing rain. Both of them lost in thoughts of long ago.

"You have troubles," Jolene said.

Johnnie closed her eyes. "I do."

"They are clouding your head. You need to sweat them out."

"I've been thinking about it."

"You're thinking too much. It gets you in trouble."

Jolene was right. She often was.

"I'm worried," Johnnie confessed. "That all I've got now... what I've worked hard for...I'm worried it's going to come crashing down."

Jolene sipped her drink and then placed it beside her chair. "You are attached to material things?"

"No, I couldn't care less about that." She knew she could live without those. "I'm talking about my home. My safe place. My safe world."

Jolene seemed to think long and hard. "We will both worry about that. Always. It has stained our insides and we can't wash it away."

"I can't go through it again, Jolene, I can't."

"You won't. You will find a way. You did last time; you will this time. And you know you have a home here."

Johnnie turned to face her. "What if it's a person, Jolene? What if it's a person scaring me like this?"

Jolene looked at her with deep, dark eyes. "Someone is trying to take something from you?"

"No, not exactly. She's trying to get in. To see me. The real me."

"Is she a danger?"

Johnnie shook her head. "I don't know. I don't know her that well. She says she can help me."

"You need help."

"Yes."

"With what?"

"To paint."

"Your troubles are your feelings for this woman aren't they?"

Johnnie clamped her mouth shut. She turned and stared out at the desert. Listened to the patter of rain.

"If you didn't have feelings for her you wouldn't care if you let her in. It wouldn't bother you because she would mean nothing to you. What would it matter what she thought? But this person, this woman, she means something to you."

"I like her."

"I know." She paused. "People like us, it's hard to let the outside in. We don't trust it. It's too much. We feel it all."

"You're the only one who understands." Jolene knew exactly how she felt, which was why they had bonded together on the streets.

"You can talk to me anytime." She touched her temple. "In here."

Johnnie reached over and squeezed her hand. "How about you? Are you getting out?"

"I don't go out unless I have a reason."

"And you can't find a reason can you?"

"No."

Johnnie chuckled. "I figured as much. Is your nephew still helping you out with supplies?"

"He is a good boy."

Johnnie blew out a breath. "I should come by more. Check on you. You never answer that cell phone I gave you."

Jolene patted her hand. "You come when we need each other. And you are doing well, Johnnie. Getting out. Talking to people."

"I'm really not out all that much. I stick to small places and avoid crowds."

"You're finding your way. Living how you need."

"And your way is here. In the desert." She smiled.

"Yes. With my mountains."

Johnnie rose and stretched. "I brought you some groceries, figured you weren't getting out much." She crossed to the truck while Jolene protested. It was hard for her to accept things, even when she needed them. Johnnie opened her cab and retrieved two large brown bags full of goods. She closed her door with her hip and hopped back onto the porch. Jolene stood and pulled open the screen door. Johnnie walked inside and placed the bags on the small kitchen stand. The house was dim and lit by two small lamps. Homemade blankets covered the windows, and Jolene only had one pulled back a bit. A small fire burned in the fireplace. A loom stood before a soft looking chair. A rug looked to be half-finished on it.

Jolene disappeared into a back room and came out with a large dream catcher. She placed it on her palm and gave it to Johnnie.

"For you."

Johnnie took it carefully. She knew the important sentimentality of it. "Jolene, this is incredible."

"All we seek can come through dreams. This you know."

"Yes," Johnnie whispered. "That I know well."

"Touch your woman friend. See what you feel, what you sense. It has never failed you and it won't fail you now."

Johnnie embraced her and held back tears. For two years, they'd only had each other. She didn't know what she'd do without her.

"Go now. You've scared off my coyotes."

Johnnie turned at the door and smiled. Jolene returned the smile.

Johnnie walked out the door and stepped back into the rain. This time she didn't cower.

CHAPTER THIRTEEN

Elaine stepped through the inner office door, smiled politely at the medical assistant, and followed her to a large room draped with curtains. The woman stopped halfway in and yanked open a curtain before pointing to a red chair. Elaine set down her purse and took a seat. She began unbuttoning her blouse as the woman closed the curtain.

"Anything change since the last visit?" she asked as she typed at a computer.

"You'll have to be more specific."

The woman looked at her. "How are you feeling?"

Elaine pulled open her blouse. "A little tired sometimes."

Her fingers flew across the keyboard. "Chest pain?"

"Some."

Elaine sighed and eased out of her blouse.

She reached back and unlatched her bra, pulled it off, and placed it on top of her blouse on the small table next to her.

The woman looked at her without a second glance. "Any medication changes?"

"No." She didn't mention that sometimes she missed her blood pressure pill and that she was often dizzy when she stood.

"Still a nonsmoker?"

"Of course."

"What about alcohol?"

She bit her lower lip. "Occasionally."

"Okay."

The woman rose and came to stand on her right side. She began pulling out cords and straightening them. Then she placed them accordingly across Elaine's lap. Next, she began peeling and sticking electrodes along Elaine's chest.

"You look better since the last time I saw you," she said, gently lifting her left breast to place an electrode beneath.

"I thought so too, after weeks of the antibiotic. But now..."

"You feel a little tired." She smiled and stuck the remaining two on Elaine's lower legs.

"Yes."

Elaine relaxed as she connected the chords to the electrodes.

"Okay, you know the drill."

She pushed buttons on the EKG machine, and after a moment, it printed out results. She tore it off to look at it. Elaine watched her, but her face was unreadable. She initialed it and placed it in Elaine's file.

"All finished." She unhooked the chords and left the electrodes to Elaine, who pulled them off quickly.

"You can get dressed and go in to room four." She smiled. "I hope you feel better."

"Thanks." Elaine heard her scrape the curtain rings along the rod to exit. She stood to dress and then pulled back the curtains and walked confidently to room four, where she found fresh butcher paper laid out for her on the examination table. She avoided it and sat in the chair instead.

Doctor's offices and hospitals were now her new kryptonite. She hated them and avoided them at all costs. She had never been a good patient, mainly because being one actually required a lot of patience. Something she had very little of. And this, this appointment was not a good start to her day. She glanced at her watch and scowled at the slim magazine selection. She had an appointment with a client soon.

She crossed her legs and pressed her palms along her skirt. They were clammy, which was unusual for her. Nervousness didn't often trouble her.

"Well, look who finally came back," Dr. Klein said as she entered the room with a smile. She extended her hand and took Elaine's softly. Elaine found it warm and welcoming, just as always. "How have you been?"

She sat at the small counter and opened her laptop. She typed a few things and then opened the file folder to retrieve the EKG reading. Her face, too, was unreadable.

Before Elaine could answer, she spoke again, meeting her eyes. "We've been trying to get you back in here. We've tried calling, sent letters."

Elaine clasped her hands. "I've just been very busy."

"I see. You're one of those huh?"

"One of those?"

"A workaholic. Using work as an excuse for everything." The corner of her mouth lifted to show she was teasing her.

Elaine tried to smile, but she felt guilty. A feeling she knew all too well. It cramped her stomach.

"I won't berate you for not coming in for your follow-up. People get scared. White coat syndrome as they say."

Dr. Klein was kind and intelligent. Beautiful in a classic way. If she weren't happily married with three children, Elaine would've let her thoughts go to a private meeting in a hotel.

Dr. Klein continued studying her computer. "How long after the antibiotics did you start feeling this way?"

"You mean tired? I don't know. I felt good for a while. Then this started...a couple of weeks ago."

She glanced up at the calendar. She looked concerned.

Elaine struggled to explain. "I didn't think anything of it at first. I thought it would take a while to get my strength back you know? And at first it wasn't bad."

"And you did finish the last treatment, right?"

"Yes." She recalled how the home nurse had come, hooked it to her PIC line, and waited until it had emptied.

Dr. Klein stood and offered her a hand. "Can you sit up here for me?"

Elaine did so carefully, the paper crinkling beneath her. She wished she were anywhere else but there. Dr. Klein listened to her heart for a long while. When she stepped away she asked, "Any fever?"

"I don't think so."

"Nausea?"

"Some."

"Can you stand in place?"

"Yes."

"How long before you need to sit?"

Elaine closed her eyes. "I'm not sure."

"But you're able to walk."

"Yes."

She again offered her hand and helped Elaine back into the chair.

"Any lightheadedness?"

"Sometimes, when I stand to walk."

She took her blood pressure sitting, then took it again as she stood. When she finished she returned to her computer. "I think we need to take a look at some things. Run some tests."

"Should I be worried?"

"No need to worry. It will only cause stress, which is something I want you to avoid."

Dr. Klein turned to look at her. "You had one hell of an infection, Elaine. I'm pretty sure it's gone, but we need to check some other things."

"Like what?"

"We need to make sure it didn't cause any damage."

Elaine breathed deeply. "Okay."

"Like I said though, no worrying. Let's just run the tests. In the meantime, take it easy. No marathons."

Elaine touched the necklace Barb, her late wife, had given her and tried to control the fear that had sparked within her. "Got it."

Dr. Klein walked to her and took her hand. "Make an appointment with me soon after the tests. And if you begin to feel worse in any way, I want you in the emergency room."

Elaine released her hand and nodded.

"It was good to see you. I'll see you soon." She smiled and left the room, leaving Elaine alone with her thoughts. The infection in her heart had been bad enough, and she thought she had it beat. But now...damage? What did that mean? Fuck.

Another medical assistant entered and tied off her upper arm to draw blood. Then she gave her the paperwork for the testing. Elaine heard the drone of instructions, but they didn't compute. At some point, she nodded her understanding and stood. She left the office and stepped into the drizzle of rain. She didn't bother to open her umbrella.

CHAPTER FOURTEEN

Johnnie pulled into the parking lot and killed the engine. Her heart raced worse than it had the first time. Then she'd been anxious over what to expect; now she knew, and it made it worse. She played with her hair in the mirror and studied her face, which still looked etched with worry, so she practiced looking calm, poised, ready for anything. She'd spent an hour getting ready, which was a long time for her. But she had to choose the right clothes, the right shoes, the right fragrance. And her hair, well, it still wasn't right.

Giving up, she popped up the mirror and popped in a mint. Rain began to fall and tap on her truck.

"Great."

She opened the door and hurried inside the office door, but not before she got plenty wet. The door chimed, and the pretty girl behind the glass waved. Johnnie waved back and ran her fingers through her damp hair and smoothed out her tight teal v-neck shirt and dark jeans. Her shoes squeaked as she approached the glass, just like before. She straightened her shoulders and offered a smile, but her breathing was quick and she was afraid it would give away her nerves.

"Riot, right?"

"Mm hm." She tapped her fingers along the counter but then caught herself and stopped.

The receptionist picked up the phone to announce her arrival. "You can go on back." She pushed the button and the door clicked.

Johnnie said thank you and squeaked across the lobby to the door. She took a deep breath and entered. The hall was lit as before, but this time a man emerged from the last door. He was well dressed in an expensive suit. He buttoned the front of it as he breezed past Johnnie.

"Hello," he said.

"Hello." Johnnie turned to watch him exit. Then she turned to look at the first door on the right. It was open, but only so far. Johnnie could see the candlelight. She walked up and stood in the doorframe. The scent was different, more like eucalyptus.

"You can come in, Riot," the woman said.

Johnnie squared her shoulders and entered. She gently closed the door behind her. The woman was on the couch, this time in black slacks with matching suspenders. They contrasted nicely with a white silk tank. Johnnie swallowed a lump in her throat and heated from head to toe.

The woman crossed her legs and bobbed her black heel confidently.

"You're wet," she said.

Johnnie again palmed her damp clothes. The woman examined her closely from head to toe.

"Your skin is glistening."

Johnnie didn't say anything; she wasn't sure if she should.

"Come sit next to me." The woman patted the cushion.

"But I'm—"

"I don't care. I want you to sit next to me."

Johnnie crossed to the couch and sat. The woman turned toward her and studied her face. Then she touched her. Ran her fingertips along her damp arm. "You smell like rain and a very tantalizing cologne."

She reached up and brushed her mussed hair from her forehead. "You know when you flush with heat, it marks your face along your bone structure. Here and here." She stroked her cheekbones and Johnnie inhaled sharply.

"Would you like to get out of those clothes?"

Johnnie wasn't sure she'd heard right.

"You feel cold. I think you'd be warmer if you changed out of those clothes."

"I have nothing to wear." Her heart rate sped up, and she searched the woman's eyes for meaning.

"I have a robe. I have towels." She rose and crossed to her desk. She opened a drawer and removed a thick towel. She returned to the couch and handed it to Johnnie.

"Thank you." Johnnie took it and patted her face dry.

"Here, let me." The woman took the towel and gently pressed her arms and ran it through her hair. Then she wrapped it around Johnnie's neck and smiled. She sat back and crossed her legs again.

"What's that cologne you're wearing? I like it."

"I don't know."

"You don't know?"

"I don't tell people what I wear."

"Why not?"

"Because I want to be the only one who smells like me."

"What if I want to smell you and you're not here?" She raised an eyebrow at her.

"I seriously doubt that would ever happen. You aren't supposed to like your clients."

The woman looked amused. "I can like my clients."

"Then where do you draw the line? Sex?"

"You're worried about sex again."

"Not worried. Just realistic."

"Do you want to have sex with me?"

Johnnie laughed. "That's the point isn't it? For me to want you?"

"Yes."

Johnnie held a throw pillow in her lap as if it would somehow shield her from the woman's great powers.

"So tell me, what did you think of the last appointment?" She wrote something with her pen and pad and then rested them in her lap.

She seemed to sense Johnnie's hesitation. "Remember, I want the truth. Nothing more, nothing less."

Johnnie shifted. "You know how I felt. I wanted you."

"You don't sound happy about that."

"I'm not. It makes me feel out of control."

"Did the questions bother you? Or maybe...the answers?"

CHAPTER FIFTEEN

Johnnie tried to hold her gaze, but it was so penctrating, so stirring. She was already reaching inside and touching her, maneuvering things.

"Both. I don't like talking about me."

"I picked up on that. What else?"

"I don't like...that you're so attractive."

The woman put the tip of the pcn to her mouth. "So if you didn't find me attractive this would somehow be easier?"

Johnnie again had to look away. "Probably."

"Why is that?"

Johnnie didn't want to answer, but she knew the woman would insist and wait her out. "Because I wouldn't be thinking about it all the time. I wouldn't be worried about it."

"Worried about what?"

Johnnie gripped the pillow. "About what you think. About whether or not you think I'm attractive." She nearly sighed at the confession. Her heartbeat was in her ears.

"I see." She wrote some more and then stopped to look at her.

"Why does it matter if I'm attracted to you?"

"It—just does."

"It makes the fantasy more real for you."

"Isn't that the point?"

"Yes."

Johnnie sighed.

The woman reached over and touched her hand. "If you know what this is and you don't like it, why did you come back?"

Johnnie stood. The feel of her hot hand was too much. "I don't know. I'm fucking insane I guess."

"Would you like to see someone else? I can suggest others."

Johnnie turned quickly to look at her. "No."

The woman was silent. "Do you want to end this?"

Johnnie massaged her forehead. "No. I want you to keep making me feel...alive."

The woman stood. She placed her pen and pad on the couch and touched Johnnie's arm. She leaned into her.

"Excited?" she whispered in her ear.

Johnnie shuddered. "Yes."

"Take off your shirt," she said.

Johnnie closed her eyes.

She hesitated, but the woman took her hands and placed them at the bottom of her T-shirt.

Johnnie peeled her shirt off over her head. She felt the woman take it from her hand. Her body heaved with excited breath.

"Now your bra."

Johnnie opened her eyes. The woman was watching her. She was looking at her like she wanted desperately to touch her.

"Don't be afraid."

"It's been a long time," Johnnie said as her voice caved with emotion and desire.

"I understand," she said. She moved behind her. "I won't look."

Johnnie breathed deeply. Her skin came to life under the woman's continued stare.

"You don't have to do it. Everything is up to you."

Johnnie turned her head to speak to her. "Help me," she said, reaching back to unlatch her bra.

She felt the woman still her hands and release the hook on the bra. It fell loose off Johnnie's shoulders.

"May I help you take it off?" the woman asked.

Johnnie nodded, noting her bated breath. She allowed the woman to guide it over her arms and hands. She took it behind her, probably placing it with the shirt. Johnnie stood very still, ample breasts puckering in the air. She felt lightheaded yet heavy. Hot yet chilled.

The woman found her hands and leaned in to whisper in her ear.

"Do you want me to touch you?"

Johnnie's knees weakened. She could feel the woman's quickened breath on her neck and in her ear.

"Can you—do that?"

Silence.

"You can. You can touch yourself and pretend it's me. Would you like that?"

Johnnie couldn't control her breathing. The room was spinning. "Yes."

The woman pressed closer. "Raise your hands," she said.

"Now, touch yourself and pretend your hands are mine. Show me how you want me to touch you."

"Oh God," Johnnie felt the hot twitch between her legs. She was wet and nearly panting.

Slowly, she moved her hands up her sides, lightly along her abdomen, up and around her breasts. Her nipples tightened, beckoning to be touched.

"You feel so good," the woman breathed.

Johnnie moaned softly.

"Just close your eyes and feel," she said. "Feel our hands together, worshipping you. Let all the bad go. Just think of now and how good it feels."

Johnnie's clit began to throb. She moved against the woman, wanting to face her. She wanted to take her mouth in hers.

She tried to turn, but the woman wouldn't let her. Instead she stilled her and held her hips.

"You must learn patience."

"I want to see you, feel you."

"No."

"I want more."

The woman struggled for breath. Johnnie felt her tremble. She seemed to struggle for words. "First you need to feel. Exist in the moment."

"I am feeling. I am existing. Christ, I'm so wet."

The woman grew silent. "You want to come."

Johnnie tensed. "Yes."

The woman released her and backed away.

"If you want to come, go ahead."

Johnnie blinked. "What?"

"Go ahead. I will be right here." She sat, her eyes burning and alive.

"I don't understand. You just told me to let that go."

"I think you will do much better if you learn to channel your desires, yes. That's what I'm trying to get you to do."

Johnnie stared into the woman's eyes. "I think I finally understand."

CHAPTER SIXTEEN

Johnnie reached past her for her damp clothes. They chilled her as she dressed, but it didn't stop the pulse between her legs.

The woman surprised her by speaking strongly again. "Did you bring yourself to climax after our last visit?"

Johnnie wasn't sure she heard her correctly. "Does that matter?"

"I assumed you did."

"Well, I didn't."

"Did you take a lover?"

Johnnie stared at her in disbelief. "No, did you?"

The woman appeared shocked at the question, but then the look was gone.

"Tell me, what did you do after our last session?"

Johnnie tried to forget the breath in her ear, the press of her body, the feel of her own hands.

"I went home and I painted."

The woman crossed her legs. A hint of a smile came.

"That's good news."

Johnnie hugged the throw pillow.

"Are you not pleased with that?"

"I'm fine with it."

The woman wrote in her notes. "You're upset now. Why?"

"I feel exposed."

The woman lowered her notes. She moved closer. When she took Johnnie's hand, she squeezed. "We don't have to do anything like that again."

Johnnie laughed, feeling crazy. "I would agree, only I liked it. A lot."

"Do you feel safe with me?"

Johnnie looked down at her beautiful hand. "I do."

"Then how can I make you feel better? Unbutton my shirt? Show you mine?" She smiled.

Johnnie rolled her eyes. "If I said yes you still wouldn't do it."

"No."

They were silent for a moment.

"You're worried that I can't handle this," Johnnie said.

"I know the things I've said and done reached you deeply."

Johnnie didn't speak.

The woman continued. "I know it's how you're built, but I need to be sure you can handle it. That you want to handle it."

Johnnie grew serious. "I handle it every day. There's no extent to what I can handle."

The woman smiled. "I would imagine not, considering you feel and experience what others can't or avoid. Life isn't easy for you."

"It isn't easy for anyone. People just have filters that I don't."

"Which is why this will really get to you."

"It already is."

"Yes."

"I'm stronger than I seem."

"I know. I don't think you always know though."

Johnnie couldn't believe how right she was. "I know how you can make me feel better," she said.

The woman leaned back and smiled. "Okay."

"Tell me what to call you."

Her hand went to her gold necklace where it toyed with a charm.

"You can call me whatever you like."

"Anything?"

"Within reason." She smiled.

"I want you to call me Johnnie."

"Johnnie?"

"Yes, I can't stand Riot. It's ridiculous."

"Okay."

"I don't know what to call you, so please just pick something. Something you like."

"I really have no idea."

"What do your other clients call you?"

"Different things."

"But what do you like? I don't want to call you something meaningless. You're real. A person. You have thoughts and feelings. I know you do because I can feel you." Johnnie closed her mouth and looked away. She'd said too much. Given herself away.

The woman cleared her throat. She chose not to respond to that, and Johnnie was grateful.

She stood and crossed to her desk. She sat behind it and wrote more in her notes.

"I've made you nervous," Johnnie said, sensing it, noting her proximity.

"Oh?" She looked up, curious.

"I think so."

"I'm fine, Johnnie. And remember we're here to talk about you."

"I thought we were supposed to tell the truth. Or does that only pertain to me?"

The woman stood and leaned on the desk. She crossed her arms. "Why don't you tell me what you painted?"

Johnnie was caught off guard by the question. "It isn't important."

"If it's not important, then it should be no trouble to tell me."

"It's private," Johnnie said a little louder than she'd meant.

"Okay." She walked closer with her eyes trained on Johnnie's. "What was it that helped you paint this private painting of yours?"

Johnnie squeezed the pillow.

"Can you answer?"

"I can't think," Johnnie confessed. She was losing control again, leaving it behind in a trail of dust.

"Why are you so afraid to look at me? Is it because I move you?"

Johnnie trembled.

"Yes."

"Why are you alone, Johnnie? Surely women want to be with you, touch you. Why don't you let them?"

"I haven't wanted anyone."

The woman met her serious gaze and then dropped her hands. "Why?"

"I haven't been drawn to anyone. Attracted to anyone. Why? I don't know."

"You want me, though?"

"Yes. But I would never let myself go there. Not really. I don't want to let anyone in. Even you."

The answer seemed to surprise her. She looked away suddenly.

"I see." She crossed her arms again. "So should I or should I not continue with things like we did today?"

"I want you to," Johnnie said. "I don't want you to stop. That is, as long as you're willing."

The woman didn't speak and her hand went to her necklace. "I will help you any way I can."

"Thank you. I know it isn't easy for you with me."

"How do you mean?"

Johnnie looked up at her. "Nothing, never mind."

For the first time, the woman looked vulnerable, exposed. She busied herself with paperwork on her desk.

"I think that's enough for today."

Johnnie stood.

"I didn't mean to make you uncomfortable."

She offered a smile. "I'm fine. Quit worrying."

Johnnie stood still, and waited. When the woman stopped, she looked over at her and appeared to try desperately for something to say. "See me next week," she said. "Tell Julia—"

"I need to see you sooner than that," Johnnie said.

The woman looked taken aback.

"If that's okay with you."

"I—check with Julia. If I'm available, that's fine."

Johnnie nodded.

"Any advice for tonight? Like go feel these feelings?"

The woman stared at her. Again, she seemed to be at a loss for words. "Yes, Johnnie. I think you should go home and feel. Think about today and see where it leads you."

She walked slowly to the door and quietly pulled it open.

She gave Johnnie a reassuring smile. But Johnnie wasn't sure if she was trying to reassure Johnnie or herself.

CHAPTER SEVENTEEN

Elaine sat in her overstuffed chair, staring into the candle-light. Her glass of scotch was half empty and about to slip from her hand. Vocal jazz from the fifties and sixties played on a loop in the background. She had the vinyls of nearly all of them, but she was too drunk and too tired to rise and choose them. So instead she allowed Pandora to do the work for her. Save for the music, her home was quiet, alive and breathing only by sporadic candlelight. It had been three days since she'd last seen Johnnie, and she'd done her best to keep her from her mind. Scotch, books, music, maga-zines, shopping. None of it helped. And Michael again suggested she end the sessions for her own sanity. Especially after she'd con-fessed what had happened at their latest session.

But Elaine wasn't a quitter and she wasn't ready to date. If she ended the sessions, there would be nothing stopping her from seeing her, feeling her, kissing her. They'd get lost in erotic bliss. She knew it.

And as tempting as that bliss was, it was dangerous and often led to more. Something she couldn't afford. Not now, not ever. She placed her scotch on the end table and looked down at the photo-graph. She thumbed the image as a tear slipped down her face.

Barb had been gone for five years now. Five years that felt like a mere blink of an eye. The pain of her loss had not faded, not even a little. It stabbed at her, ate away her insides. So much so that she often woke at night curled in a ball, crying in pain. She couldn't feel like that again. Lose like that again.

She was coming dangerously close with Johnnie. She could feel it. She hadn't been that aroused since Barb, and yet she'd kept going, telling her to remove her shirt and bra. Mentally touching her. She'd nearly climaxed from that alone. And something else was happening. Johnnie was reading her somehow. Pegging her thoughts and feelings. Putting her on the spot. Could Johnnie really be that sensitive? She'd known someone like that, one of Barb's old friends. But she'd never experienced it herself.

She placed the photo of Barb next to the glass of scotch. She rose and allowed her heart rate to catch up with her movement. She tightened her satin robe and headed for the kitchen, but the doorbell stopped her movement. It was a little after nine, and she knew Michael wouldn't call this late. She crossed to the door and looked out the peephole. Sighing, she unlocked the door and pulled it open.

"Hi," Kyle said, hands in pockets, tank top and jeans damp with rain that pattered in the background.

"What are you doing here?" Elaine leaned against the door, upset, but only a little. She reminded her too much of Johnnie to get angry. In fact, if she allowed her swirling thoughts to blur, she could imagine it was Johnnie.

"I was in the neighborhood; thought I would see how you were."

"In the neighborhood?" Her community was gated, hardly a place where one would drive casually by.

"I'm not a stalker, I swear. I just—I followed someone in and saw your lights on."

"You know this is unacceptable."

"Yes."

"You can't do this again."

"No."

"You can come in, but only for a minute."

Elaine pushed open the door and allowed her entry. She could smell the rain on her wet skin. It fueled the fire she'd tried to drink away.

"The living room," Elaine said.

Kyle stepped inside. "Should I take off my shoes?"

"Please."

Elaine locked the door and breezed by her. She waited for her in the center of the Aztec rug. Kyle removed her shoes and approached slowly.

"How have you been?" she asked.

"I don't want you to talk," Elaine said.

Kyle didn't even blink. "Okay."

"Stand in front of me."

Kyle stood in front of her. Elaine leaned into her, hoping for the cologne that Johnnie had worn. But she smelled only rain. She put her mouth to her ear. "Take off your shirt."

Kyle swept her shirt up over her head. Elaine took it and tossed it to the floor. "Now your bra."

Kyle began to reach back for the hook, but Elaine stopped her. "Ask for help."

Kyle paused. "Can you help?"

Elaine pushed away her hands and unhooked the bra. She brought it forward and off her shoulders and tossed it to the floor.

"Now," she said, growing excited. "Take my hands and touch yourself."

Kyle took her hands and guided them softly up and down her torso to just below her breasts, then she moved them across her firming nipples causing her to moan.

Elaine gasped for breath, leaned in, and nibbled her ear. "Show me how you want me to pinch your nipples."

Kyle slid her fingers alongside her gathered flesh and pinched and tugged. It caused her legs to buckle, and Elaine had to help her remain upright.

"Like that? You want it like that?"

Kyle breathed, "Yes."

Elaine moved her hands slowly up to her full breasts. She felt the puckering, the gathering of her nerves. She ran her fingertips across them, heard her moan, and then pinched as Kyle had done, causing her to cry out.

"Yes," Elaine said into her ear. "Tell me, does that make you wet?"

"Yes. So wet."

Elaine teased her like that several more times, grazing and then pinching. When she tugged her, she bit softly into her neck.

Kyle cried out again and again.

"Do you want to come?" Elaine asked.

Kyle gripped her hands, chest heaving. "Yes."

"How badly?" Elaine closed her eyes, imagined Johnnie beneath her hands, rocking back into her.

"Bad. So bad it hurts."

Elaine licked the damp rain and sweat from her neck. "Good. Now undo your jeans, slip your hand in, and stroke yourself."

Kyle hurriedly unbuttoned her jeans, slid her hand into her underwear, and groaned as she found her flesh.

"Oh fuck," she said as she leaned back into Elaine. "I'm so hard."

"And slick."

"Yes."

Elaine toyed with her nipples and continued nibbling her neck. "I want you to get off. Right here, right now, with my hands playing you."

Kyle moved her hand quicker, strained her body as she closed her eyes and stroked.

"That's it. Feel good, baby. Let it all in and then let it all go."

Kyle bucked wildly, and Elaine tugged hard on her nipples. She went over in a series of cries and fits with Elaine holding fast to her. Elaine closed her eyes and moved her hand downward where she grabbed Kyle's wrist, pulling her hand away. Then she sank her own hand into her underwear and felt her hot slick folds for herself. She groaned and Kyle spasmed.

Elaine stood like that for a long while, holding her close, feeling her flesh pulse. Then she opened her eyes and gently pulled away. Kyle, still breathless, turned to look at her.

"Can I touch you?" she asked softly.

Elaine looked away. She sat in her chair and sipped her scotch.

Kyle busied herself dressing. "You want me to go," she said, coming to stand before her, buttoning her jeans.

"Please."

Kyle nodded. She moved toward the door.

"Please lock it on your way out," Elaine said.

She heard Kyle slip into her shoes and then open and shut the door. Above the house, thunder rolled, and Elaine grabbed the photo of Barb, slid down farther into the chair, and thumbed up the volume on her speaker.

Would the pain ever go away?

CHAPTER EIGHTEEN

Johnnie slowly pulled herself from her dream state to answer the phone after several rings.

"Yeah. Hello."

"Is this Riot?"

Johnnie grabbed her head and sat up. "Yes." Her clock radio said it was after ten.

"Your practitioner wishes to meet at a different location today."

Johnnie's mind fought to wake and register the words. "Okay, where?"

"She prefers that you meet where you paint."

Johnnie swung her bare legs over the side of the bed. "Yeah, I don't think I can make that happen." She had four paintings of the woman now.

"She would like to see where you work."

"I just—" Fuck, what was she going to do?

"Do you have an address for me to give her?"

She would have to hide the paintings. Johnnie stood and gave her the address to the studio, then she jumped in the shower. After debating several outfits, she settled for a light pink tight tee and khaki cargo pants. She ran pomade through her hair, sprayed on her cologne, and headed out. She was anxious about the woman seeing the studio. She wasn't exactly an organized artist. She had several works started and off to the side. Stacks of finished canvases she wasn't happy with. Sketches. Old furniture she refused to get rid of. It wasn't exactly impressive.

When she pulled up to the plaza of office spaces for rent, she killed her engine and failed to notice that there was a person sitting in the sedan next to her. She nearly jumped out of her skin when he spoke.

"You're late," Jim said as he crawled from his BMW. "Good news is it isn't raining." He looked up at the sky as if to be sure.

"Jim, hi." Johnnie tried to act casual, but she was frazzled and surprised.

He looked at her and smiled a knowing smile. "You forgot didn't you?"

She held out her hands. "Sorry."

He joined her by the glass door. "Don't worry about it. You always were a bit absent-minded."

"Afraid so," she said, unlocking the door and allowing him to enter first. The smell of paint and turpentine and dry wall dust assaulted them, and Johnnie at once relaxed. Jim headed straight back to the large room with the big windows where she worked. He was on a mission and a longtime friend. She'd let him move in if he asked.

She grabbed a chilled bottle of iced tea from her old fridge. She cracked it open and found him in front of her latest, arms crossed, a pleased look on his face.

"You were right. She's a stunner." His jaw flexed just as it did every time he examined her work. His mind was jumping with possibilities. He took a step back, eyes still trained on the painting. "The others?"

Johnnie crossed to the far wall and uncovered the other three. Jim moved to help her and they placed them all on easels. He crossed his arms again and stood in silence.

"You know I have a Brazilian collector who would kill for these."

Johnnie sank onto a nearby stool. "They aren't for sale."

Jim paid her no mind and kept examining the paintings. "He would want them all and any more if you painted her again. He has a thing for dark haired beauties. An obsession of sorts."

"She doesn't know these exist."

"So tell her. Show her."

"Say I do. I doubt she would want some strange man drooling over her every day."

He laughed. "A woman that looks like that. She's heard it all before."

"I can't." She moved away and sipped her tea.

Jim finally turned away from the paintings. "It's personal?"

Johnnie nodded.

"Are you in love with her?"

She gave him a look, letting him know he'd gone too far.

He let it go. "Do you have anything else?"

"Nothing new. Just what's against the wall there."

He moved along the wall, lifting canvas after canvas. "I'm having my spring show soon. And as always, I want you in it." He lowered a canvas and met her gaze. "Those would be perfect."

"I can't."

"Tell me you'll think about it."

She sighed.

"Johnnie, I know you need the money."

"Some things are more valuable than money."

He stared at her. "You are in love with her."

Johnnie heated. "Jim, I'm just simply not going to sell this woman's image without her knowing."

"So tell her! My God, she'll be flattered. Who wouldn't?"

Johnnie shook her head. "It's not that simple."

"Make it simple."

He retrieved his phone and silenced a call, then walked toward her. "Johnnie, these are good. Very different for you. You're popular right now among collectors. You have to take advantage now."

She knew he was right. But so was she.

He lightly held her elbow and kissed her cheek. "I have to go. I'll call you soon."

Jim had been very good to her. He'd plucked her out of oblivion, showing her work in his gallery, which in turn got her off the street. He was always eager to see her work, eager to keep her secure in her lifestyle. Money meant more to him than it did to her, but she accepted him for who he was. And he her.

She remained sitting on the stool as he left. She studied the paintings and finished her tea. When her back ached from sitting, she stood and turned. The woman was standing behind her, face slack with shock and surprise.

CHAPTER NINETEEN

Johnnie jerked and covered her heart with her hand.
"I'm sorry. I didn't know anyone was here." She began to panic; the woman's eyes were trained on the paintings.

"I'm a bit early," she said softly.

Johnnie moved quickly and began covering the paintings.

"No, don't."

Johnnie stopped. The woman came closer. "Let me see."

Johnnie removed the covers. The woman reached out as if to touch her own image, but her fingers hovered above the paint.

"This is what you've been painting," she said.

Johnnie burned. "Yes."

"And this is what you didn't want to tell me."

Johnnie closed her eyes. "Yes."

The woman moved from image to image, thoroughly examining each one. She was silent and her green eyes were large and liquid. Johnnie noted her shuddering breath, the mark of heat along her cheekbones. She was moved. And the realization sent Johnnie's heart rate into overdrive.

Finally, the woman spoke. "We need to leave now. We need to go somewhere with—people."

"You're not upset are you?"

The woman wouldn't look at her. "Can you drive? I need to sit."

Johnnie quickly covered the canvases and led the way out of the studio. She locked the door behind them and opened her truck door for the woman. They rode in silence, and Johnnie didn't pry. It was obvious the woman was dealing with emotions, sorting her thoughts.

Johnnie wanted to apologize, to offer to give her the paintings, to promise to never paint another one of her image. But she knew it wasn't the time. The woman was fragile now, vulnerable, and she'd never seen her like this. She didn't want to add to her burden in any way.

"There's a small café up ahead," she said. "Pull in there."

Johnnie found the café and pulled in to park. They sat in the cab for a moment before the woman finally opened the door. She looked a bit pale, and Johnnie walked with her inside and sat opposite her in a back booth.

She ordered coffee with cream, no sugar. Johnnie had another iced tea.

When the woman finally looked at her, she breathed deeply and tried to smile. Her confident pose was trying to return, but Johnnie could tell it wasn't easy for her.

"The paintings are beautiful," she said, though her voice wasn't strong. "I'm not upset in any way. In fact, I'm moved. Moved beyond words."

Johnnie wasn't sure what to say. "Would you like to have them?"

She laughed and it reached her eyes. Johnnie was mesmerized.

"Absolutely not. What on earth would I do with them?"

Johnnie shrugged. "Give them to someone special. I'm sure they would love them."

The woman lowered her eyes and sipped her coffee nervously. Johnnie reached for her hand but stopped herself.

"I'm sorry, I didn't—"

"You're fine." She stared out the window. "I think it best if we talk here today."

Johnnie searched her face. She could sense her emotion, her growing feelings. The paintings had touched her deeply. Just as they had Johnnie.

"I understand. I couldn't do what you do and not—have feelings."

"Actually, it's quite easy. You just surprised me is all. I've never had a client paint me before." She looked at her. "And I couldn't do what you do—feeling everything."

Johnnie laughed and then grew serious. "Yeah, well I don't wish it on anyone."

"And I don't wish what I'm able to do on you. It would change who you are. Harden you. And that would be a tragedy."

Johnnie sipped her tea. "So what now?"

"We do your favorite thing. We talk."

Johnnie smiled. "I think you seeing those paintings exposed me enough for one day."

The woman blushed, and Johnnie wanted to touch her skin and feel its heat. But she didn't dare, for there was something between them now. Something fierce and alive and needful. If that door was opened, there would be no stopping them.

"Oh no, we're just getting started." The coy smile was back. Johnnie returned it.

CHAPTER TWENTY

Johnnie fingered the sweat on her glass. Johnnie knew she had felt something. But saying so would only cause more angst between them, something Johnnie knew they were both trying to downplay. "All I need to do is see your face. Hear your voice and I'm good."

The woman swallowed, and she fingered her necklace, a gesture Johnnie was beginning to recognize as nerves.

"I don't think I should charge you anymore."

"But it's still your time. You're still helping me. So, yes I'm paying you."

"Then we need to get you working."

"I am. And according to my friend Jim, those paintings of you could be wildly popular."

"I'm not sure what to say."

"Or how to feel?" Johnnie smiled. "Don't worry. I told him no way."

She blinked. "Why?"

"Because they are private, personal. And they are of you. Wouldn't it make you uncomfortable?"

She stirred her coffee. "Johnnie, when I was younger, I modeled."

"Oh."

"So no, I don't mind. We are here for your success after all."

Johnnie sat back against the booth. The paintings meant so much to her. Could she ever let them go?

"You seem disappointed."

"No, I'm just...I don't know. I feel possessive of them."

The woman pegged her with her eyes. She read into the words, knew what they meant, though she didn't say it.

"Do what's best for you."

"I'm not used to doing that." She sighed and looked away.

"It's time to start."

"It makes me feel selfish. Like I'm not doing the right thing."

"Really?" She sipped her coffee, looking intrigued.

"Care to tell me why?"

Johnnie squirmed a little.

"You're uncomfortable."

Johnnie nodded. "I don't like bringing up the past. I do better by just going forward."

"That's understandable. So how can I help you do that? What can I do to help make your future better?"

Johnnie half grinned. "Right, because we both know you can't keep arousing me forever."

She glanced out the window, thinking that possibility wouldn't be half bad, but then she pushed it from her mind.

"At some point in your life you learned it was safer for you to agree with people, to please them. And it sounds like you still do it to some degree."

Johnnie shrugged. "You're right."

"You live alone?"

"Yes."

"Do you get out much?"

Johnnie shifted and pushed the empty iced tea glass away. When she found nothing to distract her hands, she played with her straw wrapper.

"I like to stay home."

The woman sipped her coffee. She gave her a few moments before pressing her. "Why?"

"It's just what I prefer."

"To be alone?"

"To be safe."

The woman paused, holding her mug near her lips. She lowered it carefully instead of taking another sip.

"Do you have people over to your home? Friends?"

Johnnie wasn't able to hold her eyes. She was becoming embarrassed. She knew her life wasn't typical. She knew people didn't understand.

"I have one good friend who comes over."

"And do you go out with friends anywhere?"

Johnnie sighed in frustration. "Sometimes."

"Do you have fun when you do that?"

"Not really."

"Because you don't feel safe?"

Johnnie couldn't handle her concerned look. She didn't want her to know these things. She already knew too much.

"Johnnie?"

"I don't want to talk about this."

She reached across the table to hold her hand but stopped. Johnnie somehow felt it anyway, so warm, so caring, and her eyes were full of care and concern. Johnnie didn't want that. She couldn't count on people to care. They always said they did, but they didn't, not when it counted.

"Why does it make you uncomfortable? Do you not feel safe right now?"

Johnnie swallowed against a burning throat. "I don't want you to know these things. I don't want anyone to know."

The woman seemed to think for a moment. "You're afraid of what I might think. That maybe I will reject you."

Johnnie's heart pounded with fight or flight. She couldn't run because the woman needed a ride. No, she'd have to sit and take it.

"Johnnie, I'm not going to hurt you. Or think any less of you."

"You can't possibly know that."

"It would take trust."

Johnnie waved off the waitress, no longer thirsty. The woman did the same with her coffee.

"That is something I do not have," Johnnie said.

"Oh, but you do. You're already trusting me. Little by little."

Johnnie reached back for her wallet and set a few bills on the table. The woman dug in her purse and did the same. Johnnie slid from the booth and politely waited for the woman to walk in front of her. She was dressed more casually today. Tan linen pants and flowy blue linen shirt. She looked like she belonged on an island, holding hands with a lover as the ocean lapped at her feet.

Johnnie wished for an instant she could be that lover, but thinking such things was only torture.

They climbed into the truck and rode in silence. The woman looked out the window and pressed her dark hair behind her ear. Johnnie noted the small diamond stud and another smaller one nestled in her upper ear. The image stirred her just as nearly everything with the woman did.

"This is a nice truck," she eventually said, looking over at Johnnie. Her eyes settled on her hands.

"Thanks."

"I've been thinking about getting one."

Johnnie laughed. "Really?"

"Something funny about that?"

Johnnie pressed her mouth closed. "No, nothing at all."

"A woman like me can have a truck."

"You're absolutely right."

She laughed. "You're stereotyping me."

"Nope, not at all."

They pulled back into the office complex, and Johnnie parked next to the woman's black Audi.

"I don't think Audi makes a truck," Johnnie said, sliding out of the truck with a smile.

The woman rounded the truck. "Very funny."

Johnnie sank her hands into her pockets as they stood near the front entrance.

"Aren't you going to invite me in?"

Johnnie must've looked surprised because the woman smiled.

Flustered, Johnnie unlocked the door and held it for her. Then she followed her inside and offered her a drink, which she declined. Instead, she set her purse on the counter and eased onto a stool.

"Johnnie?"

Johnnie turned from the easels. "Yes."

"I want you to be able to trust me."

Johnnie heated at the look the woman was giving her. She began slowly unbuttoning her shirt.

"What are you doing?"

"I'm sharing myself with you. I want you to touch me."

"What?" Johnnie looked away, heartbeat in her throat.

"Can you paint right now?"

Johnnie breathed deeply. "I don't know."

"I want you to. I want you to touch me by painting me."

She stopped with the buttons and reached up and unhooked her lacy bra and draped it over her purse. Then she opened the shirt just wide enough to show the weight of her breasts without showing her nipples.

Her necklace reflected in the incoming stream of sunlight. Johnnie forced herself to breathe. She couldn't take her eyes off her. Her skin was smooth, like cream, save for a beauty mark near her navel.

"Come here," she said, voice strong.

Johnnie walked slowly toward her, feeling like she was going to float right up off the floor. She closed her eyes, wondering if she would actually reach her.

CHAPTER TWENTY-ONE

Elaine reached out and took her hand. Johnnie opened her eyes, and Elaine gently pulled her closer. She placed Johnnie's hand on her heart and inhaled sharply at Johnnie's obvious response.

"I have a broken heart," Elaine said, trying desperately to keep her voice calm. "They tell me it's fixed, but it doesn't feel like it."

Johnnie stared deeply into her eyes. "It hurts."

"More than you know."

"I can feel it," Johnnie whispered. She sucked in a shaky breath and pulled her hand away. "I'm sorry you hurt like that."

Elaine grabbed her hand again. "Johnnie, can you...sense my feelings?"

Johnnie swallowed, pulled her hand away. "Don't ask me what I can't explain to you."

Elaine covered her heart, still able to feel Johnnie's touch. She watched her walk back to the easels. She wasn't sure what had just happened, but she'd never had somebody look at her with such understanding, such empathy. So much so that she felt like crying with relief.

"Is this a bad idea?" she asked, tugging her shirt closed.

Johnnie moved a canvas off an easel, turned it, placed a new canvas on it, and began opening paint and assorting brushes.

"I've made you uncomfortable again," Johnnie said, taking a pencil and scratching on the canvas. She paused. "Do you not want to do this now?"

Elaine shook her head. "No, I'm fine. I'm just making sure you are."

Johnnie studied her body and continued drawing. "I understand things better now."

Elaine straightened her back and opened her shirt again. She hadn't modeled for someone since college. And as she watched Johnnie work, she felt her skin heat. She liked watching her face, the concentration, the clench of her jaw. Elaine closed her eyes and moved her fingertips up and down her chest, giving herself goose-flesh. Johnnie didn't complain, didn't ask her to stop.

"Do you want me to take off my shirt?" she said softly, feeling like she had when she'd touched Kyle's bare skin, imagining it was Johnnie. Like there was a very fine line stopping her from jumping in headfirst, and she didn't give a flying fuck if the line snapped or not.

Johnnie paused, looked at her closely. "No."

Elaine softened, disappointed. Johnnie was still showing control.

"Pull your shirt open just a bit more."

Elaine did, but Johnnie shook her head and approached. She reached out and moved the shirt deftly with her thumbs to where just a peek of her dark nipples showed. Elaine held her breath. Johnnie held her gaze, and with the tip of her finger, she lightly traced a line down her chest.

"This..." she said, "is beautiful."

Elaine held her hand and didn't want to let it go. "Tell me, Johnnie. Tell me what hurts you so."

Johnnie looked down at their hands. "Let me paint you," she said. "Let me capture this beauty."

"You're more sensitive than I'm aware of aren't you?"

Johnnie met her gaze. "Yes."

Elaine released her hand. She watched her return to the painting. Watched the muscles move in her forearm as she painted.

"I want you to sell this painting," she said. "Make some money."

Johnnie kept working, never breaking focus. "No. This one is special."

"What makes it special?"

Johnnie paused. "It's you showing me you."

Elaine tried to regain her composure. "Sell the others then."

"I might," Johnnie said, once again working. "But there is one in that series I will not let go of."

"Which one is that?"

Johnnie seemed to hesitate, but then answered. "The first one I painted. The one of you sitting on the couch."

"In the black skirt?"

"Yes."

Elaine had the urge to finger her necklace. "The one where I'm looking at you with desire."

Johnnie stopped. Elaine saw her flush. "Yes."

Elaine smiled. Johnnie was talking to her, admitting things that were difficult to admit to someone she knew so little. Could she admit these things to her? No. She couldn't even admit her own feelings to herself. Johnnie was open and brave in ways she couldn't possibly understand.

"Thank you for talking to me. I know you don't trust."

"I don't. That hasn't changed."

"What has?"

Johnnie sprayed the painting with a squirt bottle. Elaine assumed it was to keep it moist.

"You showed me a little of you. And I know doing that is also hard for you. We are very much alike that way."

Elaine stared into the dust motes dancing in the sunlight. "I think you're right."

"Unfortunately, I almost always am."

Elaine decided to change the subject. "Tell me about your friend. The one you let come over."

Johnnie grinned and gave a little laugh. "Eddie? He's a big pain in my ass."

"Eddie. How is he a pain?"

"He mothers me. Nags me."

"Do you need mothering?"

"He would say yes."

"What would you say?"

"No."

"He worries about you?"

Johnnie mixed some colors together. "Endlessly."

"Why?"

She shrugged. "He says I don't eat enough, or I eat too much. I don't get out enough. I don't date. I'm a recluse. On and on and on."

Elaine smiled. "Sounds like he cares."

"He drives me nuts."

"Do you take care of yourself, Johnnie?"

Johnnie paused again. Her facial expression changed. "I do fine, thanks."

"But if I were to ask Eddie…"

"He'd disagree with me."

"So how does he help? Does he have solutions?"

Johnnie smiled. "He gave me the number to your practice."

Elaine straightened. "Really?"

"Yep."

"And we were able to help him?"

"Oh yeah. He went on and on about a guy named Pedro. Thought he would never shut up about him."

Elaine laughed a little. "Pedro. Yes, he's quite popular."

"What about you?" Johnnie asked. "Are you popular?"

"I do all right."

"Men?"

"Mm, mostly."

"You prefer them to women?"

Elaine shifted a little. "Professionally, yes."

"Personally?"

Elaine gave her a crooked grin. "Wouldn't you like to know."

"What makes you think I don't know already?"

Johnnie stood, worked harder, more focused.

"How are you doing? Need to move around some?"

"I'm fine. I just don't like being under your microscope."

Johnnie smiled. "Sucks doesn't it?"

"Yes."

"Maybe you'll have mercy on me now."

"Not a chance."

Johnnie laughed. "Okay, now I need you to look at me like—"

"I want you?"

Johnnie flushed. "Like I'm the one who can mend your heart."

Elaine grew silent. She forgot to breathe. "I'm not sure I can."

"Pretend."

"I can't."

"Think about why your heart hurts and what would make it feel better."

Elaine was quiet again. A vision of Barb came, standing right next to Johnnie. Her eyes teared, and she begged her to be real. To return. To walk up to her and touch her. To take her in her arms and take her home. To never leave their safe haven again. To never cry, never hurt. Never curl into a ball in pain. Please, Barb, walk to me.

She blinked and Barb was gone. Johnnie was there, painting her, stroking her face with her brush, looking at her with such love and understanding. Reaching out to her, touching her heart and mind.

Should she break the invisible link between them? Or should she let it remain and flow with electricity, sharing each other, understanding, feeling?

A tear slipped down her cheek. Johnnie saw, but she didn't stop. She kept painting, gently wiping the tear away with a caring, soulful look. She was holding her now, suspended. Above everything that was dangerous. Johnnie wouldn't let her fall.

When Johnnie finally stopped, Elaine was lost in her own world. Johnnie was standing before her. Touching her face gently. "We're done."

Elaine blinked back tears and tugged her shirt closed. Johnnie continued stroking her face. "Are you okay?"

Elaine nodded. She held Johnnie's wrist, stilling it. She couldn't let the touching continue or she'd get lost in her. She stood and buttoned her shirt.

"Would you like to see?" Johnnie asked.

Elaine wiped her cheek, found it dry, and felt relieved. "Not right now."

Johnnie watched concerned as Elaine reached for her purse and slung it over her shoulder. When she approached, Elaine fought closing her eyes and kissing her.

"You're uh, shirt is buttoned crooked." She concentrated on fixing the buttons. Elaine breathed rapidly. "You're not okay," Johnnie said.

Elaine pushed back her hair. "I will be fine."

Johnnie looked into her eyes. "That's my favorite saying."

Elaine smiled. "Then you know it well."

"Yes."

Elaine squeezed her hand. "I need to go." Somehow hours had passed. How had she not noticed?

Johnnie stepped back. "I know."

"Thank you," Elaine said as she walked away.

"For what?"

"For making me feel."

CHAPTER TWENTY-TWO

Johnnie smiled at Jolene across the small, worn table. They were eating hot noodles, ramen noodles. For the first time, they weren't eating them dry, choking them down with tepid water. Here in the tiny studio motel room, they had a microwave and running water. Warmth from the chill of the desert night. Jolene smiled back and slurped in a large mouthful of food. Her face was wrinkled and wind worn. Johnnie had bought her a jar of Vaseline, which they both applied to their hands and faces to help soothe the sting of the dry skin.

"They have a laundry room," Johnnie said between bites.

"No," Jolene said. "I will wash them in the sink."

Johnnie nodded. All that they owned sat in a pile near the door. They guarded it like dogs because people were more than happy to walk off with their stuff. It was probably why Jolene didn't want to use the public laundry.

"We have two nights," Johnnie said. "We can get some good sleep."

"Mm, that will be good."

Sleep on the streets was never peaceful unless you were drunk. Johnnie and Jolene took turns keeping watch most nights. Even when they slept behind the beauty salon between the building and the chain link fence. It was quiet, no one bothered them, but still, they never felt totally safe.

Johnnie finished her noodles, placed the plastic bowl in the sink, and stretched. She lifted her Buck knife from the waist of her pants and placed it on the table. Jolene had one too, and they'd had to show them more than once to keep bad men at bay.

"You going to shower now?" Jolene asked.

"Yes."

Johnnie walked to the bed and sat to peel off her boots. Then she headed to the bathroom. The image in the mirror shocked her, though she knew it would be bad. Her face was chapped and hollow, eyes sunken. Her hair was long and stringy, and she knew she couldn't run her fingers through it. She had long ago stopped worrying about looking normal. When you had no money, no shelter, it grew tiring to care. And no matter how many times you tried, brushing your hair, brushing your teeth, wearing deodorant, people always knew. Homelessness had a stench one couldn't hide. And people were like sharks; they picked up on it from great distances and treated you with disdain.

Johnnie took off her two sweatshirts and the T-shirt below. Her bra was no longer white, and it was basically threadbare and useless. But she wore it for warmth. She fingered her bony ribs and her sunken abdomen. She pulled her loose fitting pants down over her hips and kicked them away. When she went for her socks, she paused. Small black specks covered them. And they moved.

She tore them off and yanked open the bathroom door.

"Jolene."

"Yeah."

"We've got fleas."

"Okay."

"Goddamn it." Johnnie hugged herself, already itching. She walked to the bed and pulled back the covers. The sheets were clean. She checked the mattress. It looked okay.

"I think they're just in the carpet."

"I will call," Jolene said, rising to deposit her bowl in the sink.

Johnnie returned to the bathroom and stepped into the hot shower. She scrubbed and scrubbed, washed and rewashed her hair. Then she saturated it with cheap conditioner. It was the only way she'd get a brush through it. Jolene knocked on the door as she rinsed.

"They brought a bug bomb."

"Great." She turned off the shower and dried herself. She pulled a brush through her tangled hair. She reentered the bedroom and found that Jolene had laid out an outfit for her. She was sitting on the bed and stroking her long braid which hung down her shoulder.

"We have to leave the room for an hour while the bomb works."

Johnnie dressed. She was frustrated. "Can't they give us a different room?"

"They are full."

Johnnie put on her boots, and she and Jolene set off the bug bomb. They sat outside their door and waited, too afraid to leave their stuff. Dusk had fallen, and the motel was hopping. Prostitutes walked by, some leading johns by the hand. Kids screamed as they ran and played, raising hell without supervision. Two cop cars pulled in, lights on. The two officers emerged and leaned against the cruiser to talk.

"You thirsty?" Johnnie asked.

"Sure."

Johnnie rose and headed for the stairs. As she walked down, she noticed a man slumped over near the bottom. When she reached him she said, "Excuse me." But he didn't budge. She said it again and got no response. She stepped over him carefully and bent to examine him. He held his empty wallet open in one hand with a single family picture inside. She pushed back on his shoulder to view his face. His eyes were open but unfocused. His mouth was slack.

She left him, unsure what was wrong and what she could do to help. She made her way to the soda machine and bought two Cokes. When she returned to the stairs, the man was weeping uncontrollably. He didn't seem to mind when she bumped him to get by.

She returned to Jolene and they sat and watched darkness bleed in completely. More prostitutes brought more johns. Then the girls would stand at the rail and smoke, looking down on the parking lot. One walked up to them and asked them if they wanted any pills. Said she'd give them a good deal.

Johnnie thanked her but said no. She returned to her friends and they laughed and carried on, hollering at potential clients down in the parking lot. When Johnnie and Jolene returned to their room, it smelled like chemicals and stale cigarette smoke. Johnnie took off her shoes and walked the carpet in her socks. Numerous fleas hopped on.

"Didn't work," she said.

Jolene shook her head.

They would have to keep everything on the bed and on the table. Jolene went to shower, and Johnnie hung things in the closet and organized as best she could. Then she walked to the couch and placed a sock on her hand to run it across the cushions. No fleas.

Relieved, she sat and closed her eyes. Jolene emerged dressed in clean clothes and joined her. They didn't bother with the television. They got enough of people and noise on the street. They preferred peace. But peace was not forthcoming. Beyond the thin walls, people shouted and laughed and cussed and banged things. Sirens wailed. Soon helicopters circled overhead. Johnnie stared at the flimsy lock on the door.

For forty hard-earned dollars, she thought they could feel safe for one night, maybe two. But it wasn't meant to be.

Jolene turned on the television, hoping to drown it out. They watched PBS and Everybody Loves Raymond. *They fell asleep leaning into each other with Johnnie's knife in her lap. Around midnight, there was loud shouting and spotlights shining from helicopters, police calling out orders. Johnnie jerked when someone tried to barrel their way into their room. She stood and unsheathed her knife, heart pounding. They tried three times, physically moving the door. Then she heard them run and soon after more shouts and footsteps.*

She remained standing, with her knife poised. She pushed back on the door and braced it with a kitchen chair. Jolene sat watching her.

"You won't sleep tonight," she said.

Johnnie shook her head. "You go ahead."

"You should ask those girls for Xanax. It helps you."

Johnnie stared out the window. "No, I need to be ready for anything."

"In the morning, then," Jolene said. "You will get Xanax and sleep while I keep watch."

Johnnie knew better than to argue with her. She simply nodded.

Jolene went to bed and Johnnie returned to the couch. She watched the door and listened keenly. She held the knife tightly. Would she ever feel safe?

As she stared at the drone of the television, she knew the answer was most likely no.

CHAPTER TWENTY-THREE

Johnnie stared into the pint of Guinness and inhaled. It smelled miraculous, and she took a small sip and thoroughly enjoyed it. This was her first and she decided it would be her only. She was in her favorite back booth, back in her hovel, sketch pad in hand. But for the first time in weeks, she wasn't worried about painting. She felt relaxed though truly awake. Memories of the past had been haunting her dreams and her waking thoughts. She wasn't sure why, but she figured it had something to do with the woman and her probing questions and deep, penetrating looks. Johnnie had let her in a little, and the realization didn't terrify her as she'd suspected it would.

Still though, she needed to be careful. Her relationship with Gail was a harsh reminder of how people could turn. Somehow though, after feeling the loss she'd felt when she'd touched the woman's chest, she didn't think the woman would act anything like Gail. But how could she be sure? She'd read Gail wrong, so who's to say she could read anyone anymore? Maybe her family was right; maybe it was all in her head.

"Ah, Johnnie, I see you're enjoying your usual," Sean said with his thick brogue. He gave her a basket of fresh bread. "Eat it and don't argue. You could use a little fattening of the arse if you ask me."

"Thanks." She took a bite and tried not to groan at how good it was. Sean grinned and wiped his hands on his bar towel.

"So you've been painting?"

"Quite a bit actually."

"Well, that's grand. Are you feeling better then?"

"A bit." She motioned at the empty seat across from her. "Want to join me?"

"Nah, I can't. But there's someone who wants to." He looked over his shoulder. "Name's Ian. Fresh off the boat. He's a good friend of mine and he's one hell of a painter."

"Really?"

Sean turned again and gave a shout. "Ian, get your sorry arse over here and meet me friend."

A small man at the bar fumbled a bit as he slid off his stool and turned toward them. For a second, Johnnie thought he was drunk. But when she saw the cane, she realized he was blind.

He walked up and felt for Sean, who took his arm and guided him to the booth.

"Is this the lovely lady?" he asked, smiling.

"'Tis. Her name's Johnnie.'

"Johnnie? Well, that's quite a name."

He removed his pageboy hat and patted down his gray hair. He reached across the table.

"Can I feel ya? So I know who I'm talking to."

Johnnie let him have her hands. His eyes, which he didn't cover with sunglasses, were dark blue and unfocused. He had purple scarring around them from some sort of accident. But when he held her, she could feel him seeing her, physical body and all.

"Aye," he said. "Sean was right about you. You've got the feelers on you."

"Sorry?"

He smiled again and squeezed her hands. "Probably why you're hiding out in this sorry old pub. Can't handle being around people."

Johnnie tried to pull her hands away, but he wouldn't let her.

"Don't fright. I'm just feeling ya. Feel me back, you'll see."

Johnnie stared into his face and breathed deeply. She felt calm, warmth, peace. He smiled and released her hands.

"There now."

Johnnie pushed him the basket of bread. "Hungry?"

"Not for food, love. No, thank you."

"What are you hungry for?"

"Same thing you are."

"Sorry?"

He patted the table and leaned forward. "Woman."

Johnnie stared at him a moment and then laughed. It seemed to amuse him.

"I'm hoping a nice one will walk in here in a minute. Take me home and have her way with me."

Johnnie sipped her beer. "I hear ya."

"Why aren't you with yours?" he asked.

"Mine? I don't have one."

"No? Hm, must've read you wrong. I coulda sworn your heart was taken."

Johnnie blushed, and she was glad he couldn't see. "No, I'm single."

He grabbed her hand. "Does your heart know?"

Johnnie stammered for words. He released her and leaned back.

"Never you mind. You'll go after her when the time is right."

Johnnie thought about arguing, but she knew it was useless. He could see her the way she felt others.

"You paint her though, don't ya? Beautiful lass like that."

Johnnie looked over to the bar where Sean shrugged and grinned.

"I have been, yes."

"I had a girl I would paint. Long time ago. Before I lost me eyes. Aye, she was a looker. I didn't know what was better. Painting her or touching her."

"I know what you mean."

"I lost my chance with mine. Don't lose your chance." He slapped the table. "Sean tells me you've done quite well for yourself. With your art."

"Somewhat, yes. I've had some luck with collectors."

"Your heart belongs to a beautiful woman, you're making money painting, tell me why the hell are you sitting in here all alone?"

"I like quiet." She squirmed a little in her seat and fingered the corner of her sketch pad.

"Don't like it too much. Life goes like that." He snapped his fingers. "And let me tell ya, when you get to being my age, you wish like hell you could go back and say fuck 'em, fuck 'em all."

"What do you mean?"

"You can't hide away, Johnnie, just because you can feel. You've got to live. Fuck people. Fuck 'em all." He gripped his cane tightly and placed his fist on the table. "Do ya think I give a fiddler's fart what people think of me? Look at me. I know I look crazy. I know I am crazy. And you know what? I'm happy. I paint what I want, say what I feel, and take step after step without knowing what's ahead. You need to do the same."

Johnnie stared into the grooves on his face. Stared into the stormy ocean of his eyes.

"Fuck 'em," she said softly.

"That's a way. Fuck 'em. Even when you're feeling them and they aren't good inside, don't let it get to ya. Just walk away. You don't owe them an excuse. You don't owe them anything."

"What if they are good?"

He smiled. "Then you've got to hang on tight and live and feel with them. Don't run. Don't hide away. Pain has a way of finding ya, no matter where you live."

"Who are you?" Johnnie asked. She squeezed her beer glass, trying to control her heart rate. Looking at this stranger, this strange powerful man, she felt like she was seeing into her future.

"A kindred spirit."

Johnnie looked around. Sean was busy washing glasses, and the two other patrons were staring into their beers.

"Did someone send you?" Did he know the woman? Was this part of her therapy?

He laughed. "Like who? An Irish fairy?"

"No, I'm serious. The stuff you're saying, it's just so relevant to my life lately."

"Life has a way of giving you what you need when you need it. You just have to know how to see it." He pointed to his eyes. "Not here." He covered his heart. "But here."

Johnnie looked at him for a long time. She could feel his goodness radiate outward toward her. She allowed their connection to mix, like a warm mist. She wished she'd met him years ago.

"Where are you staying?" Johnnie asked.

"With Sean for now. But I just bought me self a little house."

"You're staying here in Phoenix?"

"Aye, I need to dry out. And I want a tan. Get me a tan lady." He smiled.

"Can I see you again? Maybe see some of your art?"

"Of course. And you'll tell me all about yours?"

"Yes."

"We can paint together."

Johnnie touched his hand. "I'd like that."

She opened her sketch pad and wrote down her number. "Give this to Sean. Call me."

She rose, glanced at her watch, and grabbed her sketch pad. She had to meet Eddie soon and she couldn't be late.

"Will do, love."

She touched his shoulder. "Good-bye,"

"Good-bye," he said, smiling after her.

CHAPTER TWENTY-FOUR

I hope you don't mind," Michael said as he handed Elaine a glass of merlot. "But I invited another guest for dinner."

She was ready to take a sip but paused. "You're kidding."

He smiled and looked away quickly. "Just a friend of Donovan's. Don't worry. She's got it all. Brains, looks, heart."

"Michael, I don't need this tonight. I thought it was just dinner." She rubbed her temple and crossed her legs. She'd kicked off her heels at the door, thankful for a relaxing evening. Now she had to rethink things.

"She's great, honest."

"Your refusal to respect my wishes about dating is really starting to get to me." She'd told him over and over, she wasn't going to date. He knew why.

He rounded the kitchen counter and continued chopping a block of cheese. He had on his trademark apron which said *World's Hottest Husband*. It usually made Elaine smirk, but at the moment, she was in no mood.

"It's not a date," he said lightly.

"No, it's worse. It's a blind date."

"No, there are no expectations. None whatsoever."

"Then why tell me? Why tell me she has it all, as you say?"

He shrugged. "Just thought you might still have a heart in that chest of yours."

"Funny."

He sighed. "I know you won't date, Elaine. And I know things are getting somewhat serious with your client. I'm just offering a bit of a distraction is all."

"I can get my own distractions."

He popped a bit of cheese in his mouth. "You're still having your one-night stands?"

She sipped her wine, refusing to answer. He knew more than she thought. He was always so damned perceptive. She couldn't keep anything from him.

"That's a dangerous game," he said. "Say you piss off the wrong woman, or sleep with one who has a jealous lover. Or worse. You get a stalker. I know how you feel about those."

"I can take care of myself."

He finished with the cheese and scraped the small squares onto a plate where he proceeded to apply toothpicks to each one. He hummed to Michael Buble, and Elaine tried to breathe deep and relax. The smell of dinner filled the kitchen and living room. Elaine hadn't had a good home cooked meal in ages. She lived off of apples and almond butter or microwave Lean Cuisines. She enjoyed cooking but not for herself. There just wasn't any joy in cooking alone. She closed her eyes, recalling family dinners with Barb and Michael and Donovan. They'd drink two bottles of wine, talk, laugh, dance. She could almost feel her. Open her eyes and see her all snuggled in on the couch, feet tucked up beneath her. She'd be holding her glass of wine, teasing Michael about his choice in music. Barb was a classic rock woman, and she'd never been afraid to share that fact and even get up and put some on.

"You still feeling tired?" Michael asked, bringing her back to the present.

"I have a headache. I think maybe I should go."

He set down his wine as a serious look came over his face. "Absolutely not. I'm not letting you run away."

"I'm not running away, Michael. I'm going home."

He walked up to her, squatted, and held her hand. "It's just a dinner."

"Right, like a dinner we used to have with Barb."

"Oh, God, no honey. This isn't like that. No one is trying to replace Barb. No one can replace Barb."

"Then what is this? I mean you're bringing a woman here?"

He flushed. "God, I can be so stupid sometimes. Honestly, I didn't try to be so insensitive. I just—"

"You just what?" She could feel tears biting her throat.

"I can tell the artist is getting to you. And that you aren't going to end it."

"Maybe I don't want to end it," she whispered.

"You're just going to torture yourself?"

"I can take care of myself."

He stood. "You didn't answer me about your fatigue. You don't look well."

"Thanks."

"Elaine, talk to me."

He settled in on the couch across from her. "How's your health?"

She didn't want to do this. She just wanted to go home. "I'm not sure."

"What does that mean?"

"They are running tests."

His face went pale. "Your heart?"

She sipped her wine.

He read all the words she didn't need to say. She could see his mind working, racing, panicking.

"When?"

"This week."

"Do you want me to go with you?"

"No."

The interior garage door opened, and Michael's husband, Donovan, entered. He smiled, showing off his prominent dimples.

"Hey, look who's here." He knelt and kissed her cheek, then did the same to Michael. He pointed at the wine. "Ya'll read my mind. Honey, will you pour me a glass while I go change?"

"Sure." Michael rose to cross to the kitchen, and Donovan disappeared into the back bedroom of the house.

"So what are the doctors saying?" Michael asked, pouring the wine.

Elaine rubbed her head again. "It doesn't matter."

He balked. "Doesn't matter?"

"I don't want to talk about this right now, Michael."

He grew silent. "I want to know what's going on, Elaine. I'm worried."

"And when I find out, I'll tell you."

Donovan returned to the living room, wearing a Tommy Bahama button-down and khaki shorts. He rubbed his hands together in anticipation before he grabbed his wine.

He turned toward Elaine as he sipped. "Did Michael tell you about my friend?"

Elaine fought rolling her eyes. How could they do this to her? And right now?

"Um, Elaine's not too happy about that," Michael said.

Donovan appeared regretful. "Oh. Well, that's my bad, Elaine. I sort of invited her before I told Michael."

"I think I'm just going to go home. I'm not feeling well."

Donovan spoke. "I don't know if it makes a difference, but she just called and said she couldn't make it."

Elaine felt the tension leave her body. "Thank God."

Michael laughed. "I think it makes a big difference."

Elaine stood and placed her empty glass on the counter. "I was really pissed at you guys."

Michael nodded. "It was stupid. We should've told you."

"Yes, you should've."

"So you could've stayed away."

She laughed. "God, yes."

Michael exchanged a look with Donovan. "Elaine, we just worry about you. It's been five years now."

"I know how long it's been. I know every single moment of every single day."

She choked on her words. Donovan embraced her. She tried to push him away, but he held her tight. She fought him again, but he wouldn't let go. He began whispering to her.

"It's okay, Elaine."

She felt Michael hug her from behind. Comforting her with soft words. The tears biting her throat broke through, and she began to sob. She fell into them, and they held her upright in a loving embrace, letting her completely break down. Soon, they led her to the couch where Michael sat and she leaned into his chest, gripping his shirt. He held her close, tears of his own streaming down his cheeks.

Donovan, too, placed her curled legs on his lap and spoke softly. They didn't ask her questions or expect her to speak. They just held her and allowed her to cry. She thought about everything as she did. How badly the pain still hurt, how Barb had looked the last day, so happy, so full of life. And then in an instant, they were hit and Barb just looked over with glazed eyes and said, "I love you." And finally, Elaine remembered the promise she'd made her as she took her last breath.

"I will never love another."

CHAPTER TWENTY-FIVE

Johnnie was sitting at a crowded table on the patio at Amsterdam's, a popular gay club in downtown Phoenix. The night was mild and a bit breezy. She tried to relax every time it blew against her skin, but the music was as loud as her company, making her uneasy. Eddie was laughing hysterically at something his new beau had said, and the rest of the crew, men and women she'd known for a couple of years, were also laughing and drinking. They'd all been glad to see her, welcoming her with long hugs and firm embraces. It had meant a lot, but she was still uncomfortable with all the energy in the place. The second she'd walked in the door, she could feel person after person. Feel not only their stares, but their emotions, energy. It often bombarded her, nearly slamming her backward. She had to steel herself in order to remain, put up a wall of sorts. Unfortunately, this often came off as her being rude or snobbish. But her friends knew better, and they were all that mattered.

She sipped her beer and eyed her watch. She wondered how long she had to stay before she could take off without Eddie throwing a fit. It was just after ten so she knew she had at least two more hours to go. She looked forward to the walk to the tram in the quiet night. Maybe she would ride beyond her stop and back again, enjoying the soothing ride, the rushing streetlights out the windows.

"Oh. My. God," Eddie said, getting her attention.

"Oh, hell no," her friend Monica said.

Johnnie looked at them and then followed their gaze to the entrance to the patio. Her heart sank to her stomach. She actually felt herself sink down a little in her chair.

"She better not come over here."

Johnnie looked down and played with her beer, praying her ex, Gail, wouldn't see her.

"She will. She has no shame," Eddie said.

Johnnie wanted to escape. She wanted to run, hop the fence and run. But she sat frozen, trapped by the safety net of her friends. She sat and waited for the confrontation and tried to think of what she would say. Should she say hello, ask how she was doing? Or should she do the ignore and look away? Her heart raced in anticipation, and her ears felt full of cotton. She could feel a powerful stare on her, and she knew Gail had spotted her. Eddie said something, but it sounded muffled. Monica gripped her arm and smiled reassuringly. She leaned into her.

"She's gone," she said. "We got you. You can relax."

Johnnie exhaled and looked back to the entrance of the patio. A cluster of laughing men stood where Gail had been.

"Did she—see me?" Johnnie asked. She'd been the one to finally end it with Gail after numerous reconciliations. Since then Gail had tried a few times to win her back. But Johnnie, with the help of her friends, had held firm, which had resulted in Gail getting very angry. She'd gone on the attack and bad-mouthed her to all their friends and acquaintances. Johnnie could still remember the attacks and phone calls from people who'd fallen for her manipulation. People who she'd thought were her friends.

"Don't worry about it," Monica said. "I won't let her near you."

Johnnie drank her beer and tried to smile when Monica leaned in and kissed her cheek. Monica had always been a good friend, and Johnnie got good vibes from her. She was mid-twenties, attractive, educated. She was bold and fearless in ways Johnnie could only ever wish to be. Monica was a cop so Johnnie guessed it came with the job.

"You seeing anyone yet?" she asked. Her dark eyebrows rose with interest. Her equally dark hair was pulled back in a tight ponytail, taming her thick mane. She'd obviously come straight from her shift. Her hair and black watch gave her away. Normally, when they went out Monica wore her hair down and her more expensive watch. Johnnie wondered what she'd dealt with that day. Sometimes, Johnnie knew, Monica dealt with very serious stressful situations. And no matter how hard she tried to shake it and leave it behind, it clung to her like a bad smell.

"No, you know me."

Monica sipped her Seven and Seven. Her toned arm flexed as she handled her glass. "When are you going to give in and give me a chance?"

Johnnie flushed as she stared into her reflective black eyes. Monica was attractive and she had a wonderful sense of humor and purpose. But she was too much for Johnnie. Too intense. Too aggressive. She often said things Johnnie found insensitive or rude. Not to mention the feelings and trauma she brought home with her. Johnnie would have to shield herself from her words and feelings twenty-four seven. The thought alone stressed her out. How could she explain any of that to her?

"It's just not a good idea," Johnnie said. "You'd grow bored."

"I doubt that."

"You would. I paint all day long and then stay home and watch old movies."

Monica studied her closely. "I think I could get you out every now and then."

"I wouldn't want you to even try. You shouldn't have to try. You deserve someone who's more like you."

"A cop?" Monica laughed. "No, thanks. I would like someone who doesn't have to deal with the shit I do. Someone calm, caring, understanding. Someone like you."

Johnnie warmed a little. "Thanks, I think."

Monica tipped her glass to her. "Can we give it a try? One date?"

Johnnie fought shifting in her seat. Monica touched her arm lightly. She seemed to sense her discomfort.

"You know what? Don't even worry about it. I don't want to pressure you. I would never want to make you uncomfortable, and I don't want you to say yes unless you mean it. A pity date I do not need."

Johnnie met her gaze. She was being sincere. "You're pretty caring aren't you?" Johnnie asked.

"You seem surprised." She looked away. "It's the job, I know. Sometimes the attitude is hard to shake when you're off duty."

"I can imagine."

"Some things just get to you no matter how hard you try to block them out or forget."

"I can sense it sometimes," Johnnie said softly.

Monica stared down at her glass. "I thought you might."

"You're very strong," Johnnie said, meaning it.

Monica scoffed. "It's all in the attitude. Most of the time I'm scared shitless."

"That's a good thing. If you weren't scared or worried in those situations, it would probably be even more dangerous."

Monica smiled. "Probably."

"Do you sleep okay?"

Her face clouded. She took several deep sips of her drink.

Johnnie knew she'd hit a nerve. "You don't have to say."

"No, it's fine. I'm just not used to someone being so intuitive. I'm not used to someone seeing me deeply."

"I know the feeling," Johnnie said, sipping her own drink.

Monica laughed. "Then you know how weird it feels."

Johnnie nodded. "Yes."

"Would you always be like this…if we dated I mean?"

Johnnie shrugged. "Probably. It's just who I am."

Monica seemed to think for a moment. "It would be interesting," she said. "Dating you."

Johnnie laughed. "Somehow I know I shouldn't take that as a compliment."

Monica spilled some of her drink in laughter as she tried to sip. "It was, crazy. Totally a compliment."

Johnnie sat back and breathed deeply. The breeze caused her hair to tickle her forehead. The sky was only dark enough to show a handful of stars. People were sitting and chatting, enjoying the evening. Two men were kissing passionately. Eddie was tickling his guy, causing hysterics at their table. Whether she wanted to admit it or not, she was having a good time. It was nice to be out.

CHAPTER TWENTY-SIX

"What a night, huh?" Monica said, following Johnnie's gaze up into the stars.

"You said it."

"You want to get out of here?"

Johnnie thought of Gail who was no doubt somewhere inside. "What did you have in mind?"

"I don't know. Maybe grab a couple of Thirst Busters and drive up to the point. Stare up at a few more of those stars."

"You mean the scarce few we can see in this city?"

"Those are the ones."

"The city lights are prettier," Johnnie said.

"Well, you'll have your choice. The sky or the city."

"You just want to make out with me on the hood of your Charger."

Monica laughed. "Maybe."

Johnnie felt good, warm, a little buzzed from her third beer and the shots she and Eddie had done. And she would do anything to get away from Gail.

"Let's go," she said, standing.

Monica stood and they rounded the table. Eddie looked up, curious. "What's up, ladies?"

"We're gonna head out," Monica said.

"Home already?" Eddie asked, looking at Johnnie.

"Relax, Eddie. We're just going somewhere else," Monica said.

He didn't need to consider why. "Oh. Right. Good idea."

Johnnie leaned in and kissed his cheek. "Night."

He gripped her hand. "Don't let her ruin your night," he said.

"I'm not." She gave him a squeeze of reassurance.

They exited the patio and thankfully hit the street without seeing Gail. Johnnie shivered a little as the night temperature dropped, and Monica seemed to sense it and entangled their arms, walking close together. The night was quiet as the boom of Amsterdam's fell into a muted abyss behind them. People walked the night paired up or in groups. Most businesses were closed, and distant laughter and streetlights were their only company.

"Did you ride the tram?" Johnnie asked.

"No, I'm over here."

They crossed the street to a paid parking lot. Monica's Charger sat like a hulk of muscle in the dark. Sleek black with a white racing stripe, it looked ready to rumble.

"I so love this car," Johnnie said, waiting on the passenger side.

"It is a chick magnet," Monica said, grinning. She pressed the remote and allowed them entry. When Monica started the car, Johnnie's heart fluttered at the sound and the feel of the harnessed power.

"I would probably kill myself in this car," she said.

Monica pulled out of the parking lot. "Don't tell me you're a speed demon."

"I am."

She laughed. "I would've never guessed it."

"Don't judge a book by its cover."

"I guess I can't," she said. She floored it on the main road, and they raced through the sporadic light like they were running from the law. People on the sidewalks stopped and stared, as did people in the cars they passed.

"You're not supposed to drive like this," Johnnie said, loving it.

"I'm just trying to impress you." She groaned as she slowed for a stop light. "Is it working?"

"It's doing something," Johnnie said.

"Good." Monica sped through the green light and drove swiftly though safely to a Circle K convenience store. They headed inside, got Thirst Busters and sweets, and headed out. They drove in comfortable silence up to the point.

Johnnie unbuckled her seat belt as they pulled in and parked. The headlights dimmed, and the lights of the city sparkled beneath them. Monica sipped her big soda, chewed on some Skittles, and leaned back to relax.

"Now this is nice," she said. She reached up and freed her hair, sliding her hair tie around her wrist.

Johnnie stared at her dark mane, thick and wavy as it fell to her shoulders. She had an urge to touch it, to run her fingers through it.

Monica reclined her seat and looked at her. "Join me," she said. "It's nice."

Johnnie reached down, reclined her seat, and sipped her Diet Coke with a splash of Dr Pepper. Her eyes drifted to the sparkling city lights, and they hypnotized her as they danced in place.

"Music?" Monica asked.

"No," Johnnie said. "Silence."

"Skittles?" she asked with a smile.

"No, thanks." Johnnie wiggled her bag of Gummy Life Savers.

Monica watched her curiously. "Those any good?"

Johnnie looked at her like she was crazy. "Um, yeah. Where have you been?"

Monica laughed. "I guess I'm not in the loop."

"Not in the loop? You're on a different planet." Johnnie handed over a few and watched with amusement as she ate them.

"Mm, yeah okay, I've been on a different planet."

"Told you."

"It's not my fault. I don't do sugar."

"Suuure," Johnnie said. She chewed on the chewy burst of flavor and pushed away the memories that were trying to come. She and Jolene had often lived off Thirst Busters and snack goods from convenience stores. The big foam cups kept drinks cooler in the hot months, and if you found a nice manager, they'd let you refill for free. Some even gave them expired goods like chips and crackers. For as many bad people as there were in the world, there were just as many good. And learning that had surprised her.

"You okay?" Monica asked.

"Hmm?" Johnnie turned and found her looking at her softly. "Yeah, just memories is all."

"Did Gail bring you here or something?"

"No." Johnnie laughed. "This would so not be a Gail thing."

"Why? She doesn't like Gummy Life Savers?"

"No, she just isn't romantic. Or thoughtful."

"Ah."

"She doesn't like to sit still."

"God, I love sitting still," Monica said. "It's so nice."

They both stared out the windshield. "With your job I can imagine."

"Mm, yes."

"What are you thinking?" Johnnie asked.

Monica laughed. "You'll think I'm crazy."

"Try me."

She sighed. "I'm thinking about the Zodiac killer and how this probably isn't very safe."

Johnnie laughed and blushed profusely. "I actually thought about that too."

"No way."

"Yes."

"Why would you think about that?" Monica asked.

Johnnie shrugged. "Because I worry about crazy shit like that."

"I do too, but I'm a cop. What's your excuse?" She was laughing hard too.

"I'm just crazy."

"Did you scope the place like I did when we pulled in?"

Johnnie nodded, mouth full of soda.

"And I've been checking the mirrors."

Monica cracked up.

Johnnie wanted to tell her why. That when you live on the streets you become obsessive about people and their behavior and actions. You have to anticipate anything and everything. It was probably very similar to how Monica felt while on the job.

"I'm a bit of a crime buff," Johnnie said.

Monica looked intrigued. "Really? Who woulda thought?"

Johnnie shrugged. "I'm full of surprises." She looked at her seriously. "What do you know about me, Monica?"

Monica wrung her hands on the steering wheel. "I don't know. That you're kind, compassionate, talented. I know you have an anxiety disorder, and it's sometimes hard for you to get out."

"And that doesn't bother you?"

This time she shrugged. "No. Should it?"

"It's an issue for a lot of people. They think I'm crazy with a house stacked full of newspapers and cats."

"I think that would be a hoarder," she said with a laugh.

"Yes, but they tend to loop us all together when assuming."

"I see." She chewed on some Skittles and then reached for Johnnie's hand. "I know a lot about you, Johnnie. And you're okay by me."

Johnnie got lost in her eyes for a moment. She felt something stirring in the pit of her stomach. She'd spent weeks feeling so aroused, so turned on by the woman, it was a miracle she could walk upright without climaxing in her jeans. Even so, she recognized the desire for release for what it was. And she remembered she'd made a vow to harness that energy and put it to good use.

"I'd better get home," she said softly.

Monica leaned in, inches from her. "Okay." Gently, she placed a soft, warm kiss on her lips. Johnnie returned it, too curious not to. When they pulled apart she felt lightheaded. Her mouth tasted like what she'd imagine colors to taste like.

"I just wanted to give you something to think about tonight." Monica brushed her cheek with the backs of her fingers. Then she straightened, adjusted her seat, and started the engine. Johnnie fixed her seat and refastened her seat belt. They drove to her house in silence, though Monica often reached over and squeezed her hand with a sincere smile.

When they reached Johnnie's loft, Johnnie turned to her and held her forearm. She liked the strength she felt there. It caused more stirring. "I think I have a sugar high," she said.

Monica laughed. "I know I do."

"Thanks for tonight," Johnnie said. "For, you know, getting me out of there."

"It was my pleasure."

"You're really a great person, Monica."

"You sound surprised."

"No, just aware."

Monica smiled. "Go on in," she said. "Flash your lights when you're in safe."

Johnnie leaned in and kissed her cheek. They parted slowly, breathing heavy. "Night."

"Good night."

Johnnie closed the door behind her and hurried up to her loft. When she got inside, she flashed her kitchen light and smiled. She checked her phone, absolutely sure she would find that Gail had tried to call. But to her surprise she found only a text from Eddie, wishing her a good night with a hashtag party girl followed by a smiley face.

She plugged the phone in to charge and turned when she heard a knock on her door. She grinned, despite herself, knowing it was Monica. She couldn't deny that there had been a little chemistry between them.

She pulled open the heavy door and froze.

"Hey, baby," Gail said, leaning against the frame. She sank her hands into her loose jeans, showing off a red G-string riding her hips. Johnnie couldn't speak, couldn't think.

"Aren't you going to invite me in?"

Johnnie blinked quickly, and her hand gripped the door so tight it hurt. And then, without rational thought or hesitation, she stepped aside and let her in, closing the door behind them.

CHAPTER TWENTY-SEVEN

Elaine tossed and turned, the bamboo sheets cool against her bare skin. She stared up at her ceiling fan, mesmerized by the shadows of the blades. She turned on her side and hugged her body pillow, the one she'd slept with since she'd lost Barb. She hugged it close with her knee propped up on it and arm pulling it tight. When she'd first lost Barb, she'd put one of her nightshirts on it and inhaled her scent every night. But eventually, the scent had faded and she was left with just a pillow. The smell of the closet had diminished as well, and it was useless to clear out the shoes and lie inside the closet with the door closed. The soothing high of doing so had long since vanished, mixing with the fresh air of the house.

If she somehow could've bottled it. Bottled Barb. But how do you capture a soul, an aura, a truly free spirit? Sure she had her perfume, and often times that still hit her with a quick kick to the gut as she walked past someone who wore it. But it wasn't Barb. It was only a piece. She wanted the perfume mingled with Barb's moist skin, the scent of her hair at the base of her neck, the taste of the impression just above her collarbone first thing in the morning. She missed how she heated when she slept, like a human radiator all wrapped up in her covers. Elaine had often awakened cold and coverless only to find that Barb had wrapped them all around herself, cocoon like. She'd never tried to get them back or to wake her. She'd simply risen and retrieved more, loving the sound of Barb's steady breath more soothing to her than worrying about the stolen

RONICA BLACK

covers. Barb slept like the dead, and she was the only one Elaine had ever been with who fell asleep as soon as she hit the pillow.

Barb had no worries or racing thoughts keeping her awake at night. Barb lived hard and fearless, free and happy. She didn't believe in drama, and she simply walked away from it when faced with it. She'd take Elaine by the hand and say, "Let's blow this pop stand, El." And off they'd go, leaving a person standing there mouth agape. Elaine recalled leaving more than one party and even moving because Barb didn't like the drama. And as the years went by, they'd had to deal with less and less. It had become more and more common for two women to live together. Men, for the most part, left them alone. And even if they didn't, Barb set it right and Elaine felt good, safe.

Elaine turned again and saw that it was after eleven. She was going on day three with very little sleep. Insomnia wasn't new to her, but it had been a while since it had reared its ugly head. She rose and slipped into her robe. She made her way down the hallway without needing light. In the kitchen she made a cup of Chai tea and settled into the sofa in the living room. She lit the candle on the table next to her and turned on the stereo. She decided to let the iPod choose on its own, and when Led Zeppelin came on she laughed and then choked up with tears. She could still see Barb dancing in the kitchen, headphones on, using the mop handle as a microphone. Barb loved to jam out and clean, jam out and drink, or jam out and get it on. She loved music and loved to dance. She'd always catch Elaine watching her, and she'd grin and pull her in and hold her as she moved.

"Come on, darling. Shake what your momma gave ya."

Elaine wiped her tears and laughed. She could almost see her now. Hear her. Feel her. God, what she wouldn't give to hold her close and move to the music. What she wouldn't give to see her dancing with the broom or sashaying down the hallway.

Elaine thumbed up the volume as Steppenwolf came on, and she laughed and cried as she remembered being awakened on more than one Saturday morning to the loud music. Of course she'd groaned and called out and buried her head under the pillows, but

Barb always found her, crawling under the covers and nibbling and tickling her awake. She'd tug her from bed and lead her down the hallway to a hot cup of coffee and homemade pancakes.

"It's a beautiful day," she'd say. "Don't waste it in dreamland."

Elaine sipped her tea as the words replayed in her mind. "Don't waste it in dreamland."

She closed her eyes, so tired. But her mind wouldn't let her rest. No, it wanted to torture her with the past. Replay image after image of Barb. But the worst part, the very worst, was that Barb's face was becoming less defined. No matter how hard she focused, she couldn't see her face as it had been in life. So she clung to the photo, stared at it for hours, trying desperately to imprint it in her mind for all eternity. But it didn't seem to help. Her memories were firm, yes, but Barb's face, her smile, were becoming smudged.

She traced Barb's photo with her fingertip. It was black-and-white, the only kind of photo Elaine ever took. Barb was on the beach, turning to look back at her, wind whipping at her hair. Her light shone from her eyes, radiated from her smile. Elaine could feel her heat, her passion for life; she could feel it coming up through the glass of the frame.

How could she be gone but still feel so close?

Elaine touched her face and then jerked as she heard a soft knock from her door.

She wiped her eyes, placed the photo on the couch, and approached the door. As she touched the handle, her eyes drifted closed, and she wished silently for Johnnie to be on the other end. She longed to be held in her arms. To fall asleep and dream peacefully like she used to do with Barb.

She checked the peephole and sighed. She unbolted the door and opened it. Kyle stood just beyond the security screen.

"I thought you might be up," she said. "Thought you might want some company."

Elaine tightened her robe, considering her options. She knew she'd be up for hours, no doubt crying over Barb. And when she wasn't thinking about Barb, she was thinking about Johnnie.

"Come in." She unlocked the outer door and allowed her entry. Kyle was in cargo shorts and a T-shirt. Her cologne was strong but tantalizing. Her damp hair suggested a fresh shower.

Elaine closed and locked the door. She motioned for Kyle to sit next to her on the couch. Kyle studied her closely, and Elaine felt slightly uncomfortable. She rubbed the back of her neck with nerves. She wasn't used to feeling vulnerable. Perhaps this was a mistake.

"How have you been?" Kyle asked.

Elaine sipped her tea and straightened her spine. "Fine and you?"

"Good. I can't stop thinking about you."

Elaine gripped her tea mug. "I'm afraid you're wasting your time."

"Am I?"

"Yes. You know there will never be anything between us."

Kyle shifted. "Sure, I know that. But it doesn't mean I can't think about it."

Elaine met her gaze. "I'd prefer if you didn't."

Kyle nodded and rested her hand on her cheek as she leaned against the armrest.

"I get it."

"Then why did you come?"

She laughed a little. "Why did you let me in?"

Elaine set her mug down. "I can't sleep."

"Maybe I can help."

Elaine smiled at her confidence. "I don't think so."

"Then what did you have in mind?"

Elaine stood, realizing it was a mistake to let her in, lead her on. "I think I can sleep after all."

She felt lightheaded and steadied herself on the couch. Kyle stood and came to her side.

"Are you okay?" Her eyes showed concern, and from the look on her face, Elaine knew she must look really bad.

"I just need to lie down I think." But her knees went weak, and Kyle caught her.

"You're not okay." She sat her down on the couch. She retrieved her phone and dialed. "I'm calling nine one one."

"No, no." Elaine tried to smile and she touched her arm. "No need to worry."

"Too late," Kyle said, reporting the situation to the operator.

Elaine blinked and tried to focus, but stared off into oblivion. Her mouth went slack, her muscles melted, and she couldn't make out the words Kyle was saying.

"Johnnie," Elaine said, fighting to hold her head up. "Call Johnnie. I want Johnnie."

She fell back against the couch, saw Barb's perfect face above her, smiled, and let the blackness take her.

CHAPTER TWENTY-EIGHT

Y ou look good, babe, really good," Gail said, crossing her legs on the sofa across from Johnnie. She had on short khakis and a see-through threadbare tank. Her skin was golden brown and moist looking. She'd been somewhere recently. Johnnie knew it was probably Mexico, maybe Central America. Gail did love to travel. And she loved to show off her fluent Spanish.

"You look…tan." She wasn't going to tell her she looked good, even if she thought it. She wasn't going to give in. The only reason she'd let her in was because she said she'd had no place to crash for the night, which wasn't unusual for Gail, vagabond that she was. And Johnnie couldn't put anyone on the street. Not anyone. Gail, of course, knew this, and she'd played it to her cause many a time. But this time would be different. She could hear Eddie in her ear and now Monica.

"I'm seeing someone," she blurted out.

Gail looked amused, even smiled a little. "Really?"

"Yes." Johnnie sat straighter, trying to better play the part.

"Would that be Monica? The one I heard drive away in that obnoxious Charger?"

Johnnie did her best to hide her surprise. "No."

"Then who?"

"You don't know her."

She grew excited, knowing she was lying about dating her practitioner, but it felt good to say it out loud.

"Does she have a name?"

Johnnie smiled. "Not one you need to know."

"Don't bullshit me, Johnnie. You don't date."

"I do now."

She looked upset, and Johnnie knew it was wrong, but she felt like she'd scored a little victory.

She rose. "You can have the couch." She tossed her a pillow and brought over a blanket. And I assume you have somewhere to go tomorrow?"

Gail fingered the blanket as if it held memories of sadness. "I actually don't. Not yet."

Johnnie sighed. How long could she hold out? Gail could play the guilt strings of her heart so damn well. Johnnie always felt for her. Fell for her. Despite what she did to her.

But Johnnie knew what she wanted now. And it wasn't Gail and her games. Even if her practitioner was a relationship based on arousal, performance, and inner awakening, it still had changed her view on love, on what was out there. It gave her hope.

"Does she know about your past, this new love?"

Johnnie stopped, considered squaring off with her, but then changed her mind. It wasn't worth it.

"Does she make you come like I do? Do you scream her name?"

Johnnie made her way to her bed. She sat and removed her shoes and then slid off her shirt and bra and unbuckled the brown belt to her worn jeans. She was sliding out of them when she felt soft hands on her back. She flinched at first but then relaxed. Gail always knew just how to touch her. She was massaging her now, and Johnnie nearly groaned. Her body took over and melted in her hands.

"She doesn't touch you like this, does she?"

Johnnie's eyes drifted closed. She stepped from her jeans and fell to the bed. Gail was nude behind her, very small bikini line showing. She crawled atop her. "I know you missed me." She took Johnnie's hands and placed them on her tiny breasts. The thick nipples were erect, teasing Johnnie's palms.

Johnnie felt herself grow wet with desire. She could make Gail come, slip her fingers up deep inside, and let her ride them until she fell over after a few orgasms. Then she could hold her down and suck her pink flesh until she begged her to stop, yanking at her hair, scratching at her shoulders. Then she could turn her over, bite her on the ass, and fuck her from behind, lick her spine, twist her hand so her knuckles hit her G-spot just right, and cause her to whip her head back and scream until she went hoarse.

She could do so many things. Stay up all night long. Pretend it was the woman of her dreams, the one she painted. God, it was tempting. And as for her own needs, they'd yet to be met, and she hadn't forgotten that. Her body wouldn't let her. She was wound like a pissed off rattler, ready to strike. Her clit felt heavy and full, and Gail, riding her bare thigh, was getting to her.

So she did something she never thought she'd be able to do. She pushed her off.

"What the fuck?"

Johnnie stood, pulled back the covers, and crawled in. She set her alarm and reminded herself to make sure Gail left before her so she couldn't get back inside.

"I need to sleep," Johnnie said. She sank into her pillow and breathed deeply. She'd been thinking about a new painting lately. The tree she'd been drawing was developing. Maybe she'd dream about it tonight.

"What's with you, Johnnie?"

Johnnie knew she was standing there, nude, with a pissed off look on her face.

She decided not to look at her.

"Good night," she said.

Gail was still for a moment. Then she heard her move and settle in on the couch.

Johnnie felt content and was just about to fall asleep when her phone rang. She sat up, ready to silence it. But when she saw the name, she answered it at once.

She moved without thought. Dressed without knowing. She floated out the door, leaving Gail calling after her.

CHAPTER TWENTY-NINE

Elaine awoke to beeping and something squeezing her arm. She winced in pain and opened her eyes. A blood pressure cuff was reporting her vitals, and the monitors next to her showed the rest. She groaned and shifted, her ass and lower back aching. She blinked heavy lids, taking in the hospital room. She lifted her hand to scratch her nose but found a pulse ox attached. She used her other hand, but the tug from the IV hurt so she let it go. She looked through the glass wall at the numerous medical personnel moving from here to there working. She licked dry lips and pressed the call button.

She looked back to the window at the light angling in through the vertical blinds, and she recalled a little from the night before. Panicked, she shifted her gown near her chest and trembled. A fresh bandage ran the length of her sternum, and she felt a tightness and pain.

"Good morning," a woman said, breezing in in light blue scrubs. She pushed buttons on the monitors and adjusted her pillow. "How are you, sweetie?"

Elaine cleared her throat. "Why am I here?"

The nurse continued fidgeting, rounding the bed to work the other side. "Your heart nearly gave out."

Elaine grimaced, suddenly angry. "What?"

"The doc will be in soon to explain."

"Can I go?"

She laughed. "Not a chance."

"I want to go." She tried to free herself from oxygen and wires. The nurse grabbed her wrists.

"No, no, honey. You need to stay. We need to fix you up." She held her until she stilled. "There you go, just relax." She offered a gentle smile. "You have some people dying to see you."

"People?"

"Oh, yes. Been here all night."

Elaine knew about Michael, he was her emergency contact, but as for who else, she was at a loss.

"What time is it?"

The nurse checked her watch. "Nearly noon. If you promise to remain calm, I'll send a visitor in."

"Can I get some water?" She was dying of thirst.

"Sure." She poured some from a pink plastic pitcher and handed her the cup. "I'll be back soon."

She left Elaine alone. The water was nice and cold and felt like a godsend against her parched mouth. Just as she was reaching for the tray with the pitcher for a refill, the door opened and Michael hurried in.

"Hey, gorgeous," he said, peeking in at her.

"Hey, yourself."

He smiled and came toward her, whipping a bouquet of flowers from behind his back. "For you, me lady."

She rolled her eyes. "My knight in shining armor."

He placed the flowers on the table with the water and kissed her. "You look so pitiful." He stroked her face and pointed at all the wires. "What all are you hooked up to? I'm almost afraid to know. Can you launch the space shuttle?"

Elaine laughed. "Possibly."

He pulled up a chair and settled in. Elaine noted his scruffy cheeks and wrinkled flannel and jeans. His ball cap also screamed casual. He had indeed been there all night.

"Michael, what happened?"

He took a deep breath. "Your heart went kaput. They had to do emergency surgery."

"Oh God. There was damage from the infection wasn't there?"

He nodded.

He held her hand. "I got the call, they said you were unconscious, I rushed here and have been waiting ever since."

She closed her eyes. "I just remember seeing Barb. I saw her so clearly. And then...I woke up here."

"She was watching over you."

Elaine teared up, but it hurt her chest to do so. "Don't make me cry," she said.

He wiped the tear with his thumb.

"Am I—going to be okay?" When could she go? When could she get back to her life?

"She said the surgery went well."

Elaine glanced around, feeling claustrophobic. She was a prisoner, held in place by wires and beeps. Her body was suddenly a machine. A real live working machine, and it needed maintenance. To think of it like that panicked her.

"You're freaking out aren't you?" Michael said, looking around as well. "I would too." He patted her hand. "Try not to think about it."

"What am I supposed to think about?"

"Well, you could sleep and heal. Or...you could think about those two lovely women out there in the waiting room."

She felt her eyebrows furrow. "What?"

He couldn't help but smile. "Yeah, I wasn't sure how you were going to react to that."

"What women?"

"Well, they are both blonde. Short hair. Built about the same."

"Oh, Jesus." She covered her heart with her hand.

Michael looked at the monitor as the beeping increased. "Maybe this isn't a good idea."

She took deep breaths and calmed herself.

"They are both here?" Could it be?

"Kyle?"

Michael nodded.

"She was the one who called me."

"Oh, fuck. She was at my house."

"Yes."

Elaine closed her eyes, wishing it away.

"And as for Johnnie…" Michael said.

Elaine opened her eyes with a start. "Johnnie?" She searched his eyes. "Johnnie's here?"

"Yes."

"Oh, my God."

"Who did you think the other blonde was?"

"I wasn't sure. But I never expected Johnnie. She doesn't even know who I am."

Michael grew concerned. "Is this the client you've been telling me about?"

Elaine tried to sit up. "Johnnie's here?"

He steadied her. "Easy, El. Lie down. I can tell her to go."

"Johnnie? But how? When?"

He eased her back against the bed. "You need to calm down or I'm calling it quits for today."

Elaine closed her eyes again and tried to focus on relaxing. But she knew it would be impossible until she found answers to her questions.

CHAPTER THIRTY

M ichael, please tell me," Elaine said.
He sighed, filled up the cup with water, and handed it to her.

"Apparently, you told Kyle to call Johnnie just before you lost consciousness. She found her number in your phone."

Elaine sipped the cold water, but it did little to calm her. She knew she shouldn't have Johnnie's phone number in her phone. But she'd put it in there the day she'd gone to her studio in case she got lost. Of course she could have erased it. But truth be told she liked pulling it up and looking at it. Knowing that she was just a push of a button away sometimes excited her, despite knowing it was wrong.

"So Johnnie is here? She came?"

"The only time she's budged is to pace."

"And Kyle?"

"She was scared. She said she didn't really know you. She didn't even know your name."

"No, I suppose she wouldn't."

"You know for two women who hardly know anything about you, they sure seem to care." He smiled. "Of course, I'm not surprised."

"My life is crazy," she said aloud but more to herself.

"With women, yes, a bit so. Would you like me to ask them to go?"

Elaine looked at him, felt the love and peace in his eyes. "I think I need to say some things to Kyle."

He pulled off his cap and ran his fingers through his hair. "Okay."

"And as for Johnnie…"

"Have you slept with her?" he asked, replacing his cap.

"No."

"But you want to."

She looked away. "I can't talk about this, Michael."

"If your feelings for her are strong, you need to face it. Maybe now isn't the time, but it needs to be dealt with. I know you're not sleeping; you're still breaking down over Barb. You've got a lot going on inside, El. And all this, this stress, isn't good for you."

"I'll deal with it."

"Good, but not today."

"Michael, don't get bossy."

He held up his hands in innocence. "Okay, okay." He stood then gave her a kiss. "I'll be back tonight with the hubby."

"'K."

"I'll send Kyle in."

Elaine watched him go. Then she braced herself to face Kyle. When she entered, she came with a soft smile. She stood at the foot of the bed, hands in pockets. She looked uncomfortable.

"You okay?"

Elaine laughed a little. "I'm fabulous, thanks."

"I, uh, was really worried."

"I know. I'm sorry for that, Kyle. You should've never been put in that position."

"I'm glad I was there."

"Well, yes, I am too. But as far as being there in the first place… that was wrong. So I owe you a huge thanks for probably saving my life and a huge apology for the way things have been going between us."

Kyle leaned on the bed, staring at her hand for a moment. "I accept the thank-you, but the apology is not necessary. You've been straight up with me about what goes on between us. I just really like you, so I pushed things. I guess I hoped to wear you down."

Elaine watched her fidget with nerves. "I can appreciate that. And once upon a time, I was young and got caught up in the same thing. It never works, Kyle. You deserve someone who feels the same as you. As nice as you are...and caring...I find it hard to believe that you can't find someone."

She looked up. "It just hasn't happened. Not yet."

"It will."

She laughed. "Promise?"

"Yes. But don't expect it to happen on that dating app."

"Yeah, okay." She rubbed her upper arm. "Why don't you have someone?"

Elaine swallowed with difficulty. "I do."

Kyle looked defeated. "Right. Yeah. The woman in the waiting room."

Elaine wanted to disagree, but she stopped herself. "I'm sorry, Kyle."

"No, no need. Thanks for being honest from the get-go."

She gave a wave and left the room, leaving Elaine alone with her thoughts. Anticipation began to build in her gut, and the beeping heart rate monitor increased. She breathed deeply and tried not to think about Johnnie just a short distance away. Probably pacing the hallway, wondering if she should come or go. Maybe she'd already made up her mind when she saw Kyle come in. She was probably assuming all sorts of things about her.

"Christ," she said, palming her forehead.

What was Johnnie going to do? More importantly, how was she going to react to whatever Johnnie chose? She sipped more water and pressed back into the pillow. She listened to the machine, felt the pinch of the IV in her hand. Imagined the drip of the saline into her bloodstream. She felt the cool air, the starchy feel of the sheets, the tight tucking of her feet beneath a blue blanket. She focused on everything she could to keep her mind off Johnnie. But eventually, after several minutes that felt like an eternity, she heard a knock at the door and the sound of it opening.

Johnnie.

CHAPTER THIRTY-ONE

The room wasn't as bright as the hallway, and Johnnie was thankful as she entered Elaine's room. She could see slivers of sunshine pushing through drawn vertical blinds. Though her heart was in her throat, she kept moving, putting on a small but completely intimidating smile. She saw the foot of the bed first, then her gaze traveled up Elaine's tucked in body to her face. Her smile nearly faltered at the sight of her pale skin with darkening around her eyes. She fought a look of deep concern and instead smiled brighter, holding out the flowers she'd brought for her.

"These are for you," she said, coming to stand next to her. Her hands shook holding them so she laid them on the bed. Elaine took them gingerly and brought them to her nose to inhale.

"Yellow roses," she said. "Thank you."

Johnnie rubbed the back of her neck. "You need some yellow right now."

"I believe you're right." She smiled, motioned for Johnnie to sit, and lightly touched the petals, visibly reacting to the softness of them. "I could touch them for hours," she said.

Johnnie watched her graceful hands and recalled just how soft and perfectly spiraled the petals were. "I know what you mean," she said.

A nurse came in before they could say much more. She checked the machines and silenced the beeping. Elaine thanked her profusely and asked for pain medicine. Johnnie felt a stab in her chest at hearing the request. She didn't like the thought of Elaine in pain.

She could hardly stand to see her as she was. She just wanted to yell at someone to fix her so she could take her in her arms and take her home. The yearning was surprising; she'd only ever felt that way about Jolene. It was a protectiveness, a compassion. An empathy. And she couldn't believe how strong it was.

Johnnie pressed her palms to her denim-clad thighs as the nurse left and came back. She injected something into the IV line. Elaine thanked her again and she left them, but not before she let Johnnie know that her visit should be short. Elaine needed her rest.

Elaine unwrapped the roses, plucked one from the banded bunch, and set the rest on her tray. She held the one she'd chosen to her nose, allowing it to linger before it drifted to her lips where it lightly caressed.

Johnnie swallowed with difficulty, and she could feel her skin flush with heat. The sight was almost as erotic as it was absolutely beautiful.

A nearly broken beautiful woman, drawing strength and comfort from a perfect rose.

"I suppose you know all about me now," Elaine said, glancing over at her. The look was calm, pleasant, as if they were having an everyday conversation.

Still, Johnnie felt a bit of shame. Elaine had not intended for her privacy to be shared.

"I know your name," Johnnie said. "And Michael."

Elaine refocused on touching the rose. "How do you feel now that you know those things?"

Johnnie thought for a moment, a little surprised at the question. "I guess I don't think anything. I'm just glad you're okay."

"Yes, now you know. My heart truly is broken." She smiled at her own humor.

"Was," Johnnie said. "They said they fixed it. Gave you a new valve."

Elaine closed her eyes and inhaled the rose. "No, it still is. I'm afraid it always will be."

Johnnie didn't argue. She recalled the other woman who had waited with them. Who was she? An ex? A current lover? Johnnie hadn't liked the jealous feeling she'd felt in meeting her. She'd acted possessive of Elaine and defensive toward Johnnie as if she were a threat.

Was Elaine referring to her or someone else? Who had broken her heart?

"You want to know why, right? Why my heart is broken." She looked at Johnnie with wide eyes. Seeking eyes.

"Only if you want to tell me." She grew nervous. She was unsure of Elaine's motives.

"You aren't curious?"

Johnnie felt nailed to her chair, on the spot. Elaine had pegged her with her fiery gaze.

"Tell me," she said.

Johnnie gripped the armrests just as she'd done at their first meeting. "Yes, I want to know," she breathed.

Elaine didn't let up, but she began twirling the rose with her fingers. "My wife died," she said.

Johnnie felt as though she'd been slapped she was so shocked at the matter-of-fact statement.

"I-I'm sorry," she managed.

Elaine looked at the rose as if its twirling dance were giving her messages.

"You don't have anything to be sorry for," she said. "You haven't done anything wrong."

They sat in silence, and Johnnie's mind went into overdrive as she thought about Elaine losing her spouse. It explained all that had happened back at her studio. It explained the tightly harnessed desire she'd seen in her, the well-manicured control she had.

"And you want to know about the other woman," she said. "She looks similar to you don't you think?"

She blinked, and Johnnie saw that her eyes were glossed over, and her lids open and shut too slowly. The drug had kicked in.

"I guess," she said as she stood.

Elaine reached out and grabbed the belt loop of her jeans. "Where you going?"

"You need to rest." Gently, Johnnie unhooked her fingers and held her hand.

"No, you need to stay. I have things to tell you."

"I'll come back."

"No, you won't. You're too uncomfortable. I know you, remember?"

Elaine tugged on Johnnie's hand.

"You know who that woman was?" she asked. "She was you."

"Sorry?" Elaine was more drugged than Johnnie had thought.

"She was you. I pretended she was you. I let her in my house and touched her because I wanted you."

Her eyes drifted closed and then tried to open again but failed. Johnnie stood there like a statue holding her limp hand. She was burning from the words but trying desperately to calm herself since they were drug induced. Even so, Elaine had managed to stir her even in an incapacitated state. How could this woman cause so much reaction in her?

Johnnie watched her slip into sleep. Watched her mouth mumble a bit before it too gave up and gave in to the drug. Johnnie lifted her hand, her beautiful hand, and kissed it. Then she placed it on her chest and took the rose from the other hand. She placed that on the tray along with the bouquet. She stood mesmerized by the sight of Elaine sleeping. She wished she could curl up next to her and embrace her, bury her face in her dark mane. It was something she would think about the rest of the day. Something she'd dream about at night.

For now, she had to go. She had to let her sleep.

Beautiful Elaine.

CHAPTER THIRTY-TWO

Johnnie drove home without the radio. Her eyes burned from lack of sleep, and her bones felt as though they were melting beneath her skin. The stress of the previous night and morning was finally taking its toll, and she knew it was useless to fight it. Elaine was going to be okay and she couldn't be more thankful. And even though she wasn't sure what to think of the other woman who had called her and been there, she owed her a thanks as well.

She pulled into her covered parking space and headed for the stairs to her loft. She needed a hot shower and something to eat. Hopefully, she had some yogurt in the fridge. Feeling like a ragdoll, she unlocked and pulled open her large door. She blinked a few times to make sure the image she was seeing was real.

"Where have you been?" Gail rose from the couch wearing nothing but boy shorts. She held Johnnie's face in her hands. "I've been worried sick."

Johnnie felt like collapsing in fatigue and defeat. She'd completely forgotten about Gail.

"I told you you could stay the night," Johnnie said, mainly to remind herself.

"Yes." She grinned and wrapped her arms around Johnnie's shoulders. "But we didn't get to the good part." She kissed her and tried to plunge with her tongue.

Johnnie pulled away in reflex. She closed the door and headed toward the fridge.

"What's with you?" Gail followed.

"I'm tired."

"Why didn't you answer your cell?"

Johnnie opened the fridge, unopen to drama. "Did you eat all of my yogurt?"

"It was all you had here, so yeah."

Johnnie retrieved the orange juice, screwed off the lid, and downed several large gulps.

"You still didn't tell me where you were or why you left."

Johnnie replaced the juice and sighed. "A friend of mine was in the emergency room."

"Really?"

"Yes."

"Monica?" Gail had always been jealous of Monica. And seeing Johnnie and her together at Amsterdam's obviously set something off in her. It was probably why she'd shown up. Johnnie knew this, but she'd still let her in. She never could get over the look in her eyes when she pleaded. She'd said she had nowhere to go. That she missed her and wanted another chance. She'd said all the right words. The words Johnnie always wanted desperately to believe.

"No, not Monica."

"Then who?"

Johnnie crossed to her bedroom where she sat and removed her boots and socks. She crawled up to her pillows and curled up on her side. Her bed felt unbelievably good. So good she could stay there for all eternity. She closed her eyes as she sank farther into the feather duvet.

"Johnnie?"

Johnnie startled and felt movement on the bed. Gail had crawled up next to her. Johnnie felt her spoon her from behind. It was an unusual move. Gail was hardly ever affectionate. It meant she wanted something.

"I need to sleep," Johnnie said.

Gail groaned. Then she pulled closer and whispered in her ear. "I'll give you a good night kiss."

Johnnie closed her eyes and felt her flesh break out in goose bumps as Gail teased her ear with her lips and tongue and lowered her hand to her waistband. Too tired to fight, Johnnie relaxed and then moaned as Gail's fingers found her center.

"Oh, yeah, that's it," Gail whispered in her ear.

"Don't talk," Johnnie said, mind already on Elaine and her powerful words. She tried to imagine how Elaine touched the other woman while pretending she was Johnnie. Had she stroked her like this? Spoken in her ear? Milked her until she was as wet as she could get? She groaned and rolled onto her back. It was no longer Gail touching her, pleasing her. It was Elaine, and Johnnie wanted to make it good for her. She moaned louder, pumped her hips, lifted her shirt, and lifted her breast above her bra to pinch her own nipples. She was lost in a world of Elaine, and when she came, she came hard and loud and violently, holding Gail's arm to her, coming up off the bed and crying out for her. She called her from the depths of her soul until her voice was raspy and spent.

Again and again, the wave of pleasure came and she rode them as hard as she could for as long as she could. When she finally stilled, she fell back onto the bed and shivered with aftershock. Her hand was still gripping Gail's arm. She let go and Gail pulled it away quickly. She looked angry, but Johnnie was too fucking happy to care.

She sank into her pillow and grinned. Her eyes fell closed with fatigue.

"Who the fuck is Elaine?" Gail demanded.

Johnnie heard her and felt the sharp nudge to her shoulder.

"Johnnie? Johnnie?"

"Sleep now," Johnnie said.

She felt Gail climb from the bed, heard her dress, and then heard the door close behind her when she left. Johnnie once again turned to her side and curled up. She drifted off to sleep with thoughts of Elaine.

CHAPTER THIRTY-THREE

Elaine opened her eyes and focused on the elevated television in front of her. It was on a DIY home show, and the volume was low and coming through the handheld nurse remote near her side. She arrowed through the channels and frowned when she found nothing interesting. She'd been in the bed for days, and she was antsy and uncomfortable. She wasn't used to being away from home and the bed she'd shared with Barb.

"How are we feeling today?" a nurse asked as she came in the room, rubbing her hands together with hand sanitizer. She checked Elaine's machines, changed out the IV, and snapped on some gloves. "Let's check your incision." She opened Elaine's gown and removed the bandage. Elaine refrained from looking. When she saw the staples and the red of the cut, she felt like Frankenstein, and she hated thinking about her chest cavity wide open and her heart being handled. In fact, it terrified her, and she was rarely afraid of anything.

"I'm not afraid to die," she said, surprising herself. She wasn't. She would be with Barb, and with her heart trouble, it was something she'd had to face before. What she was afraid of was living through all of this. The staples, the scar, the manhandling of her heart, the beeping of the damn machine, keeping track of every beat, driving her mad. If the beep fell and went long with a flat line, would she hear it or would she already be gone?

The nurse, who smelled like baby lotion, bandaged her back up and patted her arm. "You don't need to worry about that." She played with the blanket and the sheet. "Are you comfortable? Do you need anything?"

"I'd really like another pillow. And a shower."

"We can do that. Give me a second, sweetie." She winked and left the room.

Elaine stared at all the flowers she'd been sent from friends. Michael and his husband had come every day. The others kept their distance per her request. She didn't want people seeing her like this. She felt vulnerable, imperfect. Image was everything in her business, and she had to maintain her strong confident self. Doing so also helped her. Knowing she was down at the moment frightened her a bit. She needed a shower, a change of clothes. And maybe tomorrow she could go.

Maybe tomorrow she could go home and make sure Johnnie knew she could come for an appointment. Though she'd tried not to get her hopes up, and despite the fact she didn't like Johnnie seeing her like this, she'd secretly tensed each time the door had opened, thinking it might be her. Something inside her sparked each time Johnnie was around, and it was becoming more and more difficult for her to ignore. She knew the line had been drawn as far as dating her or touching her, but it was her little secret that she enjoyed pushing everything right up to that line.

Michael, however, could see it. And he'd brought Johnnie up each time he visited, offering to call her, et cetera. And he'd known at once that Kyle was a one-night stand kind of deal. He didn't say anything about her, just made his point with his grunts and faces. The message had been clear; he didn't like her messing around with random people for sex. He thought it was useless, harmless to her emotionally, and dangerous to her physically.

"Here we go." The nurse returned with a pillow and a shower kit. Then she covered her wound for the shower. She turned on the water and freed Elaine from her IV. Then she helped her to the shower. Elaine had been walking every day, and she was pretty good on her feet, so she was able to shower on her own. The nurse left her, and Elaine relished the hot water and lathered herself again and again. She needed to shave and she needed more conditioner, but she would have to hold off until she got home. Right now, she was just thankful for the soap, small bottle of shampoo, and hot water. It revived her and brought a smile to her face. By the time she dried off and slipped into a fresh gown, she was in a brighter mood, looking forward to the future. And she'd just crawled into the fresh sheets the nurse had provided for her when the door opened.

"Michael, really, you don't have to come twice a day," she said. "But I love you for doing so."

"Hi," a voice said. Johnnie peeked around the corner. She looked unsure and nervous.

Elaine's heart fluttered. "Johnnie, hi." She was breathless.

"Is it a good time to visit?"

"Of course." Elaine shifted in the bed and fingered her wet hair. She must look like a drowned rat with her wet head and pale skin, dark marks beneath her eyes. She felt better, yes, but she'd been weak for a while, and she knew her body showed it.

Johnnie crossed the room with a large wrapped basket. She set it on the foot of the bed and wheeled the food tray so that it was in front of Elaine. Then she placed the basket on the table.

"Open it," she said as she sat down next to the bed.

"You shouldn't have," Elaine said. "Can't you see I'm already spoiled?" She looked at all the flowers.

Johnnie, however, didn't look away from her. She was taking her in, inhaling everything about her. Elaine could feel it.

"Forgive me," she said. "I know I must look a sight."

Johnnie scooted closer. "You look amazing," she said. "You look like you. The real you. And I can't seem to take my eyes off you."

Elaine felt a blush coming on. How long had it been since someone made her blush?

"You're very kind," she said, unsure what to say. She wanted to stare back, but she didn't dare for fear that Johnnie would feel her or read her. Or maybe she already was.

"Open your gift," Johnnie said with a smile. She seemed excited, and her eyes danced in the angled sunlight coming through the window.

"Really, you shouldn't have."

"I couldn't help myself. I wanted to give it to you yesterday, but you were asleep when I stopped by."

Elaine stopped her hands from opening. Johnnie had come; she'd been there. Her fluttering heart warmed. She smiled and willed the tears to remain in her throat. She swallowed them down and continued opening the gift.

"Wow," she said as she handed the paper to Johnnie who wadded it and threw it in the trash bin. It was a basket full of scented lotions, candles, and bath accessories, including shampoo and conditioner. Are these floating candles?" She held up a small rose-shaped candle with a flat bottom.

"Yes. I took a guess at what you might like. And I know the doctor said less stress…so I got you candles and bath salts and oils, for once you get home."

"It's…" Elaine looked at her and teared up, "perfect." How could Johnnie possibly know?

"Are you okay?" Johnnie leaned in, seeing the tears. Elaine held them back, got control.

"Yes, I'm just not used to…"

"Gifts?"

Elaine laughed. "Gifts from the heart," she clarified. "You put thought into this."

"I did. I handpicked everything. Smelled the lotions, tried the bath stuff."

"Really?"

"Yes."

Elaine put down the candles. "Why?" She met her eyes. Johnnie seemed to physically melt beneath her gaze, and Elaine knew in that instant that Johnnie felt it too. Really, truly felt it. It was so thick right now they could cut it with a knife.

Desire. Love. Connection.

Which one was it, she didn't know.

Perhaps all of them.

CHAPTER THIRTY-FOUR

I care," Johnnie said.

Elaine looked away. Willed herself not to cry. Her emotions were closer to the surface since the surgery. Even Michael had noticed.

"Thank you," she managed.

"You're welcome."

They sat in silence for a moment. Then Johnnie did something Elaine didn't expect. She took her hand and a bottle of lotion from the basket. She squeezed some out and began massaging it into her hand. Elaine's breath hitched and she closed her eyes.

"Just relax," Johnnie whispered. "Don't think about anything."

"I can't," Elaine confessed. "I can't stop what I'm feeling."

Johnnie used her thumbs and massaged her palms. "I can't either," Johnnie said. "I know I should, but I can't. And the truth is...I like it."

Elaine opened her eyes. Johnnie moved up to her wrist and arm. Elaine was melting in her hands. The gesture was so kind, so generous, so tender. Dear God, she couldn't hold back.

"I like it too," she said. "A lot."

Johnnie stopped and brought her hand to her mouth. She kissed the back of her hand.

"My ex-girlfriend came back," Johnnie said.

Elaine was so turned on, so relaxed, she didn't even blink.

"Yeah?"

"Yes." Johnnie began the massage all over again. "I let her in and everything. And last night, I let her touch me."

Elaine heated but not in jealousy. She imagined what Johnnie looked like in the throes of passion, what she sounded like when given pleasure.

"I let her, but I thought of you. I imagined it was you."

Elaine turned to look at her. "You did?"

"Yes." Johnnie's cheeks were flushed with what could only be desire.

Elaine stared at her face, watched her upper lip tremble just as it had done that first day, that first appointment. "Did you come?"

Johnnie swallowed but did not look away. "Yes, so hard. So long. I cried out for you. Did you hear me?"

Elaine shook with desire. "I do now."

Johnnie brought her hand to her mouth again. She kissed it and then angled it to breathe upon her wrist. Elaine made a small noise, and the heat rushed to her clit. Johnnie seemed to sense this and she kissed her wrist and inner arm. Then she leaned in and kissed Elaine on the lips.

The press of her beautiful flesh to hers was all Elaine thought it would be. Warm, soft, tender. Yet strong and powerful. She kissed her back, and they explored each other, tasting and taking. Johnnie held her jaw and took in her lips again and again. Elaine did the same and scouted with her tongue. Johnnie groaned when she felt it and groaned again as she welcomed it and explored with her own.

Elaine clung to Johnnie's shirt, tried to come up off the bed. But Johnnie held her down and kept the kissing, gentle and controlled. Elaine wanted to pull away and taste her neck, feel her breasts.

"Let me," she breathed, trying.

Johnnie kissed her. "No. You need to stay calm."

"I'm far from calm," Elaine laughed, teasing with her tongue.

"I know; this is not good for you."

"Oh believe me, it's very good for me."

Johnnie pulled away, struggling for breath. "We can't, not now."

Elaine reached for her and then let her arms fall. Her heart raced and her entire body screamed to be touched.

She bit her lower lip in frustration.

"I'll ask if I can go home." She pressed the call button for the nurse.

Johnnie laughed softly and returned to the chair. "You need to rest," she said. "Even if you go home."

She held Elaine's hand.

"Will you come?" Elaine asked. "To my home?"

Johnnie nodded. "Of course. If that's what you want."

Elaine eased back, palmed her chest, and took a deep breath. "It is."

Johnnie squeezed her hand. A nurse walked in, a different one from before. She hooked Elaine back up to the machines.

"When can I leave?" Elaine asked.

"I don't know offhand, and the doc's gone for the evening."

Elaine sighed.

"But you're doing very well. Should be soon." She smiled. "You've got quite the gift basket there. I wish somebody would deliver one of those for me."

Elaine smiled. "I'm very lucky."

"I'll say." The nurse patted her leg and left.

Johnnie grinned. "She likes my gift," she said.

"Mm." Elaine looked at her, wanting to taste her. She wanted out of that bed so damned bad.

"She can't have it."

Johnnie kissed her hand again. "No, she can't. It's just for you."

The door opened again and Elaine sighed. "I have no more blood; you've taken it all."

But it was Michael who peered around the corner. "Knock knock."

He had a bottle of wine in his hand and he tiptoed inside.

"Here, take it." He handed Elaine the bottle, and she tucked it beneath her covers.

"What is this? You're crazy."

"You're going to think I'm crazy when you see what that is."

Elaine took a glance and her mouth fell open. "Michael Anthony!"

"I told you."

"Oh my God, you mad man." Elaine looked at Johnnie. "He just spent a fortune on a bottle of wine." She eyed the bottle of D'Oliveira Vintage Madeira 1957. He'd easily spent four hundred dollars.

Michael interrupted. "But what you don't understand and what she's not telling you is that she's a bit of a wine snob. Only vintage for her."

Elaine grimaced at him. "I've been better. Been settling for less."

Johnnie squeezed her hand and rose, most likely to be polite and let Michael visit. Elaine warmed at her kindness but already felt hollow at imagining her leaving.

"I should get going."

Elaine loved looking at her in the v-neck white tee and worn jeans. Such simple attire held such beauty. It awed her.

She protested her leaving, as did Michael. But Johnnie insisted, and Elaine knew she looked weak, tired. And they very well couldn't get it on in the hospital. If Johnnie's heart had raced like hers had, it was probably a good thing she was leaving. Otherwise, no one would be able to pull them apart.

"I have work to do," she said. Elaine imagined her painting. So focused and intense. A strand of hair falling across her brow to brush back. It made her want her all the more.

She held fast to her hand. "I'll call you," she said softly.

Johnnie nodded. She knelt and kissed her tenderly on the lips. "I look forward to it."

Johnnie left her breathless, looking back once before she rounded the corner.

She and Michael were silent for a long moment after she left. Elaine stared at the spot where she'd disappeared, somehow hoping her presence, her essence would remain.

"She's very kind," Michael said, breaking the silence.

Elaine kept staring. "Yes."

"She's cares very deeply for you."

Elaine closed her eyes. "I think so, yes."

"You care very deeply for her."

Elaine breathed deeply. "I do."

More silence, and Elaine opened her eyes to study the gift basket. It was as if she chose each item herself. It was so thoughtful, so intimate somehow. Now when she bathed, she'd think of Johnnie and long for her presence. Johnnie would know what she smelled like, what her bathroom would smell like with the candles. She would know these intimate things about her, and the thought excited her. It would be between them. Their little secret.

"I'm very happy for you," Michael said. She looked at him and saw the tears. "I'm just so happy."

Elaine teared up, thinking of Barb. A sensation gnawed at her insides, and she knew it well. Guilt. It killed her excitement and desire, devouring it like a quickly growing cancer. It blackened her, bled through her body until she was completely dark. She cried then, hating herself for feeling anything but love for Barb, hating that she felt such guilt.

Michael inched closer and held her, allowing her to sob. "It's okay," he said. "Go ahead and cry." He held her gently, yet he felt so strong. She smelled his spicy after-shave, and she clung to his muscular form. It was an embrace she could only ever have imagined. She'd never had that embrace as a child. A loving fatherly embrace, telling her it was going to be okay. Protecting her. Harboring her.

But she had it now with Michael, and though it was a long time coming, she clung to it and took it, trusting that it was true and right and good. She cried until she tired and he released her and wiped her tears. Then he tucked the covers in around her. His own cheeks were wet with tears, and his eyes were glossed over. He smiled at her despite it and tapped on the hidden wine bottle.

"Too bad we can't open that now."

Elaine laughed, wiping her eyes. "No kidding."

Michael seemed thoughtful. "Nah, that needs to be shared with someone very special."

Elaine swallowed against a tear torn throat. "Barb's not here," she said.

"I know," he said. "Johnnie is."

Elaine glanced at their entwined hands. "I'm not sure I'm ready."

"No one ever is. You just have to open your heart and try."

"I'm not sure I can. Not completely."

"Uh, you looked to be doing a damn good job of it when I walked in."

Elaine couldn't help but laugh a little. "That's just it. She moves me so, and I lose my head and my desire takes over. She just completely floors me, Michael. And leaves me feeling things I've never felt, not even with Barb."

"And that's what's bothering you. You feel you're betraying Barb somehow."

Elaine nodded. "I guess I am. How can I lose the love of my life only to find that she may not be the love of my life? What kind of person am I?" Her eyelids grew heavy as she spoke, and her last few words were difficult to get out.

"A human," Michael said. He leaned in and kissed her forehead. "Now, don't think. Just rest."

Elaine's eyes fell closed, and they were too heavy to open. She breathed deeply and fell into the peaceful realm of sleep.

CHAPTER THIRTY-FIVE

Johnnie was in her studio painting with her palette knife, creating a rainy cityscape for a client when Eddie walked in, calling out his presence like a Viking winning a battle. It made her jerk, and she cursed him under her breath.

"Must you scare the absolute shit out of me every time you walk in?" She straightened from her focused stance and placed her palette knife on her tray. She wiped her hands with the moist cloth she kept next to it. The sun was sharp coming through the large windows, and she had to squint to look at him.

"Is that how you greet someone bringing you prizes?" He breezed behind the counter and deposited several plastic grocery bags, sunglasses on, new haircut worn with a bounding excited confidence.

"It depends on the prize." She moved to the counter.

He smiled devilishly as he unpacked the groceries.

"Nice haircut," she said as she found a cherry tomato to pop into her mouth. She hadn't realized it, but she was starving.

"You like?" He framed his head with his hands, like a spokesmodel trying to sell it to viewers. It was shaved on the sides and back with the top slicked down to the side. Somehow he made it look good.

Johnnie reached for another tomato, and he slapped her hand. "Rinse first, you Neanderthal."

Johnnie shrugged and popped it anyway. "What's all this?" She noted bag after bag of vegetables and fruits.

"This is my new thing." He removed his shades and leaned on the counter. "I'm going vegan."

Johnnie laughed. "Bullshit." Eddie was always jumping into fad after fad. "I give it a week. No, three days."

He gave her the finger. "I'm serious, John John."

"What brought this on?"

"I went to the doctor."

"And?"

He continued unpacking and then began organizing. "I have high blood pressure."

"Why? I thought I was the one who was too intense."

He shrugged. "I don't know. I'm getting older I guess. Both my folks have it, and I do tend to worry about things. Present company included."

Johnnie watched him work, and she felt a twinge of guilt. "I'm really doing fine, Eddie."

He didn't speak, just kept busy. "You are now, yes." He shook his head. "It's not just you. It's the dating, the men, and the lack of relationships, my folks, my job. I'm just too stressed. And..." He gave her a sheepish look. "I'm getting a little thicker around the middle."

She stole another tomato. "That's easily fixed. You know I've lost a lot more weight than that."

He widened his eyes. "I don't know, girl. I'm not going to be able to go as extreme as you do."

"This isn't extreme?" She pointed at all the vegetables.

He placed his hands on his hips. "Oh, my God. You're right. What the hell do I do with all this?"

"And why in the world did you bring it all here?"

"Because you're doing it with me."

"What? No. No way."

"Yes, you are." He turned and began placing the food in the fridge. "And since you're mostly here now, I brought you some things to help you get started."

"Eddie, this is crazy. I have no idea how to be a vegan. And this is more than just a little."

"I plan on visiting you a lot. The less I'm alone, the less I'll stress. You're my sounding board."

"That's fine. But…"

"I know. I don't know what to do with it all either. Which is why we're jumping into it together."

"But I don't have high blood pressure. So technically, I don't have to do this."

He turned hand on hip. "You have no idea if you do or don't. You avoid doctors like the plague."

Johnnie rounded the counter and helped him finish putting things away, having no idea what half the stuff was. But she played along. Eddie was always there for her, and this honestly probably wouldn't last. They finished, and Eddie handed her a Naked Juice and they headed for the old sofa where they sank into comfort and familiarity.

"This was such a good thrift store buy," he said, rubbing the soft green fabric of the sofa.

"Mm," she agreed, sipping her berry blended juice.

He looked around, not as enthusiastic about his green colored juice. He took small sips and seemed to be heavy with thought. "You've been busy."

She took a big breath. "I've been steady. Lucky I guess."

"If that's what you want to call her."

Johnnie lowered her juice and watched the dust motes dance in the sunlight. "Elaine," she said.

"Your drop-dead gorgeous muse."

Johnnie smiled, but inside she felt uncertain.

She hadn't heard from her in days. Elaine left the hospital a while ago, and Johnnie couldn't help but feel anxious over the situation. She'd said she'd call, and Johnnie had been waiting patiently. She'd pushed off Gail again and again, but it was getting more and more difficult to do so. Monica had called as well, wanting a date. She'd put her off, but she didn't want to hurt her or play games.

"She hasn't called has she?" Eddie asked.

"No."

He sighed and crossed a leg over his knee. His shoes were expensive and shiny. She didn't know the brand or the price, but she knew him. His black slacks were pressed perfectly along with his white tee and black paisley patterned vest. His fingernails were also black, probably to match his Wayfarer shades.

"What are you going to do?"

She leaned back and crossed her ankles in brown lace up work boots. Paint splattered her work jeans and her green Lucky T-shirt.

"I don't know."

"Yeah, that's a tough one."

"I'm worried for her health. What if she's not okay?"

"Wouldn't she be back in the hospital?"

Johnnie didn't answer, considering his comment. He was right. Unless Elaine was at another hospital.

"Why don't you call that Michael guy? He would know, right?"

Johnnie nodded. "Yeah."

Eddie nudged her. "So call."

"What, now?"

His eyebrows rose. "Why not?"

Johnnie stood as her nerves got the better of her. She paced. Eddie sighed.

"Sweetie, don't have a panic attack, just call."

"I'm not having a panic attack."

"No, you're just going over what-ifs and torturing yourself. Stop it."

She stopped, knowing he was right. She reached in her back pocket for her phone and stared at the illuminated date and time.

CHAPTER THIRTY-SIX

The bell on the door rang as someone entered. Johnnie turned, expecting to see Gail, who had been showing up at the studio whenever she felt like it. Her heart jumped to her throat when Elaine appeared. She stood in a pair of jeans and a red sleeveless blouse. She was clinging to a black purse.

"Hi," she said.

Johnnie couldn't help but stare.

Eddie, however, hopped up and crossed the room to introduce himself. "Hi, I'm Eddie, the BFF."

She smiled and took his hand. "I'm Elaine," she said.

"The muse," he said for her.

She cocked her head and then agreed. "I guess I can own up to that."

"Oh, you should," he said.

He gave Johnnie a look and then gave the gesture to call him. "I'm off, ladies," he said. "Elaine, it was a pleasure and I hope to see you again soon."

Johnnie waved him off and they heard the bell sound as he left.

Elaine stepped farther in, and Johnnie felt nailed to the floor.

"I, uh, was just going to call Michael. To check on you."

Elaine looked away. "I'm sorry I haven't called. It's just been difficult getting back into the swing of things."

Johnnie wasn't sure what to do. What her presence meant. She could feel her tentativeness.

"Are you okay?"

Elaine again met her eyes. "Yes."

"Well, that's good news."

"Yes."

Johnnie watched as she glanced around, studying the finished canvases.

"You've been working a lot I see."

"I'm just trying to keep busy really."

"It's working."

Johnnie couldn't take the small talk anymore. "Did you want to sit and talk?" She motioned toward the couch. "Would you like a drink?"

Elaine held up a hand. "No, I'm fine, thank you."

She didn't move and Johnnie felt sick. She wasn't there to see her, to be with her. She was there to say good-bye.

"Don't," Johnnie said, clenching her jaw so she wouldn't tear up. She looked away and put up her wall. It was just another person pushing her away. Saying they cared but really didn't. She could handle it. It was all she knew when it came to love.

"Johnnie, I—"

"Just please go. I don't want to hear you say it." She met her eyes. "Not you," she whispered.

Elaine moved closer with pain etched on her beautiful face. "I just can't," she said. "I don't want you to get hurt."

Johnnie nodded. "Yeah, okay."

"I'm not ready," she said.

Johnnie laughed, so angry so hurt. "Right, because I'm so dangerous." She shook her head. Her phone vibrated, but she ignored it. "Please, leave me be. The more you say, the worse it is."

"I didn't mean for this to happen," Elaine said. "I should've just stopped the sessions."

"What is this exactly? And what the hell is so bad about it? I for one, like it, whatever this is. It has taken my world and turned it upside down and shaken it. It has seriously shaken up the snow globe of my life, and I know it has yours too."

Elaine felt the words; Johnnie could see it on her face. But her body held firm, and Johnnie knew the words hadn't penetrated her heart.

"Johnnie, I'm not over Barb. And that isn't fair to you."

Johnnie moved closer and Elaine's breath quickened. "Do you think I'm over the people or things that I've experienced in my life? No. I'm not. But I go on. Day by day. And I open up, even though I know better, even though I'm afraid. I opened up with you. Not completely, but enough to know this hurts like a motherfucker."

"I'm sorry," she said.

"You feel it too," Johnnie said, standing before her. She touched her arms, felt her tremble. She touched her face and felt her skin heat.

"Johnnie…"

"Kiss me," she said.

"We can't. It isn't wise."

"Fuck wise."

The bell on the door rang again, and Johnnie took a step back, the moment gone. Gail walked in like she owned the place and stopped. She looked at the both of them, and her face contorted in anger. Elaine turned and straightened herself.

"Who the hell is this?" she demanded.

Johnnie was furious. "Gail, get out."

"No, I want to know who this is."

Elaine looked to Johnnie. "I should go." She crossed the room.

"No, please don't go," Johnnie said, going after her.

"Is this her?" Gail asked. "Is this Elaine?"

Elaine stopped and turned to look at her.

"It is, isn't it?" Gail moved toward her, and Johnnie hurried to get between them.

"Gail, you know you aren't welcome here. You need to leave."

Gail ignored her, her angry gaze focused on Elaine. When she spoke she spat venom. "She calls your name when she comes," Gail said.

Elaine blinked as if she couldn't believe what she'd heard. Johnnie wanted to die, and her heart jumped from her mouth and lay beating helplessly on the floor.

Elaine moved toward the door with her purse now slung over her shoulder.

"But it's me making her come," Gail shouted after her. "It's all me."

Elaine pushed through the door, and Johnnie ran out after her.

"Elaine, please. Please stop."

Elaine opened the door to her Audi sedan. She slid on designer black shades, but they didn't hide the stone of her face.

"It's over with Gail," Johnnie said. "She just won't leave me alone."

Elaine looked up just before she climbed into her car. "Well, if you're fucking her, she's not going to go away. Trust me on that one."

Johnnie watched helplessly as she climbed in and started her engine. After she backed out, she peeled away, leaving Johnnie in the late afternoon sun. It never felt sharper as it pierced her eyes and Elaine's words pierced her heart.

CHAPTER THIRTY-SEVEN

The desert was blooming with life, and Elaine was sitting on her back patio taking it all in. Baby birds were chirping, mothers and fathers leaving the trees to search for food. The air was crisp after a short rain, and Elaine could smell the earth and the trees. She eased back in her lounge chair and stared at the swaying palms in the breeze, letting them talk her into a quick nap. Her eyes grew heavy in response and she fell limp. The magazine she'd been reading slid from her lap, and she startled awake. She retrieved the magazine and settled back in, but she was no longer as relaxed as she was before.

Her recovery had been going well for the most part. But her insomnia had worsened. The doctor said her heart was fine and doing well, and she was proud of Elaine for exercising daily and eating a proper diet. But the sleep problem, that was a different story. Dr. Klein recommended a psychiatrist, and Elaine had fought her on it. But Dr. Klein knew her history; she knew about her loss. And she also knew that Elaine had done very little to deal with it.

"Hello!" Michael called from the side gate.

"Come on in!" she replied.

She heard the squeak of the gate and then the tornado rush of his new little Yorkshire terrier, Maximus, tearing through the yard. Donovan had adopted him as a surprise for Michael, who had been thrilled. He'd been begging Elaine to come meet him. Michael rounded the corner with a smile, hand in the pocket of his khaki shorts, with the other carrying magazines. He plopped them down on the small table next to her and groaned as he settled in on the opposite lounge chair.

"It is a goddamned gorgeous day," he said, soaking up the clean sunshine. He placed his hands behind his head and looked over at her with one eye closed. "So," he looked to the tiny dog, "what do you think? He cuter than me?"

She laughed. "Mm, you might have some competition."

"Sha, you sound like Donovan."

They both watched the dog hop through the grass. Then Michael looked at her once again.

"So how you doing, El?"

She raised her eyebrows and watched Maximus make his rounds to her bushes and trees. "Okay, I suppose."

"Liar. You look like a ghost. You haven't slept much have you?"

She shrugged.

"Did you make an appointment with that shrink?"

She glared at him. "I'm going to pretend you didn't say that."

He laughed. "My God, you are stubborn."

"I'm a psychologist. I do not need a shrink."

"What you need," he said, "is to sleep. You can't fully recover without sleep."

"I'm well aware of that, thank you."

"So call."

"I've made an appointment with my general practitioner."

He laughed again. "Oh, if Barb were here now."

"Yeah, well, she's not."

"I wish she was because she'd have your ass in that shrink's office in a nanosecond. Dragging you in by your ear if necessary. She couldn't stand to see you suffer just because you're stubborn. She thought it was ridiculous. Remember?"

Elaine didn't say anything.

"Am I going to have to do the dragging?"

She gave him a look. "I dare you to try."

He sighed. "I think you should see the psychiatrist. You need to deal with more than just the insomnia. You need to deal with your loss. Grieve properly. You know this, Elaine."

"Of course I know, Michael. It's just not so easy to recognize things when it's yourself."

"Okay, then let's step out of you."

She chuckled.

"No, I'm serious. Pretend I'm talking to you about a client. She's middle-aged, widowed, kind of a lone wolf, has casual sex, doesn't date, rarely comes out to see her friends, overworks, over drinks, hasn't gone through the stages of grief, can't sleep, keeps her emotions bottled up—"

"Okay. I get it. I'm a little fucked up."

"You're not fucked up; you're just sad." He took her hand. "And you miss her. And that's okay."

She couldn't look at him. If she did she knew she would cry.

"Let someone help you with that. If not me, then someone. Please. I want you back. I want the laugh back, the dancing green eyes, the fearless wit."

"What if she's gone for good?" Elaine said.

"She's not. She may have changed a little, but she's still in there."

Maximus jumped up near her feet and then balanced his way up to her. She scratched his head and sealed her mouth as he showered her with kisses.

"See, Maximus agrees."

She laughed. "I bet he agrees with anyone."

Michael released her hand and stared at the sky. "You know what we need?"

"A margarita with salt?"

He laughed. "Besides that. We need a trip to Sedona."

She stared at the sky with him while scratching Maximus on the chest. He made a noise of pleasure and rolled onto his back on her chest.

"As soon as you get some sleep that is," he said.

"Maybe." She had to admit Sedona did sound nice. Maybe stop off at Oak Creek, have a picnic lunch. Do a little hike. Visit the shops. Take photos. It sounded nice. Really nice. "I might just take you up on that," she said.

"I'll hold you to that," he said.

He grabbed the magazines and perused through them.

Elaine noted the *Time, People, National Geographic, Photography*. He'd brought them for her, which was nice. She looked at the one he chose.

"*Men's Health*?" she asked.

He shrugged. "I like the articles."

She laughed. "Oh, I do too."

"Leave me alone," he said, flipping through it.

She opened the *Time* and skimmed through, searching for an interesting read. Michael was still doing the same.

"So have you seen any of Johnnie?" he asked nonchalantly.

Elaine froze and her heart sank into a deep pit. She tried to regain her composure by flipping pages, but it was too late, he'd seen it.

"El?"

"No, I haven't." In fact, it had been a couple of weeks since she'd last seen Johnnie at her studio. The memory of it was all too real. All too painful. She preferred not to think about it. But honestly, it was eating her up at night, causing her to toss and turn, driving her to madness. She'd finally give in and get up, open a bottle of wine, sit and stew in the living room with vocal jazz saturating her mind with Johnnie and Barb until she was so damn deep in it she was drowning with no one there to save her.

He raised an eyebrow. "I figured the two of you would be seeing a lot of each other."

She tossed the magazine aside. Searched for the *New Yorker*. It wasn't there.

"Did you bring me a *New Yorker*?"

"Nope."

She grabbed the *People* and tore through the pages. Why did he have to bring up Johnnie? Couldn't she just relax outside on a beautiful day?

"I think you should call her," he said softly.

"I think you should mind your own business."

He smiled and tilted his head as if he'd taken a blow to the face. "I think you'd better call her before someone else scoops her up. She's quite the catch."

"I think you should know that she already has someone else. Her ex. So there."

"Really?" He put down his magazine and stared at her.

She put hers down as well. "Yes."

"When did this happen?"

"I don't know. But she admitted to sleeping with her and then the ex showed up at the studio while I was there. She was not happy. Which leads me to believe that Johnnie is not being honest with either one of us."

She knew that probably wasn't the case. What she saw in Johnnie, felt in her kiss, was all too real. And Johnnie had told her she'd only thought of her, and the ex had even confirmed it. But it sounded like a good enough reason, and maybe it would keep Michael at bay. Her insane jealousy at the sight of the two of them... that was more difficult to keep at bay. She didn't like the feeling, and honestly, she had no right to feel that way. Yes, she and Johnnie had shared a kiss and their feelings, but Johnnie had slept with her ex before that. And she and Johnnie weren't exclusive or even dating. But even so, knowing that Johnnie had been with someone else while they were navigating their way toward each other...it gave her pause and made her think. Maybe Johnnie wasn't really so into her after all. Why else would the ex show up at studio and act so possessive? Had Johnnie already sunk back into a relationship with her ex just because she hadn't heard from her in a few days?

The possibility stung, and it only added to the madness of her feelings and the thoughts of Barb and everything else swirling in her mind late at night.

Michael had stopped turning his pages. He was focused now, but she doubted he was really reading.

"Are you sure about all that? Have you discussed it with her?"

"She tried to tell me it was over between them."

"Then maybe it is."

"I doubt it. The ex seemed pretty pissed. Acted like I was an intruder."

He scoffed. "Right, and that's never happened to you, right? Unwanted one-night stands hunting you down when you had already told them to get lost?"

She adjusted her sunglasses and took a sip of her iced tea. His point had hit home, and she recalled Johnnie telling the ex to get lost. Maybe he was right. Then again maybe she was. Either way, she was keeping it as far away from her as she could.

"But the nights are a bitch," she whispered to herself.

"Hmm?"

"Nothing."

She sat up and placed Maximus on the ground. He took off into the grass and chased a lizard to the wall and then barked as it escaped by climbing upward. She needed to move, to get out of the stagnation she was in. Michael was stirring things up in her just like always. Maybe she should go to Sedona on her own.

She stood and stretched carefully. Her incision wasn't so tender anymore, but she still imagined it could easily tear open somehow.

"Let me take you to dinner," Michael said, rising with her.

She moved toward the back door. "I'm not up for it tonight. Thank you, though."

He stood still with his hands in pockets, trying to fend off defeat. "I could make you something."

She blinked slowly. Her body felt like lead. She needed to lie down and at least try to sleep.

"Not today, okay?"

He nodded.

He came to her and hugged her. She leaned into him but kept her arms slack. If she held him she might never let go. She knew he was her anchor in her increasingly tumultuous sea. But she needed to try to stay afloat on her own. At least for now.

"You coming in tomorrow?" he asked, releasing her.

She nodded.

"You don't have to you know."

"I know."

"If you don't show I'll assume you're sleeping."

"Okay."

He kissed her cheek and called to Maximus. She watched as they walked through the grass to the back gate. He let himself out with the Yorkie on his heels. She went inside and collapsed on the couch, television on mute. She stared at the ceiling fan praying it would lure her to sleep.

If only she could be so lucky.

CHAPTER THIRTY-EIGHT

Johnnie lay haphazardly on the old green sofa in her studio. She flicked a wet brush with her thumb while staring out the window. The day should be dreary, dark, brooding. But that was just the way she felt inside. No, the world outside was bright and sunny. Everyone having a grand old time.

She grimaced and tossed the brush. She crossed her bare feet along the top of the couch and placed her hands behind her head. Her eyes grew heavy, as they often did lately. She didn't fight it, knowing it would lead to a land of laudanum, a numb, pleasant land of Elaine. Often times, she'd sit and stare for hours, in a half stupor, just thinking of her or staring at the paintings of her. She'd sold some, but the one where she had that look, the one that wanted Johnnie, she'd kept that one. And the one where she was touching her broken heart, she'd kept that one as well. She'd wanted to bring them home, but Gail wouldn't allow it. In fact, Gail kept turning them to face the wall.

Johnnie laughed a little at her ridiculousness. Nothing could erase Elaine. Not now, not ever. But Gail was possessive, and for some reason she wanted Johnnie back. It was a mystery to Johnnie, but she just assumed she was flat broke and waiting for the next free ride to Costa Rica or someplace similar. She had a lover there. And they were volatile, on and off. At the moment they must be off. Johnnie wished she cared, but she just really didn't give a damn.

She was still painting, but she had slowed dramatically. Her friend Jimmy was just grateful she still had enough for his show. Commission requests were still coming in, and Johnnie tried; most of them were easy. But her heart wasn't in it, and her new friend Ian had noticed, offering to give her a good kick in the arse. She'd go to his house and they'd drink a few pints and paint. She was really enjoying her newfound love for abstract. At Ian's she didn't even pick up a brush. It was all palette knife, and it made her feel free, fierce, fiery. He often commented on the sound of her strokes and her breathing. He knew she was working shit out when she painted at his house.

He just laughed and encouraged her. Told her the only thing worse than a woman was the paint. It was an addiction, a desire, a fucking menace, and it would drive you mad whether you put it to canvas, wall, or nowhere at all. A woman could walk in and out of your life, but the paint, it would always be there, waiting for you to do something with it.

Johnnie eyed her phone as it vibrated. It was Jolene. She could always feel when Johnnie was off. And she'd been bugging her since Gail had been back. Jolene did not care for her by any sense of the word. She found her fake. And that was not a good thing at all when Jolene said it. No, she wanted Johnnie to go up north to her brother's house to sit and sweat all these issues out. Johnnie had been putting her off, too depressed and lethargic to even consider it.

The doorbell chimed, and she didn't bother to look over.

"Don't get up. It's only me," Gail said, coming over to sit, placing Johnnie's legs atop her.

"Don't worry. I won't."

Gail rolled her eyes. "Why are you so depressing? God, you're so negative it's driving me crazy."

Johnnie didn't bother to look at her. "Then go."

"I will."

"Good."

"I'm serious, Johnnie. You're really a downer."

Johnnie didn't answer. She just stared at the wall. She could smell Gail's lotion, and it stirred things in her whether she wanted them too or not.

"I'm sorry about Elaine or whoever, but she's just not for you. She'd doesn't love you like I do. No one does." She took her hand and tried to sound sincere. But Johnnie was learning her moves, her technique. She said all the right things. She even seemed to mean them. But it was only skin deep. Inside, who knew what she was thinking? How to get what she wanted, how to get ahead, how to outplay the person…who knew? But it wasn't love. It wasn't caring. It wasn't sincerity.

Yet Johnnie was putting up with it and playing along in a way, while feeling her out in return. What else did she have to do? Elaine didn't want her, and as far as she was concerned, Elaine was the one. And when the one walks away, nothing else seems to matter. You go on, one foot in front of the other, but you're not really awake. You're a zombie with a mechanical heart, it beating whether you want it to or not. Besides, what if Gail was right? What if Elaine couldn't really love her with her past and her issues? How badly would that hurt to fall for her to have something and then to have her jump ship because she didn't have the capacity to love unconditionally? Or worse, what if they had something and it terrified Johnnie…leaving her to fear Elaine would wise up at any moment and walk away, turning her back on her? Like her own family had?

She grabbed her head. It was all too much. It was just easier not to care, to ignore if she could. But the thoughts and the images were a constant barrage, like a bad film stuck on the reel.

"What is it, baby? Your head hurt?"

"No." She sat up and stroked Gail's face. Gail moved a little as if uncomfortable. She looked into her eyes. "Tell me how you feel about me," Johnnie said softly. She leaned against the couch and relaxed. If Gail loved her, she'd be able to tell.

But Gail looked away and laughed nervously. "What is this?"

"Come on, talk to me."

"I tell you all the time."

"But not like this. This is intimacy." This was what she had with Elaine. Gail looked at her, eyes full of fear.

Johnnie raised her eyebrows, waiting. She stroked her face again, and Gail caught her hand.

"This is seriously freaking me out," she said.

Johnnie didn't move as Gail rose and went to the fridge and pretended to be thirsty. "Want something?"

"No." She sighed. "Can you come back please?"

Gail opened the water and drank. "Babe, you know I love you. But that closeness crap makes me feel trapped or something."

"You can't sit here and look in my eyes?"

Gail laughed. "Can't we just forget it?"

Johnnie felt the hair on her neck stand up like she did when she sensed a person with untruthful energy. Someone that wasn't authentic. A predator. She sometimes felt it with Gail, but Gail always covered.

"Come here. I'll help you wrap up these canvases for the show."

She was always so helpful when Johnnie needed it. According to Gail, that was her showing love. Johnnie rose, defeated, and began wrapping the canvases she was going to display. When they got to Elaine's, Johnnie stared, lost in her gaze.

"Please tell me you're selling those or getting rid of them."

"Neither," Johnnie said. "But I am showing them."

"You're kidding?"

"No." Johnnie wrapped them carefully. Gail huffed next to her and began throwing stuff around rather than placing it nicely back in place.

"I won't have her in the loft," Gail said.

Johnnie continued wrapping. "It's not your loft."

"Johnnie," she said, hands on hips. "Don't you care how I feel?"

Johnnie thought about it a moment. "No. I only care how I feel right now. I know that sounds selfish and unlike me, but it's where I'm at."

Gail stared at her, shocked. She dropped her hands in disbelief. "I don't need this shit, Johnnie."

"I don't either. If you can't handle it, you can go. I would understand."

Gail remained still. Then she approached and held Johnnie's hands. "We'll do whatever you need." She embraced her, but the hug was stiff. Johnnie could never melt into her form like she could Jolene or Eddie or anyone else who offered a loving hug.

They continued to wrap and pack up the canvases. Johnnie didn't bother thinking about whether Gail meant her words or not. She knew she was only biding her time. Using Johnnie. But again, Johnnie just couldn't find the energy to care. Maybe Gail was the only kind of person she deserved. Maybe a person like Elaine couldn't love her. Maybe she just wasn't good enough.

She was too sensitive and too anxious. She over thought and felt people. She was so different and she'd stuck out like a sore thumb in her family. Just as she did in society and in relationships like this.

Maybe Gail was what she was only ever going to get. She might as well accept it.

CHAPTER THIRTY-NINE

Elaine crossed her legs and then crossed them again the other way nervously. She shifted in the chair. The office was so nicely decorated she half expected Dr. Hannibal Lecter to walk in buttoning an Italian suit. At this point, she'd settle for Hannibal the Cannibal in order to just get it over with. He would let her live, wouldn't he?

The door opened, and a woman in her sixties entered, wearing jeans and a sweater and white Chucks. She smiled and eased into her chair across from Elaine.

"Hello," she said.

Elaine felt at ease. "Hello."

"You're Elaine, I presume?"

"Yes."

"I'm Dr. Susan Redmond. But please call me Susan."

She smiled again, crossed her legs, and reached for her notes and a nice fountain pen. Elaine relaxed and took in the Tiffany lamps and the comfortable but imported furniture. Elaine realized she had some work to do on her own office.

"Do you mind if I call you Elaine?"

"No, of course not."

"Tell me, Elaine, why are you here today?"

Elaine found herself shrugging. "I don't really know. I've just been told I need to come."

She flipped through some papers. "Ah, Dr. Klein. Love her. She says you're having trouble sleeping and that you've just recovered from heart valve surgery."

"That's right," Elaine said, smoothing down her skirt.

"That sounds pretty heavy," she said. "How are you feeling right now, physically?"

Elaine readied herself to exaggerate. She straightened her shoulders. "I'm—"

But Susan's look was so soft, so understanding.

"I'm exhausted."

Susan studied her a moment. "Thank you for the honesty. Is it important for you to always appear strong?"

Elaine blinked, surprised. "Yes, yes, it is."

"Since when? Can you remember when that started?"

Elaine blinked again, taken aback by the quick insight. "I guess I was a child. Ten, eleven maybe."

"Can you remember why?"

Elaine closed her eyes. "My father. He was a tough love sort of man. He told me to never show weakness. That the world would eat me up."

"Tell me about him. Was your relationship good?"

"For the most part. I know now that he did things that weren't right, but on the other hand, he did things that were really great. He was just a man."

"How was his treatment of you?"

"Well, that was often confusing. I never knew when he was going to be upset with me or not. Or for what reason. He'd just stop talking and start avoiding. He would lie when I asked if he was upset with me. Many times it hurt me deeply and confused me. I felt like I was always walking on tiptoes around him, never knowing what would set off a silent mood."

"You didn't feel unconditional love?"

"No. If he was happy with me, I was on top of the world. He would joke around, do really nice things, very thoughtful things. But if he wasn't pleased with me, it was ice. Just total ice."

"So you were always trying to please?"

"Yes."

"Do you have siblings?"

"Yes. Two sisters. One of them half."

"How did he treat them?"

"I guess you'd have to ask them. I do know that he favored his biological daughter."

"Why? What makes you say that?"

Elaine pushed out a breath. "I was an overachiever, always trying for his approval, his attention. With his daughter, I felt like I had to downplay that. He—did things. Said things. For example, he asked me if I would give her some of my trophies."

Susan's eyebrows rose. "Really? Did he say why?"

"Because she wanted to pretend she had earned them. To make her feel better."

"She wasn't athletic?"

"No. So he always compensated for that by saying how she was the smart one."

"And you weren't?"

"I was. He just always said I wasn't. I wanted to be a doctor. He said I wasn't smart enough, but she was. He didn't believe it until we both took our SATs. After that, he didn't say it again."

"Did your mother know any of this was going on?"

"No. These were things he said not to tell Mom."

She wrote and looked at her with concern. "Were there lots of things he said to keep from your mother?"

"Yes."

"Anything inappropriate?"

"No. And honestly, once I reached college, I stopped caring how he felt about me. It was just too exhausting, and I had learned it wasn't healthy. So I let it go."

"But you still feel you have to exert a certain stature."

"Absolutely. I feel like I still have to prove I really am the best."

"Who are you trying to convince?"

Elaine paused. "I—I don't know."

"Yourself?"

"I guess, yes."

"Can you accept that you are the best? Will you ever believe it?"

Elaine thought for a panicked moment. Was she the best? Was she strong? Capable? Deserving of everything she had earned herself? Or was she just not quite good enough, only there to give what she earned to someone else?

"I don't know."

"You are good enough, Elaine." She smiled. "Those trophies were yours, the grades were yours. Your talent...it is all you. I'm sorry you were never given approval or told how fantastic you really are."

Elaine found tears forming. "It's silly really. I wasn't abused. Mistreated."

"Emotional abuse is a tricky subject, as I'm sure you know."

She nodded. Fought tears.

"Think about that for some time," she said. "Now, tell me about your health. Are you disabled in any way?"

"No, I just have to take it easy for a while."

"Good."

"And your heart feels okay?"

Elaine wanted to shatter, to show her the shattered pieces of her heart. "Physically, yes."

"But emotionally we're struggling aren't we?"

Elaine could only nod.

"Can you tell me what has you crying?"

"Just realizing things I've never thought of."

"Ah." She again looked at her notes. "Dr. Klein says you're having trouble sleeping."

Elaine wiped a stray tear. "Yes."

"What keeps you up?"

They sat in silence for a long moment while Elaine composed herself. Who was she kidding? She'd convinced herself she could walk in here and give her answers, thank her for the advice, and then walk out unfazed. But here she was not even ten minutes in and she was on the brink of falling apart.

"It's a lot of things," she finally said. "Mainly my wife."

"Oh, you're married?" She smiled and made a note.

"No, my wife, Barb, passed five years ago."

Susan's face clouded, and she passed her some tissue. "I'm very sorry to hear that."

Elaine nodded and took the tissue but swallowed down the tears. "It was sudden. An accident."

Susan wrote some more in her notes. "Tell me, Elaine, where are you in the process of grief?"

Elaine wasn't sure how to answer because she wasn't sure where she was at. "I have no anger, but I still have a hard time accepting that she's gone. And I—I feel like whatever I do in my life still affects her somehow."

"So you're feeling guilt?"

"Yes."

"Can you tell me why? What is it that has you feeling guilty?"

Elaine bit her lower lip for strength. And then something miraculous happened. She thought of Johnnie and she smiled, despite the deep sorrow. "I've met someone and I am developing feelings for her."

Susan smiled. "That's a wonderful feeling. Are you allowing yourself to enjoy it at all?"

"Sometimes. Honestly when it happens I don't even think about it. I'm just so—overcome."

"That's sounds beautiful."

Elaine smiled. "It is. But as soon as she's gone I think of Barb and the whole cycle starts over again."

"Have you been intimate with anyone since Barb?"

Elaine looked down at her hands. "I have, yes."

"And how did that go?"

"Fine, actually. They were strangers, one night stands."

"You had no feelings for them."

"Other than physical attraction, no."

"But this new woman, I'm sorry, what's her name?"

"Johnnie."

"Johnnie, you care about her, like you did Barb."

"Yes." She stared at the wall, her emotion climbing up her throat again. "It—feels—the attraction I mean, feels stronger than it did with Barb."

Susan relaxed her hand and looked at her softly. "You know that's perfectly normal. We feel differently about each person we meet. You being strongly attracted to Johnnie does not mean you love or loved Barb any less."

Elaine sucked in a shaky breath. Hearing it aloud nearly knocked her over. Michael had told her the same thing, and she knew it in her head. But she just couldn't allow it to seep into her heart.

"Can you accept that, Elaine?"

Elaine covered her mouth. "I'm trying."

"Take deep breaths."

Elaine did as instructed. She kept replaying her words. "I don't love her any less. She's still my Barb."

"Yes, and she always will be." Susan shifted in her chair. "Does Johnnie know about Barb?"

"Yes."

"Is she understanding?"

Elaine grew quiet. "I've pushed her away. Told her it was because I wasn't over Barb."

Susan looked at her in thought. "How did she take it?"

"Not good. She tried to talk sense into me."

"Do you feel like you're not ready?"

"I think—I think I'm just scared."

"Of what?"

She thought deep, dug it out. Cried before she could talk. "Of loving that hard again and losing."

Susan soothed her as she cried. When she finished, she allowed her some time to compose herself.

"These are all perfectly normal feelings, Elaine. You're beating yourself up for no reason. Everyone has to grieve, even someone like you, who strives for strength and perfection. These thoughts, feelings, it's the process."

Elaine gave an exhausted laugh. "When is it going to end?"

"When you let it."

"When I let it?"

"Right now you're fighting it. Let these feelings and thoughts come. Feel them. Experience them. Don't drown them out with meaningless sex or alcohol or anything else."

Elaine laughed again. "Feel. That's what I tell my clients."

"You're a smart lady. You know this. It's just difficult to see when the client is you."

Susan made some more notes. "You say here in your forms that you don't run a typical practice. What do you mean by that?"

Elaine cleared her throat. "I'm a creative coach of sorts. A creative practitioner. I help people find their inner strength, creativity, and ambition."

"Interesting."

"It is. It's very rewarding."

"Why the secrecy? You didn't put a name for your practice."

Elaine sat straighter. "We offer unique techniques to help the person grow. Sometimes it can be intimate in nature."

"Sex?"

"Sometimes sexual, yes. It depends upon the client. But as a rule, we do not touch our clients."

"You guide."

"Yes."

"Do you enjoy your job?"

"Very much so. I love helping people discover their inner desires, talents, feelings."

"I take it you are successful?"

"We are."

"You need stimulation and visual results in order to feel that you've done a good job."

"Yes."

"A typical practice would bore you."

"It did, yes."

"This Johnnie, how did you meet her? Was she originally a one-night stand?"

Elaine stared at her, having no idea what to say. "She actually was a client." Her chest tightened at the judgment she feared might come.

"Oh?"

"Yes, she's an artist."

"She good?"

"Very."

Susan smiled. "And you ended things because of your feelings?"

"Yes."

"How did that feel?"

Elaine relaxed a little. "Awful. She's so talented and I know I can help her so much more. But the feelings, they were mutual. It wasn't right."

"Can't you still help her? Just not in a doctor client atmosphere?"

"I suppose I could. But—"

"You've told her no because of Barb."

Elaine nodded.

"Elaine, tell me, at night when you can't sleep what are you thinking about?"

"Barb. My empty bed. My empty house. Johnnie. Guilt. Loneliness. Longing for both Barb and Johnnie."

"Do you take anything? To help you sleep?"

"No. I've tried. It didn't help."

"What about drinking?"

Elaine closed her eyes. "I do do that, yes."

"Do you get drunk?"

"Yes."

"Do you sleep?"

"Eventually. But fitfully."

Susan made more notes. "Are you currently able to work?"

"I do, but I've cut back on clients."

"Would you like to get back to work?"

"Yes, very much."

She rose from her chair and walked behind her desk. "I think you'd benefit from a low dose of antidepressant and something for anxiety to help you sleep."

Elaine thought about arguing. Susan watched her.

"Will you give it a shot?"

Elaine felt the heaviness of her eyes, the fatigue in her limbs. Her chest still burned from surfaced emotion. Eventually, she nodded.

"In the meantime," Susan said, "have people over to your home. You might even want to invite Johnnie. See how it feels."

"Oh, I don't know. I mean—"

Susan held up a hand. "When you feel ready."

Elaine nodded.

Susan sat and typed on her laptop. She asked for Elaine's pharmacy information, sent the prescriptions, and then folded her hands and looked at her.

"Cut back on the drinking," she said. "Can you handle that?"

"I suppose I have no choice."

"Not if you want to feel better."

"I want to see you in two weeks. And please call if you have any questions or problems before then."

Elaine rose and Susan came to shake her hand. She took her hand in both of hers. "I lost my husband eight years ago," she said. "The pain never goes away, but it does soften."

"Thank you."

Susan smiled, saw her out, and Elaine left the office with a lot on her mind. Mainly, Johnnie.

CHAPTER FORTY

*T*he night was black, hazed so that the streetlights looked like smudges of light. Johnnie had hit just about every cheap pay-by-the-week motel there was in her area. She'd been driving for two hours, crying, angry and confused. Her father had just run her out of her business, and her parents had put her on the street. Gail wouldn't answer her phone, but she had a new lover and wouldn't give Johnnie the time of day. Johnnie knew this, but she kept trying to reach her, desperate.

Being on the street with agoraphobia was a nightmare she couldn't form into words. People morphed into demons, lights turned to strange orbs of evil. She jerked when horns honked. She had trouble breathing when stopped at a stoplight. And when she pulled over at a motel, it took her twenty minutes to work up enough nerve to go inside and ask about a vacancy.

Her head began to spin with a cracking headache from stress. Her stomach was clenched, but it still growled. She had eight hundred bucks. That was it. The rest had gone to the business to pay off the bills.

Why had she trusted him when others had warned her? Because she'd wanted to believe in him. Believe in his integrity, the integrity he always talked about and bragged about. Johnnie struggled to make sense of it. Gail had been in business with her. Could it have something to do with her? She'd kicked her out three weeks before, claiming a new lover. Johnnie had been staying at her folks', hoping to work it out with her.

But nothing was working for her. She was panicked and beyond terrified. She pulled into Gail's neighborhood, where she lived off alimony from her ex-husband. The library sat off to the right in the desert. Johnnie eased her vehicle in and parked near the back. A No Dumping sign sat next to the Dumpster. A hump, a form, moved. It stretched upward. It was a person. The night was chilly so the form drug a blanket over its shoulders. It moved toward the car.

Johnnie cranked the car and locked the doors. But the figure held out a blanket. A beautiful hand-woven one. Johnnie squinted and saw her wide face, and long braid. Johnnie powered down her window.

"It's cold," she said. "Even in the car." She pushed the blanket forward.

Johnnie struggled for voice. "Thanks, but I'm okay."

The form lowered the blanket and turned to walk away.

"Wait," Johnnie said. "What are you doing out here?"

The woman pointed at another sign that said No Urban Camping.

"I'm camping out."

Johnnie rubbed her temple.

"You've got nowhere to go," the woman said.

Johnnie nodded.

"You've been crying."

Johnnie wiped her face, embarrassed.

"This place is safe. Only the cops come to run you out. I just hide at the dog park till they're gone."

"How long have you—been out here?"

The woman shrugged. "Two weeks."

"Where is your home?"

"Ain't got one. Can't keep a job so I got evicted."

Johnnie clenched the steering wheel. Anger rose within her. "Get in the car," she said.

The woman just looked at her.

"We'll find a place to stay."

The woman came close, then reached out and touched her hand. They felt one another in silence. A calm came over Johnnie.

A kindred feeling, an understanding. She knew the woman was a recluse. That she had suffered abuse. She also sensed her goodness. She also sensed fear.

"I'm Johnnie."

The woman nodded and removed her hand. "Jolene."

She walked around the car with a few more blankets and climbed in. Though she'd been on the street for a couple of weeks, she looked decent. She appeared to be fed and clean. When she spoke, it was with purpose and monotone in pitch.

"Where are we going?"

"Home." Johnnie put the car in reverse and headed toward Gail's. A strange car was in the driveway. Johnnie pulled up next to the house. "I'll be right back." She walked up the front walk, staring at the paint she'd chosen. She looked at the neglected rose bushes she'd planted and saw the sun pot she'd chosen for the front porch.

She rang the doorbell. It was midnight. She didn't care. A light came on over the stairway. The door cracked open a few seconds later.

"Johnnie," Gail whispered. "What do you want?"

"I want to come home."

Gail looked behind her, panicked. "You can't."

"Tell her to go. I belong here. This is our home. We made it together."

"Johnnie...you have to go."

"I have nowhere to go. Dad, he ran me out of the business. It's over. The whole thing. He took it all. All that we built, they gave it to someone else."

She sighed.

"Did you say something, do something?" Johnnie asked.

"I just talked to Dean, like always."

"Gossiped with him? Did you say something about me? About my father?"

"Look, Johnnie, I can't do this. You can't stay."

Johnnie tried to see past her. "Is this the woman you've been having lunch with? Telling me I can't meet her? Let me guess, you're telling her I'm treating you like shit, right?"

Gail sighed. "I'm closing the door now, Johnnie."

"Gail, don't do this."

"Gail?" A voice came from behind. A woman appeared and pushed open the door.

Johnnie inhaled sharply. "Are those my pajamas?"

The woman said something, but Johnnie turned and walked away. She punched the stuccoed wall as she walked into the gravel. It hurt so bad she had to stop and bend in pain. She wretched. Something crunched when she tried to move her hand, bones. She made it to the car. Jolene had climbed out, concern on her face.

"Are you all right?"

Johnnie couldn't answer. She crawled behind the wheel, hand throbbing, tears and anger biting her throat. She put the car in gear and sped away.

Johnnie drove to the only dive available for rent, the one she'd been avoiding. She squealed into a parking space.

"I know you don't know me. But I'm a good person. I'm really fucking lost right now and I'm—I can't handle being out in public. I'm going to get a room here. If you like you can stay with me. I hope you do, because I think I'll die inside if I'm alone."

Jolene stared at her for a long moment. "I am sorry, Johnnie, for your troubles. I will stay with you."

Johnnie nodded and then broke down in tears. She didn't let them flow easily because she was angry, embarrassed. She fought them tooth and nail, and they tore through her like daggers, stabbing her everywhere on their way out. Jolene held her shoulder and whispered something in a different language. A chant of some sort. She took her limp hand and did the same. Her hands grew very hot, and soon Johnnie's pain was a dull roar.

"Now let's go get our room," Jolene said. "Tomorrow will be better."

Johnnie laughed. "You're crazy."

"I've been called worse."

They exited the vehicle, paid forty bucks for a room, and walked in to a dusty, dank smelling, cave-like dwelling. Johnnie pulled off the paper thin comforters and turned them and spread them on the floor. She checked the sheets to make sure they were clean. She did the same with the towels. Next door, the television screamed and someone called out in sexual ecstasy.

On the other side, there was moaning, but it sounded painful. Jolene turned on the television to help drown it out. Then she stood on a chair and disabled the smoke alarm.

"I'm going across the street to Walgreens. Candles will help with the smell."

Johnnie nodded.

"Ice your hand. You've broken it."

She returned with a small bucket of ice and wrapped Johnnie's hand with a bath towel.

"Sit and prop it up."

Johnnie felt dizzy and fought her way to the bed. She sat and eased up against the headboard. She elevated her hand and closed her eyes. Darkness overtook her. Warm, deep, soothing.

CHAPTER FORTY-ONE

Johnnie opened her eyes and jerked. The room was unfamiliar. She blinked. Snoring came from next to her.
"Jolene?"

Gail turned and tried to spoon her. Johnnie, recalling her dream and the past, shoved her away and rose. She walked to the fridge where she found a Naked Juice and took a few cold sweet swigs before she collapsed on the couch. She looked down at her panties and her thin tank. She hadn't been able to wear pajamas since the night she'd seen the other woman in them. Gail had just let her take over everything, including everything that was Johnnie's.

She held out her hand, opened and closed it. It still popped, but thankfully, Jolene knew someone on the street who knew an underground doctor. He serviced patients with no questions, cash only. He'd taken care of her hand as best he could.

Johnnie had had to spend months rehabilitating it on her own. Learning how to write, turn keys, everything. And she'd never thought it would lead to a career in art. Who knew she could draw? Paint? Maybe in some strange way she wouldn't have been able to had she not injured it and had to do it all over again.

She lay down and covered herself with a throw blanket. Gail snored on, and Johnnie had half a mind to wake her and kick her out, but she didn't want to fight. She just didn't have the strength. And she knew what it was like to be on the street and she couldn't do it to her. Not even Gail.

She closed her eyes and was just about to sleep when she heard her phone ding with a message. Normally, she'd ignore it or silence it, but something told her to rise and check it. The light illuminated her skin as she checked it. Her heart jumped to her throat when she saw it was from Elaine.

She called her. Elaine answered quickly.

"Are you okay?" Johnnie asked, worried about her heart.

Elaine was silent. "Not really. Can you come over?"

"Now?" She checked the clock. It was after midnight, but she didn't mind.

"Yes, is that okay?"

"Of course. Do you need help? Should I call someone?"

There was a pause.

"You're the only one who can help."

Johnnie swallowed with difficulty. When she spoke her voice was strained. "Okay. Give me your address and I'll be right there."

"I'll text it. See you soon. And, Johnnie?"

"Yeah?"

"Thanks."

Johnnie ended the call, tossed her phone down, and dressed.

Gail shifted and sat up. "What's wrong? Where are you going?"

Johnnie pulled on some lose jeans. "Out."

"Out where?"

"It doesn't concern you."

Gail threw off the covers to reveal her nude body. "The hell it doesn't."

Johnnie pulled on a soft tee sans bra. She wanted to hurry. She was worried about Elaine. She'd sounded different. Soft, worried. She'd barely recognized her voice.

She hurried to the bathroom, brushed her teeth, and ran watered down fingers through her hair. She sprayed on some cologne. Then she crossed to the counter, grabbed her keys, made sure she had her phone, and slid into her work boots.

"When will you be back?" Gail asked with her hands on her hips.

"I don't know."

"You're going to her aren't you?"

Johnnie hesitated. There's was no telling what Gail might do to her place if she was ripe with jealousy.

"A friend needs me. Go back to bed. I have to hurry."

She unlocked the door, looked back at an angry, crestfallen Gail, and then closed the door behind her. She didn't give Gail a second thought as she hurried down the stairs.

The only name in her mind was Elaine.

Chapter Forty-two

The house was quiet. Elaine had just turned off the stereo, unable to take the vocal jazz. Tonight it sounded too scratchy, too loud. It irritated her rather than soothed. She eyed the clock. It had been twenty minutes since she'd called Johnnie. She was anxious, confused, uncertain. Feelings she rarely experienced, especially in her own home. She sat on the edge of the couch. She was in her satin nightgown and matching robe. She hadn't even thought about changing.

That was one of the things she liked about Johnnie. She felt like home. Like she didn't have to impress her.

She wrung her hands together. She'd taken her pills hours ago, and they had relaxed her, but now she was wide awake and eyeing the wine. Barb had crawled into bed with her, whispering in her ear. She'd allowed it to happen, imagined it, felt it. Cried over it. But she felt like hell. Then she'd thought about Johnnie. How would she feel in her bed, in her home? Was Susan right? Should she try it?

Having nothing else to lose and secretly wanting to see her, Elaine had called her. To her surprise, she'd answered right away. She seemed eager to come help. Trouble was, Elaine wasn't sure how she could help. How she could even go about asking for something she was unsure of?

The doorbell rang. It chimed beautifully. One that Barb had chosen and installed. It crept along behind her as she rose to answer the door. Johnnie stood beyond the security screen, hand in pocket, sexy casual as always, like she'd just stepped out of a photo session with James Dean and a bunch of artists.

"Hi."

Elaine was breathless. She never thought she'd see Johnnie on her front stoop. "Hi."

She unlocked the screen door and allowed her entry. Johnnie studied her as she passed, face-to-face. Elaine inhaled her cologne and felt a rush of heat race to between her legs. She closed her eyes to get control and then closed and locked the doors.

"Please, make yourself at home," she said, offering Johnnie her choice of furniture.

"You have a very nice home," Johnnie said. She sat on the couch, taking in the room.

Elaine sat too, in a chair across from her. She sat perched, unsure. "Would you like a drink?"

Johnnie shook her head. "No, thanks."

"Are you hungry? I could heat up this soup Michael made—"

"Elaine, are you okay? I mean, why am I here?"

Elaine stood. "I'm sorry, I know it's late, and I—"

Johnnie stood too. "Are you sick?"

Elaine pressed her lips together then breathed deeply. "No."

Johnnie waited. She came closer. "Has something happened?"

Elaine took a step back. "No—yes."

She held up her palm to keep Johnnie at bay. She couldn't handle her close proximity at the moment. She knew she would lose it. She would kiss her, fall into her arms and cry while begging her to make love to her.

"I needed to know—" She grabbed her head in frustration.

Johnnie looked worried. "What?"

"I needed to know what you felt like in my home."

Johnnie stood in silence. She searched her face with wide, seeking eyes as if she couldn't believe what she'd heard. "What— How does it feel?"

Elaine felt for her necklace and toyed with her charm for comfort. It was a small shamrock, one Barb had given her for luck. "Like you've always belonged here."

Johnnie wanted to come to her. She took another step forward. But Elaine stopped her. "Please, can we just sit for a while?"

Johnnie retreated back to the couch. "Sure." She sat carefully on the edge, waiting for Elaine to sit again as well.

"Please relax," Elaine said. "Take off your shoes if you wish."

Johnnie reached down then hesitated.

"Please, I would like for you to make yourself at home."

Johnnie removed her shoes and set them aside, then she sat back against the couch. Elaine stared at her white cotton socks and felt a warmth go through her. Seeing Johnnie so comfortable in her home made her heart sing. Like it was always supposed to be.

"Can you not sleep?" Johnnie asked softly.

Elaine leaned back and crossed her legs. "No."

"Have things been difficult?" Johnnie asked, appearing truly concerned. It was odd having the tables turned, but she liked having someone other than Michael care.

"A little. You?"

Johnnie laughed and shook her head. "You could say so."

"Why is that?"

Johnnie looked away. "You have to ask? Isn't my coming here past midnight at a last-minute request obvious enough?"

"Because of me."

Johnnie met her gaze. "Mostly."

"What about your ex?"

"She's around."

"But it's not what you want. Why?"

"She treats me badly. Uses me. Toys with me."

"Why do you put up with it?"

"I don't know. Maybe you can tell me. Why am I here in the middle of the night just so you can decide how I feel in your home?"

Elaine took a deep breath. Johnnie looked away in obvious pain.

"I guess because I'm nice. I care about people more than they care about me."

Elaine felt her heart tighten, squeeze with tension. In no way whatsoever did she want Johnnie to think she didn't care about her. But she was right. Her request was selfish, one-sided. She was using her to find out how she felt about things. It wasn't fair.

"I'm sorry, Johnnie," Elaine breathed.

"Yeah, you say that a lot. It never ends well for me."

Elaine nodded. "You're right."

Silence fell over the room. Elaine thought back to late nights with Barb. How they'd sit and talk, and Barb would always fall asleep on her, head tilted toward a shoulder. Then an image of Kyle came, standing there all wet, while Elaine did things to her pretending she was Johnnie. None of it comforted her, made her okay inside. The only thing that did was to stare at Johnnie sitting and feeling on her couch in her socks.

"Would you prefer to go?" Elaine asked. "I would understand."

Johnnie scoffed. "No, I don't want to go, you impossible woman. I want to stay. I want you in my arms." She leaned forward and dropped her head in her hands.

Elaine heated at the strong words. What was she doing messing with this poor woman's emotions? She either had to sink or swim. She couldn't keep doing this to her.

"I can't make love to you, Johnnie."

"Of course not."

"Not yet."

"Because I don't feel right in your bed."

Elaine blinked. "I—I don't know. I just know I'm still working through pain, and I wanted to know how someone I cared about felt in my home. I haven't had any—many—women here since Barb. It always felt wrong somehow. But you—I want it to feel right."

"You want me to wait while you work it out."

Elaine didn't speak. Was that what she was asking? Was that fair?

"Don't bother answering," Johnnie said, slipping into her shoes.

"Johnnie, wait."

"I can't. I can't do this. I can't let people do this to me anymore." She stood. "Not even you." She clenched her fists, clenched her jaw. "I'm worth more than this. And if you can't see it, then you don't deserve me."

Elaine stood, flabbergasted. "You're absolutely right, Johnnie."

"I'm sorry if I sound like a bitch, but it's where I'm at. I'm sorry you're still struggling over Barb. I hope you can work that out. But I can't be your pawn until you figure it out."

"I'm so sorry. I should've invited you for dinner, invited you and had a session of sorts. Off the record of course, no charge. I do care about you and how you're doing."

"Just not enough to see if I feel right in your bed, right?"

Elaine fought off dizziness. Jesus, she'd even had Kyle in her bed. But she couldn't have Johnnie, not now. They'd fall into passionate pieces and then come together again and again forming a whole that didn't yet make sense. She wanted all the pieces to fit, never to fall loose. God, was Susan right? Did she want perfection?

Regardless, Johnnie had things to work out with her ex. Boundary issues, treatment issues. It sounded like she was on the right track, but was she really? Could she say those words to her ex? The one that had the obvious hold over her?

Johnnie didn't seem to want to wait while she thought and processed. She crossed to the door, and Elaine hurriedly followed. When she grew close, Johnnie surprised her by turning quickly and pinning her to the wall. She kissed her then, warmly, deeply, melting Elaine into a rag doll of sorts. She went limp against her and moaned, and Johnnie slid her hand deftly up her nightgown and found her panty-less, wet, slick, and easy to glide against.

Elaine clung to her shoulders, shocked but overtaken with instant pleasure.

"Johnnie," she whispered.

"You feel so good," Johnnie said into her ear, nibbling on her lobe. "How do I feel now? Do I feel right?"

Elaine gasped for breath as Johnnie's fingers milked her engorged clit. "Mm."

"Because you feel so right, Elaine." She bit softly into her neck, fingers gliding expertly, bringing her closer and closer to climax. Elaine hadn't been touched in years. Not since Barb. She was so wet, so ready, she exploded into her, screaming and tensing and clawing at her shoulders.

The orgasm was long and powerful, and suddenly, it stopped as Johnnie pulled her fingers away and dropped to her knees. She shoved up her nightgown and found her eager flesh and took her into her mouth. Elaine banged her head back against the wall as she felt her hot mouth take her in and suck out the rest of the orgasm. She squirmed, the power almost too much. She clawed at her scalp, tugged at her hair, sank down against her strong form. She screamed into the night as another wave, more powerful than before, rose and crested and then rose again as Johnnie plunged fingers deep inside her and fucked her while she sucked her.

Elaine, lost in powerful bliss, lost all control, all thought, all concerns and cares she had. She came and came and came, like fireworks that kept shooting up one after another, a grand finale of eroticism. All she could do was feel, the hot mouth, the strong body, the thick hair on Johnnie's head, the long, talented fingers, the moaning into her. The world spun, and she was orbiting Johnnie, her core so hot and fierce, Elaine couldn't help but be drawn into her gravitational pull. She pulsed against her and eventually gave up everything. Including all muscular control. She slid down the wall, hung from Johnnie, hinged on her fingers, wrapped around her shoulders.

Johnnie quietly comforted her, kissing her face delicately. She carefully removed her fingers and lifted her easily into her arms. Elaine snuggled into her as Johnnie carried her down the hall to the bedroom. She found the bed in the near darkness and laid her down gently. She kissed her lips and began to pull away. But Elaine clung to her.

"Lie with me," she said. She couldn't let her leave. Not now. She was caught in her web of seduction and ecstasy. Now she wanted to feel what it was like to lie in her arms, to inhale her neck, feel her full breasts pressed up against her.

Johnnie kissed her again. "When you're ready," she said and backed away. Elaine lay limp, spent, and too exhausted to rise to chase after her. She heard her door close a few seconds later, and it was then that she turned over, hugged her body pillow, cried softly, and fell into a blissful sleep.

CHAPTER FORTY-THREE

How do I feel now?" Johnnie said as she started her truck and drove away. She sped through a late yellow and by-passed the freeway entrance that would take her to her loft. She considered going to Ian's, but she didn't want to trouble him so late. He was often awake at night, but she knew what he'd say. He'd just tell her that women were like the paint. Fucking impossible, relentless, gut clutching, and the most incredible high you could ever hope to obtain. And the motherfucker was right.

God, she could still taste her, feel her. Hear her cries. How would she ever move beyond that? Could she ever even hope to paint through that? No way. There was no getting through Elaine, over Elaine. She would just have to plow on.

The bottom called to her just as it did each time she felt low. The bottom, the gutter, the streets. She could see the haziness of that first night. The fucking orbs of streetlight evil, waiting to devour her. She sped into the parking lot of the seedy motel. The Anchor. The Anchor. Ha. Not a body of water in sight, not even in drops from a dry wicked sky, and they called it The Anchor. She killed her engine and crawled out, and walked into the cave-like office that smelled like cigarettes and mildewed carpet.

"I need a room."

"How long?" He was balding and had on a stained collared shirt. He was sucking down wet Chinese noodles from a worn carton container.

"I don't know."

"Fifty. And twenty deposit for the towels."

"You shitting me?" She shook her head and fished out the money. He took it without a word and handed her a key.

"Is this the shittiest room you have?" she asked.

He looked up. "It's pretty shitty."

"Perfect."

She took the key and the towels and headed for her room. The door squeaked as she opened it, and a wall of stale scents hit her. She identified cigarettes and food and the slight stench of piss. Nothing dead and rotting so she relaxed. She got to work, tossing the towels on the table, tearing off the comforters, putting them on the carpet and heading to the Walgreens. She bought supplies. Beer, Advil, a sketchbook, pencils, soup, and plastic spoons. When she got back to the room, she bolted the door and cracked open a beer. She kicked off her shoes and absorbed the loud moans and fighting couples, pimps, prostitutes, television, and traffic. She took it all in and curled up and fell asleep, comfortable for the first time in weeks.

She awoke some hours later to bright light peeking in through the heavy, blackout curtains. She walked across the comforters and yanked them further closed. Her head was splitting so she downed some Advil with a handful of water from the sink. She checked her phone and found several missed calls, mainly from Gail. She ignored her voice mails and deleted them, and instead listened to the ones from her friend Jimmy the art dealer. He said Gail was blowing up his phone with craziness and threats so he'd stopped by the studio and taken the paintings to his place for safekeeping. He wished her well, knowing she was on one of her quests. He reminded her of the show and the crowd expected to be there. He told her to make sure to drag Jolene along with some of her own work.

She sank into a chair and stared at the phone. No more messages. No call from Elaine. Fuck. What did she expect?

She rose and stepped into her shoes. She locked the door behind her, and headed to Sean's with the sketchbook in hand. She found the pub in the bright sun. It seemed to be cowering like a sun-shy animal. She pushed open the heavy red door and squinted in the darkness.

"Hey, Johnnie," Sean said, waving from behind the bar. "A pint?"

"Please." She made her way to her booth and slid in and opened her sketch pad. She began to draw before Sean had a chance to bring over her Guinness. She drew the tree she'd been drawing for months. But this time she made it more ornate, one side twisted and gnarled. The other side stretching, healthy, young. She drew another across from it. She shaded the sides with the twisted gnarled trees. Then she drew rays of sun in the center and a big beautiful tree in the center.

"That's amazing," Shawn said as he slid her a frosted glass. He sat across from her. "Ian's been looking for you. Says he has someone he wants you to meet. Said she sounds gorgeous. And better yet, she likes his paintings and some of your abstracts as well."

"I'm not interested," Johnnie said, not looking up. "Not right now."

Sean watched her draw. "You in the gutter again, Johnnie?"

She looked up. "Maybe."

"Don't stay too long this time. Life passes ya by ya know."

"Maybe I want it to."

"No, no, my friend, you definitely don't."

He rose and disappeared. Johnnie sat and drew for over an hour. She didn't bother with her beer until it was warm and the sketch was complete. She finished her drink and left cash on the table. She left the pub to head to her studio. She knew she might run into Gail, but she honestly had nothing to say to her. If she did she would light into her, and with Gail's temper it wouldn't be pleasant. Gail liked to throw things, bang her head on things, come after her with angry claws, grasping for clothes, delicate skin, and hair. Johnnie always managed to escape, but today, she knew she'd stay and take it. Just absorb it, close her eyes and take the pain. She knew it wasn't a healthy thought so she knew it was best to avoid it.

She found her studio locked and nearly empty. She grabbed a Naked Juice from the fridge, downed it, and then retrieved her large canvas. She took it outside and placed it in the back of her truck before returning inside for supplies. She placed those in her truck and then turned to look as someone pulled up in a loud car. Monica waved from the driver's side.

She climbed out with a smile. All Johnnie could do was stand and stare. She was exhausted with no reason to be. Torn to bits inside but healthy looking outside. To the world, she was fine. Fit as a fiddle.

"Hi." Monica walked up and kissed her cheek.

Johnnie flinched, unable not to. She was keyed up and intense.

"Hey, what's wrong?" Monica held her shoulders.

Johnnie shook her head. "I can't talk about it. Don't want to talk about it."

"Okay," Monica said gently. "Let's get you inside."

Monica took her hand and led her inside the studio. She left her on the couch and searched the fridge.

"Juice?" she asked

"No, nothing."

Monica returned and sat next to her. She delicately stroked her face. Johnnie couldn't help but close her eyes. The touch felt so good, so soft and wickedly tantalizing.

"You look okay, but you're not," Monica said. "You've been drinking, and your eyes are different. Like the lights been switched off behind them.

Johnnie clenched her hand, stopping her.

"Is it Gail?" Monica asked.

Johnnie looked away. "She won't go away."

"Have you told her to?"

Johnnie closed her eyes. "I'm too tired to care. Too beaten. I just want to lock myself away and paint."

Monica inched closer and turned her chin with her fingertips. Johnnie looked into her dark eyes.

"Don't you know how special you are?" She leaned in and kissed her. Her thick lips felt warm but nothing else. There was no passion, no intensity. Still, Johnnie kissed her back, not caring, trying. Trying for any sort of feeling.

Monica pressed against her and climbed atop her. She kissed Johnnie's neck, licked her earlobe.

"Ah, Johnnie, do you know how long I've waited for this?" She straddled Johnnie's thigh and rocked against her. She took Johnnie's hands and placed them on her breasts.

"Pinch me," she said, arching her back. "Pinch my nipples and make me hard."

Johnnie felt the fullness of her breasts, saw the hungry look in her eyes, and felt the damp coming through her shorts against her leg. She closed her eyes and a flash of Elaine came, doing the same thing, riding her thigh, begging her to make her hard. Her green eyes flashed, and she called out just as she'd done when Johnnie had made her come for the first time.

Johnnie warmed, but then opened her eyes. It wasn't Elaine; it was Monica, and it was all wrong. Johnnie pushed her aside and stood. She held her head in her hands.

"I can't," she said. "It's not right."

She headed for the door. Monica chased after her. When they exited, Johnnie turned to lock up with shaky hands.

"Johnnie, what is it? What's wrong?"

Johnnie walked away and unlocked her truck. "It's me, Monica, it's me."

She climbed in and drove away, leaving a confused Monica behind. She headed back toward the hotel and began to calm down. She shoved both Monica and Elaine from her mind and toyed with the radio. She refocused on her mission and felt better. Her stomach growled, despite her intense mood, and she pulled into In-N-Out for a burger and Coke to go. She would just have to keep it from Eddie who was still going vegan. Or at least it was what he was saying.

She bit into the greasy burger and nearly died. Zucchini and squash casserole from Eddie had had its moment. Meat was what she wanted. Her phone rang as she drove. Eddie was calling, as if he knew what she was sinking her teeth into. She let it go to voice mail. When she was at the bottom, she didn't want to talk to anyone. Even Eddie. He knew, but Gail was probably even calling him, and he was worried. She'd have to text him.

He'd given her nothing but shit since she'd let Gail back. And Monica, obviously, was really concerned. She knew Gail's games.

It seemed everyone did. Now she could even count herself among them.

She pulled into The Anchor as she finished her burger, threw the trash away, and then retrieved her stuff. She carried it into the room in two trips and locked herself inside. She cracked open a beer and sipped. Then she set up her easel and canvas before throwing open the curtains and squinting into the sunlight. She squeezed paint from the tubes and grabbed her brushes, her squirt bottle, and wet down the canvas. Then she started to work, but Elaine reentered her mind. She downed the beer and met the buzz. Elaine was still there. Finally, after half an hour of trying, Johnnie made a decision. Since she couldn't paint through her, or around her, she was going to have to use her and paint for her.

CHAPTER FORTY-FOUR

E laine sat on her new sofa and settled in. It was soft and deep, and she pulled her feet up and wrapped her arms around her knees. Outside, a light sprinkle teased her windowpanes. The wind gusted and bent palms. She sipped her coffee and tried to drown out the work the men were doing in the kitchen. She was doing a total overhaul. Getting the kitchen she always wanted. She could afford it, and no one was there to argue with her about nostalgia. Barb liked antiques, nostalgia, said things had lives. Elaine had found it cute, endearing, but when it came to decorating, they'd often butted heads.

She was leaving all that behind this week. She'd called into work, told Michael her plans, and set to work. Out with the old, in with the new. The night with Johnnic had helped her with that. If she wanted her, wanted a new life, she couldn't hang on desperately to the past. She had to remove her claws and let it fall. With Susan's help, she could see that some things would fall heavy and fast never to be thought of again, but others would drift, float, and come into her vision again and again every so often. And that was okay as long as she would just look and appreciate and not cling to them for dear life.

"Ma'am, the bed?" The two men were sweating despite the sprinkling rain. It was humid even with the breeze. They had her old bed turned sideways and were sliding it on a blanket out of the house.

"Do with it what you want," she said, looking away, throat tight.

They continued and she breathed deeply. Her bed was now gone. Along with her body pillow, which she'd donated the night before, along with the bedclothes. She'd slept on her new couch, her room smelling too much like paint to sleep in anyway. She'd had it painted over the weekend. A soft light green. She'd already had the workers hang her new artwork in it. And now in came her new bed. A queen instead of a king. She wanted to snuggle now. And not with a pillow.

She imagined Johnnie's full breasts beneath the T-shirt and how warm they would feel against her body on a cold night.

"Ma'am?" The bed men were back with the new one. "Where do you want this one?"

"Head against the wall with the art."

He nodded and off they went. She placed her mug on her new coffee table. She stared into the backyard. She was looking past the photo of Barb. Those she kept and she would always keep that one up. No one would fight her on it. She knew that. If they did, they didn't belong in her life. She stared at her lounge chairs. Michael was still bugging her about Sedona. But she needed to finish this first. She needed a fresh home, a fresh start. She needed to rise from the ashes, ready to start again.

It was amazing how clearly she could think with a little sleep. She still wasn't getting a lot of good sleep, but four or five hours straight beat none at all. The nightmares were going, replaced of dreams of Johnnie, of flying, of laughing. She often awoke upset at having awakened in the first place. She walked to her wall table where candles burned and unplugged her phone. She knew if she wanted Johnnie she needed to act. Johnnie was making up her mind about her life as well, and Elaine was someone else going back and forth with her. It wasn't fair.

Elaine needed to talk to her. To explain. But no matter how many times she rehearsed it, it still sounded selfish. It still sounded like she wanted her to wait. She closed her eyes. What could she do? She had to see her. She couldn't leave things as they were.

She found her name on her phone and called. It went to her voice mail. Elaine did the only thing she could think of. She invited her to lunch.

She returned to the couch and sipped her coffee. She'd showered and dressed before the workers arrived. She'd chosen a pair of jeans and a sleeveless blue blouse. She checked her watch and noted it was nearing eleven. She thought of Johnnie and considered whether or not she'd return her call. It had been days since Johnnie had given her what no one could've since Barb. And she hadn't called her afterward. She sighed. The way Johnnie had acted, the things she'd said. It was doubtful she would call.

Should she leave her alone? Was it better for Johnnie if she did? No.

She knew how Johnnie felt. And she knew those were feelings and words Johnnie didn't take lightly. She texted her.

Please call. I need to see you.

If she didn't return that, then she could feel anxious and worry. Goddamn it. She was already feeling it. Not since Barb had she cared so much. She remembered waiting up all night for Barb to text, or like something on her Facebook page. It had been butterflies, heavy and metal, slamming around her insides. It was a feeling she'd never experienced before, and she honestly thought she never would again.

She found her Kindle. She perused the latest romance books and then realized they would only fuel her fire. She tossed it aside and stared at her phone. Her message had been delivered. When her phone vibrated with a new message, she nearly jumped out of her skin.

Then it rang.

"Hello."

"I don't think this is a good idea. For either one of us."

Elaine smiled, despite the words. The voice was smooth, confident, concerned. It was Johnnie, and the metal butterflies went insane inside her.

"Lunch. Downtown. The new place. Green."

She heard Johnnie sigh.

"Is that because of the restaurant or the company?"

"Nothing. It's fine. What time?"

"Noon?"

Johnnie agreed and they quietly ended the call. Elaine jumped up and hurried to her bedroom to do her hair and makeup. She wanted to look good, damn good. Irresistible. Something about looking good for Johnnie turned her on, and she recalled the other night and the passion in which Johnnie had taken her. She felt a twinge between her legs and tried to get control of herself. No one had ever made her come so hard. Not even Barb.

A stab of guilt came, but she closed her eyes and forced it away. She finished getting ready, left the bathroom, and stared at her new bedroom. The new mattress sat bare but beckoned. The new paint made the artwork pop. She'd bought new lamps, new furniture. She couldn't wait to tie it all together with the new bedclothes she'd purchased. She wondered how Johnnie would feel about it. After all, she was the artist.

Elaine left the bedroom and told the guys in the kitchen she was leaving. The foreman had a key so he said he would lock up if she wasn't home when they left. She locked the front door and then went out through the garage. She climbed in her Audi and headed out. She wanted to arrive early, to watch Johnnie walk in. She loved watching her move. And she knew the crowded place would set off her anxiety.

This time, for the first time, she wanted to show her what it was like to have someone really be there for her.

CHAPTER FORTY-FIVE

Green was packed full, and Johnnie had to circle the parking lot several times before she found a parking spot. She thought more than twice about just speeding off and forgetting the whole thing, but she couldn't imagine leaving Elaine alone at the table, checking her watch, wondering where she was. She just couldn't do it. She said she'd be there, so here she was.

The sprinkling rain had stopped, but thick thunderheads formed overhead, hanging in her favorite colors of gray and midnight blue. She climbed from her truck, didn't bother smoothing out her paint splattered clothes, and headed inside. If Elaine didn't like her now, like this, she never would. She'd been staying at The Anchor, lost in her latest piece, sleeping and dreaming. She was wrinkled with paint cracking on her fingers and her hair tousled. At least she managed to get the shower to work. Even she couldn't stand going days without a shower. She might look a sight, but she smelled nice.

She entered the restaurant and clenched her fists as her heart rate sped up. The place was crowded, loud, and she was slammed with all the energy all at once. She fought closing her eyes, shutting it all out. Instead she checked in and asked for Elaine. The hostess smiled graciously and showed her where Elaine sat near the back. Johnnie took a step, then hesitated. There were dozens of tables to pass. So many faces, eyes, all on her. They were thinking, feeling, protruding into her space.

Elaine caught sight of her. She waved. Johnnie looked back at the door. She could still make a run for it. Besides, what did Elaine want to say? The same old thing? She wasn't ready?

Her cell phone rang. It was Elaine, who was still looking at her with gentle concern.

"Hello."

"Just look at me," she said softly.

Johnnie did so, then took a step.

"Just lock on to me and walk. I'm right here. There's no one else but me."

"You're not really there," Johnnie whispered. Elaine would disappear. Vanish. She would tell her so once she sat down.

"Yes, I am. I'm here. I'm right here. Look at me, Johnnie. Now, come to me."

Johnnie swallowed with difficulty. The words moved her, clenched her heart, and squeezed it to beat. She had help, she was there, she could do this. Her heart wouldn't fall to her feet or be besieged by others, arrowed, pierced, and bled dry.

She held the phone to her ear and walked, keeping her eyes focused on Elaine's. She could see the pop of green against her blue shirt. Elaine smiled as she grew closer. She stood as Johnnie reached the table.

"You made it," she said into the phone.

Johnnie lowered the phone. "I did."

Elaine rounded the table and touched her face. She smiled softly, and embraced her. Johnnie felt the weight of her body and inhaled the scented lotion she'd bought for her. She hugged her back, nearly fell against her she felt so right.

"Thank you for coming," Elaine whispered into her ear.

She pulled away to touch her face again, and held out her hands. "You've been busy," she said, returning to her seat.

Johnnie, suddenly self-conscience, hid her hands in her lap.

Elaine laughed softly. "Remember, Johnnie, I don't care about the paint on you. In fact, I like it."

Johnnie felt herself heat. Elaine's gaze was burning into her. She seemed different today, more in control, self-assured. She seemed happy.

"I drove by your studio yesterday, hoping to see you."

Johnnie sipped her water. "I haven't been painting there."

"No? You've been painting at home?"

Johnnie returned her glass to the table. "Not exactly."

Elaine looked down. She seemed embarrassed. "I'm sorry. I'm prying."

Johnnie cleared her throat. "I've been at this motel. It's where Jolene and I stayed the first night I was, uh—on the streets."

Elaine didn't blink. She just took in her face and her words and didn't miss a beat. "Does it comfort you to go back there?"

"It does." Johnnie confessed the rest of what she didn't want her to know. "I was homeless," she said. "Almost two years. Jolene's my friend, my savior. We stuck together, made it out together."

"I understand," Elaine said.

"Do you? Do you hear what I'm saying?"

"Yes, Johnnie, I do. Do you think it's supposed to bother me?"

Johnnie pushed out a long breath. "I don't know. Doesn't it?"

"No. It just explains some things for me. And mostly it makes me feel for you. And it makes me realize just how strong you are."

Johnnie stared at her in disbelief. Elaine continued.

"And returning to that motel is understandable. It was a roof over your head at a very scary moment. And you've also conquered it, moved on. But it was a first step, and sometimes it helped to get perspective by returning to a first step."

"You're really fucking amazing you know that?" Johnnie whispered, overtaken with emotion. No one had ever understood her like this. Other than Jolene, no one had cared to.

Elaine laughed a little. "I just see you, Johnnie. Just like you see me."

"Jolene calls it the bottoms," Johnnie said. "When I get like this. I just go off and hide there, sleep, work, get my thoughts together."

"Is it a place you'd like to show me?"

Johnnie laughed. "Um, no."

"Why not?"

"It's pretty bad."

"So? You think I can't handle it?"

"No, I'm afraid I can't handle it. You, seeing me there like that."

"At your bottom?"

Johnnie again sipped her water. Her nerves were showing. Elaine knew it all and she was still sitting there, looking at her like she was the sun and needed her to orbit and survive.

"I just realized I've never seen your home," Elaine said. The waitress brought small salads and took their drink order. Elaine ordered freshly squeezed tomato juice with lemon and Johnnie preferred the water. She ordered an extra glass, knowing if her nerves kept up, she'd finish the first one in no time. Around her, the people and the energy pressed into her, trying to penetrate. But it was as if there was a protective orb around their table. It was only Elaine's voice she could hear, feel.

"Maybe soon," she said. She didn't want to talk about Gail. It was a situation she'd been avoiding, and she could tell it got to Elaine, despite her trying to hide it behind her reserve. "So is this a session of sorts?"

Elaine sipped her tomato juice. "I'm not charging you if that's what you mean."

"I'm not worried about that."

"Good, then we won't talk about it. You're someone I wanted to have lunch with. Not a client."

Johnnie felt the crook of her mouth rise. "You'll still analyze, give your thoughts, perceptions. You won't be able to help it."

"Does that bother you?"

"No." Johnnie stared into her. "I love how you are. How your mind works."

Elaine flushed a little, and Johnnie was reminded of her heated skin a few nights before. The way it felt against her lips, tongue, the way it gave slightly when she bit softly. She could still smell her lotion and feel the pulse in her neck against her mouth.

"What are you thinking?" Elaine asked, watching her. "Right now."

"I'm thinking of you and how you felt beneath my mouth."

It seemed to amuse her. "Mm." She touched her neck, pulled her hair down over her shoulder.

"Did I leave a mark?"

Elaine laughed but it was a nervous laugh. "Yes."

Johnnie watched her closely. Elaine was moved by her, just as she was by her. She could feel the sexual tension coming across the table. Elaine was nervous because she was turned on. She was recalling Johnnie's mouth on her. Johnnie could sense it, feel it. Her own heart pounded at seeing Elaine react to it.

"We should've done this at your place," Johnnie said, ready to come across the table and take her.

"No," Elaine said, leaning on her elbow, palm covering her neck. "I wanted to talk. And there, we wouldn't get much said."

Johnnie eased back in her chair. "True."

Elaine smiled and changed the subject. "I can't wait for you to see the house. I've redone so much."

"Redone?" It had only been a few days.

"New furniture, new paint, new kitchen in progress."

"What brought that on?" Johnnie was shocked.

"You."

"Me?"

"I need a new beginning, Johnnie. A fresh start. I want to start that life with you."

Johnnie felt her breath catch. Elaine smiled, moved by her own words. Her green eyes filled with tears, but she swallowed them back.

Johnnie felt her own throat tighten. The goddamn woman of her dreams was telling her she wanted her in her life. Why couldn't she speak? Why couldn't she get up and carry her away?

"Say something," Elaine pleaded.

"I don't know what to say," Johnnie said. She felt so vulnerable. Elaine would have the ability to hurt her, turn on her. It would kill her. She wasn't sure if she could come back from Elaine.

"Say yes," Elaine said.

"I want to," Johnnie said. "Oh my God, I want to."

"Then say it."

Johnnie felt panic threaten. What-ifs flooded her mind. "Are you sure you're ready?" It was a valid question, an important one.

Elaine laughed a little. "No, I'm not. But you're right. I need to take a chance. Put the past behind me. Jump in."

Johnnie recalled saying those very things, but at the moment, she couldn't apply them to herself without the overwhelming fear bombarding her. Elaine wasn't sure. Johnnie was scared of abandonment, betrayal, God knew what else.

"Johnnie, hi," a voice said from her right.

Johnnie turned, startled. She almost raised her voice at the person for interrupting their moment. The moment. The most important one of her life. The one she was bombing.

"Monica," Johnnie breathed. Oh fuck. She was standing there in dark jeans and a tight-fitting button-down. Her dark hair was worn down and glistening against the bright light. She looked pissed, confused, possessive.

Monica forced out a hand at Elaine. "Hi, I'm Monica."

"Elaine," Elaine said, smiling politely. She then looked to Johnnie. They both did, and Johnnie felt like melting and oozing right off her chair. Motherfucker.

"Are you a friend of Johnnie's?" Monica asked, feeling the waters. She was wearing her cop watch and standing firm. She was either going into work or coming off. Either way, she was in cop mode with her questioning. She was acting as if Johnnie were hers. It was plainly obvious, and Elaine's beautiful face fell.

She stood and reached for her purse. "It seems as though you two have more important things to discuss than you and I do, Johnnie."

Johnnie stood. "Elaine, no. Monica's a friend. That's all."

Monica scoffed. "How can you say that? I thought we were giving things a chance? You know how I feel about you, and you up and disappear. Is she why?"

Elaine touched her necklace, forced back forming tears. The sight tore Johnnie's heart out. "You have things to work out, Johnnie. Women. Here, there. Who knows where." She burned a pain-filled look into her and turned and walked out.

Johnnie stood frozen, all the beautiful feelings she had for her being sucked from her chest up through her mouth, to follow Elaine out. When she disappeared, Johnnie fell into the chair, limp, exhausted. And then all the energy around her attacked.

CHAPTER FORTY-SIX

Elaine sat in her Audi outside Green with the air on, radio turned down low. She couldn't bring herself to leave. She had to see for herself what she didn't want to believe. But to her surprise, Johnnie exited alone, head down, walking slowly. Before she entered her truck, she looked up into the sky and held out her arms as if to ask why. When she eventually dropped her arms, she leaned against the vehicle for a long while. Elaine wiped her eyes, knowing Johnnie was most likely fighting tears. When the woman, Monica, came out, she tried to approach her, but Johnnie turned and yelled at her. The woman seemed startled. She backed up. Johnnie climbed in her truck and sped off. Elaine sat a bit longer, watching Monica. She watched her walk to a black Dodge Charger. She was on the phone, shaking her head in disbelief.

Elaine drove off, no longer interested. She drove home in silence, preferring to hear her windshield wipers working than anything else. It was obvious Johnnie was upset, but why exactly? And who was this woman, this Monica? How many women did Johnnie have hanging on? And why couldn't she get rid of them if she wanted to be with Elaine?

Was she just keeping them around for safekeeping? In case things didn't work out with her? Or was it because she thought things would never work out? In reality, she didn't own Johnnie, and Johnnie owed her nothing. Every time she'd seen her, she'd told her she wasn't ready. What was Johnnie supposed to do?

Elaine was expecting Johnnie to fend off others while she waited for her. It was what she had done, but Johnnie wasn't her. Still, something felt off. Johnnie couldn't hide the expression on her face when Monica had surprised her. She was pissed. She wasn't embarrassed, and she didn't act like she got caught. She was angry.

Elaine pulled up to her gated neighborhood and pressed the remote for entry. Her head hurt from trying to work it all out in her mind. One thing was painfully clear, Johnnie needed to take care of some things. Monica, and what about Gail? She'd said she wasn't staying at home. Was Gail still there?

Elaine's stomach clenched at the thought. She still recalled Gail's painful words about making Johnnie come. She could only imagine what that was like. She wanted more than anything to find out. And to think that Gail knew what that was like, how it felt... it angered her. She knew from Gail's behavior and attitude that she wasn't really in love with Johnnie. You don't talk about someone like that if you love them. You don't disrespect them by coming into their space again and again.

She pulled down her street and slowed to a stop. Kyle was in her driveway. Her little VW Bug was parked there like it was at home. Elaine clenched the steering wheel, opened her garage, and pulled in. She sat in her car for a moment, trying to control her breathing. She was angry but not just at Kyle. She was upset at everything. She was trying so hard to fight her depression, her grieving, and it seemed as though the universe was against her, telling her she belonged in that comfortable rut.

She climbed from the car. Kyle was leaning against the rear, hands in pockets. Her hair was a little damp and her shoulders were spotted with rain.

"Hi."

"What are you doing here?" Elaine closed her door and slung her purse over her shoulder.

"I just wondered how you were doing." She sounded innocent, hurt even.

What gave her the right?

Elaine hurried to the door to the house. "You can't call?" She opened it, found her kitchen half finished with things covered with plastic. She didn't bother to wait for Kyle, who she knew would follow her inside. She wasn't sure what she was doing or what she was going to do, but she was so angry and felt so damn hopeless she just moved, discarding her purse and retrieving a bottle of wine. She saw the one Michael had bought for her while she was in the hospital. It made her heart ache.

"Have you been feeling okay?" Kyle asked from behind.

Elaine grunted, opening the bottle with the corkscrew. She tossed the cork and corkscrew aside, grabbed a glass, and headed for her living room. The guys were gone for the day, leaving a note about tile. It was just as well; she would've told them to go home regardless. She didn't feel like listening to anything other than Nora Jones.

She turned on her stereo, found Nora under artists, and pressed play. She stopped in her movements as she heard her voice. It turned her blood to hot lava, and she loved the way it felt running throughout her body. She walked to the sofa, sat, and filled her glass on the coffee table. Kyle remained near the new chair.

"Is there anything I can do for you?" she asked.

Elaine sipped heavily. She laughed. "Knock it off, Kyle. You're here to fuck, nothing else."

Kyle looked shocked and then a little embarrassed. "I really just—"

"Please don't talk," Elaine said. "I'm not in the mood."

Kyle watched her closely, and then as her confidence grew, she spoke. "What would you like me to do?"

Elaine eased back, crossed her legs, and sipped her wine. She looked Kyle up and down. She looked so much like Johnnie.

"Nothing," she said. "You can go."

Kyle walked toward her. "I don't think that's what you really want."

Elaine smiled, feeling devilish. "How could you possibly know what I want?" How could you possibly be Johnnie? It was impossible; there was only one.

The doorbell rang. Elaine set down her glass and rose. Kyle remained by the chair, but disappointment marked her young face. Elaine pulled open the door. Johnnie stood staring at her with red-rimmed eyes. She'd changed clothes, and her wet head suggested a shower. The paint was gone from her fingers.

"Johnnie," Elaine breathed. She inhaled deeply as if she could finally breathe, as if she'd been holding her breath since the restaurant.

CHAPTER FORTY-SEVEN

C an I come in?"
Elaine looked back. Kyle was upset; she could hear the conversation.

"Yes, of course. Kyle was just leaving."

Johnnie entered, saw the young woman, and her face reddened. "Jesus, you think I'm bad. You've been gone what, an hour? And she's here?"

Elaine struggled for words. "She's just leaving. She's just here to check on me."

"You've fucked her," Johnnie said. "I can feel it." She was staring Kyle down who wasn't doing much to hide her feelings.

"Kyle, please go," Elaine said sternly.

Kyle pushed off from the chair and walked to the door. She faced off with Johnnie. They turned together as Kyle pushed out the door.

Elaine closed and locked it. Then turned to Johnnie.

"How can I help you, Johnnie?"

"What were you about to do with her?" Johnnie was angry, crestfallen. Elaine could see her heart tearing, trying to jump from her chest. She felt the same way at having seen Monica. And goddamn it, she was so tired of it. The back-and-forth over Johnnie. She walked to her sofa, sat, and brought her feet up.

"You sure you want to know?" she asked, feeling a little numb from the alcohol. How could Johnnie be demanding the answers to these questions when Elaine had just felt the same and had gotten none?

Johnnie came closer, face still red. "I don't know, do I?"

Elaine sipped slowly. Now she had the real thing right in front of her in her new home with the new insides. Johnnie was here, in the flesh, but she was upset. They both were. Elaine thought of Monica, wondered what all they'd done together in the dark. What all had the stars seen? Would she ever see it? Would she ever have Johnnie?

Johnnie came closer. "Were you going to fuck her?"

Elaine blinked at her forwardness. "No."

"Then what?"

Elaine set down her glass and leaned forward. "I was going to try real hard to pretend she was you. Just as I have always done with her."

Johnnie obviously wasn't expecting that answer. She reared back a little and tried to regain her composure. When she spoke it was a whisper. "How so?"

Elaine held her gaze. "Take off your shirt."

Johnnie looked incredulous. "What?"

"You want to know, I'm showing you. Take off your shirt."

Johnnie stood very still. The red from her face crawled lower, flushing her neck. And then she did it. She pulled off her shirt and stood in a black bra and loose jeans with a thick belt. Her chest heaved with quickened breath and her jaw flexed as she stared into Elaine.

Elaine matched her breathing, despite trying to control it. Johnnie was so strong, etched with muscle. One of those women who didn't need to lift weights to look strong. She was just built that way, with full round breasts held back by a shiny black bra.

Elaine struggled to speak. "Now your jeans."

Johnnie glanced down, then met her eyes again. She looked fierce, as if it were a dare and she was determined to meet it head-on. Slowly, she unbuckled her belt, unfastened her jeans, and lowered them with little help. She stepped out of them in matching black panties and kicked them aside.

Elaine stared at her in disbelief. Kyle couldn't even compare. Johnnie was curved in all the right places, legs shapely with muscle. Her panties were high-cut, and Elaine was almost positive they were a thong.

"Is this what you wanted?" Johnnie asked. "Her, like this?"

"No," Elaine said. "You, like this."

"Well, here I am."

"Yes." She forced herself to ease back as if she were relaxed. She crossed her legs. Hid her trembling hands in her lap.

They stared at one another for a long moment. Johnnie started to speak, but Elaine once again took control.

"Sit down in the chair," she said.

Johnnie looked back at it. She hesitated, then moved. She sat.

Elaine spoke, trying to control her voice. "Scoot back."

Johnnie did. She looked so incredibly sexy in the white chair. Elaine wanted to rise and straddle her. Kiss her madly, deeply. But she held back.

"Now, rest your legs over the armrests."

Johnnie didn't move, just stared. "You want me to spread my legs?"

Elaine swallowed. "Yes."

Johnnie did it, one leg at a time, painfully slowly.

Elaine couldn't tear her gaze away if she had wanted to. But the sight was almost too much to process. She felt her heart beat against the cage of her ribs. Ricocheting throughout her.

"Now," she managed. "Slide your hand into your panties."

Johnnie rested her hand on her chest and then allowed it drift downward. She eased it into the front of her panties.

"Don't move," Elaine said. "Don't touch yourself, not yet."

Johnnie stilled, watched her.

"I want you to imagine me doing things to you. I want you to imagine I'm sitting behind you and it's my hand in your panties, touching you, stroking you, making you wet. Can you do that?"

Johnnie struggled for breath. "Yes."

Elaine watched intently. "Now, slowly, frame your clit with your fingers and stroke up and down."

Johnnie began, moaning softly in the process. "I'm already so wet," she said, igniting a strong fire within Elaine who was watching her hand move slowly beneath the black fabric. "Fuck," she said, closing her eyes.

"Does it feel good?" Elaine asked.

"Yes."

"Are you pretending it's me?"

"It is you," Johnnie said. "Only you can make me feel like this. Touch me like this."

"Slide your fingers lower. Coat yourself with your slick wetness."

"So wet," Johnnie moaned.

"Now, circle your clit, around and around." Elaine stood, unable to help herself. She moved closer.

"Frame it again, up and down."

"Oh God," Johnnie groaned. "Please."

"Please what?"

"Touch it."

"Touch what?" Elaine lowered herself to her knees. "Tell me what you want touched."

"My clit," Johnnie breathed. "Fuck." She jerked as Elaine leaned in and breathed on her skin.

"Mm." Elaine moved up her thigh, lightly breathing, then moved to the other. Her own clit began to throb as she watched Johnnie react, jerking and thrusting her hips.

"Now move from side to side. Jerk yourself off."

Johnnie's hand moved quickly; her eyes were clenched.

Elaine watched her face, mesmerized. Then she leaned farther in and kissed the pale flesh of her thigh. Johnnie jerked with surprise. Held her breath, opened her eyes. Then she exhaled with quick moans as Elaine continued to kiss up her thigh. Elaine could feel her quiver as she moved to the other leg, kissing slowly upward.

Her thighs were firm with muscle, soft and silken to her eager lips. When she reached her panties, she kissed Johnnie's moving hand and then bit it softly, sending Johnnie into a mad series of movements and pleadings.

"What is it, Johnnie?" she asked. "Tell me what you want."

"I want you—your mouth."

"You want my mouth on you? You want me to suck you off, make you come?"

Johnnie pushed her hips up toward her lingering mouth. "Yes."

"Yes what? Say what you mean, Johnnie. Don't be afraid to say it."

"Fuck," she breathed. "Suck—me off. Please—hurry."

Elaine groaned with pleasure and ran her hands up her legs to her panties. Johnnie stilled her hand, removed it, and helped Elaine pull the fabric to the side. Elaine took in the heaven below her. Glistening, hungry, pink flesh, waiting for her to take it in and feed, suck, devour.

Elaine closed her eyes and lowered her mouth. She felt the warm flesh on her lips and heard a noise. It didn't register at first; she didn't want it to. But Johnnie jerked, both in wanting and in surprise. She pulled away quickly and sat up.

Elaine opened her eyes as the noises grew louder.

"Someone's here," Johnnie breathed, eyes wide.

Elaine pushed up and stood. There were voices in the kitchen, movement. Men.

"Shit, the workers." She hurried back to the coffee table, grabbed Johnnie's clothes, and brought them to her.

"Dress. I'll go hold them off." She hurried into the kitchen where the men were carrying in more boxes of tile.

"You surprised me," Elaine said, hand to chest. Her heart was still racing, her head dizzy with a blood rush.

The foreman, who wore jeans, a dirty T-shirt, and suspenders, ran a hand through the strands of thinning hair on his head.

"We lucked out. Found a place that had more in stock." He smiled. "I figured we'd come back and get as much done as possible." His eyes crinkled. "I called, left you a message."

Elaine nodded. "Great. Good idea." Her phone was charging. She had no idea who had tried to call. "I'll leave you to it then." She returned to the living room and found Johnnie standing near the door. She was dressed, hands shoved nervously in her pockets. She looked thoroughly embarrassed.

"I'm so sorry," Elaine said, walking up to her.

Johnnie shrugged. "Not your fault."

Elaine touched her arms. "You don't have to go," she said. But the mood had changed. Johnnie had pulled away, and Elaine was flustered beyond belief. The men had almost gotten quite the eyeful.

"I, uh," Johnnie struggled for words.

"Say what you want," Elaine said softly. "What you mean."

Johnnie looked into her eyes. "I'm upset that she was here. That you were about—"

"I don't want her," Elaine said. "Just so you know."

Johnnie looked away.

Elaine thought of Monica. The look she'd seen pass between them. "Did you sleep with Monica?"

Johnnie wouldn't meet her eyes.

"You did," Elaine said, feeling her stomach clutch.

"I was drunk," Johnnie said. "Hurt. Confused. We kissed."

"You touched her?"

Johnnie's eyes filled with tears, and she still refused to look at Elaine.

"I should go," Johnnie said.

Elaine stepped back, crushed, nearly floored at thinking of Johnnie touching the attractive dark haired woman. Moaning for her, thrusting for her, just as she'd done for Elaine. It seemed every woman Elaine met had had Johnnie the way she wanted her.

"I just can't seem to have you," Elaine whispered.

Johnnie opened the door. "I'm sorry," she said and pushed open the security door.

"I am too. I'm absolutely devastated," she choked out, turning away. She heard the door swoosh closed and she closed the front door without looking back. She couldn't bear to watch Johnnie walk away.

"I want you—your mouth."

"You want my mouth on you? You want me to suck you off, make you come?"

Johnnie pushed her hips up toward her lingering mouth. "Yes."

"Yes what? Say what you mean, Johnnie. Don't be afraid to say it."

"Fuck," she breathed. "Suck—me off. Please—hurry."

Elaine groaned with pleasure and ran her hands up her legs to her panties. Johnnie stilled her hand, removed it, and helped Elaine pull the fabric to the side. Elaine took in the heaven below her. Glistening, hungry, pink flesh, waiting for her to take it in and feed, suck, devour.

Elaine closed her eyes and lowered her mouth. She felt the warm flesh on her lips and heard a noise. It didn't register at first; she didn't want it to. But Johnnie jerked, both in wanting and in surprise. She pulled away quickly and sat up.

Elaine opened her eyes as the noises grew louder.

"Someone's here," Johnnie breathed, eyes wide.

Elaine pushed up and stood. There were voices in the kitchen, movement. Men.

"Shit, the workers." She hurried back to the coffee table, grabbed Johnnie's clothes, and brought them to her.

"Dress. I'll go hold them off." She hurried into the kitchen where the men were carrying in more boxes of tile.

"You surprised me," Elaine said, hand to chest. Her heart was still racing, her head dizzy with a blood rush.

The foreman, who wore jeans, a dirty T-shirt, and suspenders, ran a hand through the strands of thinning hair on his head.

"We lucked out. Found a place that had more in stock." He smiled. "I figured we'd come back and get as much done as possible." His eyes crinkled. "I called, left you a message."

Elaine nodded. "Great. Good idea." Her phone was charging. She had no idea who had tried to call. "I'll leave you to it then." She returned to the living room and found Johnnie standing near the door. She was dressed, hands shoved nervously in her pockets. She looked thoroughly embarrassed.

"I'm so sorry," Elaine said, walking up to her.

Johnnie shrugged. "Not your fault."

Elaine touched her arms. "You don't have to go," she said. But the mood had changed. Johnnie had pulled away, and Elaine was flustered beyond belief. The men had almost gotten quite the eyeful.

"I, uh," Johnnie struggled for words.

"Say what you want," Elaine said softly. "What you mean."

Johnnie looked into her eyes. "I'm upset that she was here. That you were about—"

"I don't want her," Elaine said. "Just so you know."

Johnnie looked away.

Elaine thought of Monica. The look she'd seen pass between them. "Did you sleep with Monica?"

Johnnie wouldn't meet her eyes.

"You did," Elaine said, feeling her stomach clutch.

"I was drunk," Johnnie said. "Hurt. Confused. We kissed."

"You touched her?"

Johnnie's eyes filled with tears, and she still refused to look at Elaine.

"I should go," Johnnie said.

Elaine stepped back, crushed, nearly floored at thinking of Johnnie touching the attractive dark haired woman. Moaning for her, thrusting for her, just as she'd done for Elaine. It seemed every woman Elaine met had had Johnnie the way she wanted her.

"I just can't seem to have you," Elaine whispered.

Johnnie opened the door. "I'm sorry," she said and pushed open the security door.

"I am too. I'm absolutely devastated," she choked out, turning away. She heard the door swoosh closed and she closed the front door without looking back. She couldn't bear to watch Johnnie walk away.

CHAPTER FORTY-EIGHT

Johnnie and Jolene drove in silence. Jolene sipped from a can of V8 and then fidgeted with her thick weathered fingers. It had taken three Xanax to get her to agree to the trip away from the house. Unlike Johnnie, Jolene didn't like to take medication every day in order to conquer her fear of the outside world. So to get her to go, it took a hefty dose of Xanax and the promise of something great. Today it was her brother. They were going to his home in Sedona, and Jolene was looking forward to it, regardless of her anxiety.

"He said he's been making something new," Jolene said, picking at her loose red cotton dress. Her braid was hanging down her left shoulder, almost like a pet snake. Johnnie watched her finish with her dress and then twist her turquoise rings.

"Can't wait to see it," Johnnie said. Jolene's brother, Henry, was an artist, though his medium was different from Johnnie's. Henry made things out of metal, and he was really popular, especially with the Sedona tourists. Johnnie took Jolene up a few times a year, and Henry often came down to deliver a piece to a customer or a gallery. Johnnie loved going and often took advantage of his sweathouse. He'd been trained in the ways of medicine by Jolene's father who was a medicine man. Henry knew a lot, and he practiced the old ways, but only with specific people. He didn't advertise, and didn't usually share his services with tourists. A true medicine man, according to Henry, didn't advertise for profit.

"I need this sweat," Johnnie said, running a tired hand through her hair. She was so torn up inside, so confused. Her heart wanted what it couldn't have, and Gail's aggressive tactics were beginning to wear her down. She was always showing up, either at the studio or at her loft. Then she'd disappear for a day or two. And no matter how upset Johnnie seemed to get with her, Gail always knew exactly what to say to calm her down. She'd even calmed her after she'd last seen Elaine. Johnnie had been a wreck, yelling at her, throwing blank canvases around, collapsing on the sofa in the studio to cry. Gail had sat next to her and soothed her. Telling her she deserved someone who really wanted her, who was really there. Johnnie had pulled away, insisted they leave the studio. She drove quickly, straight to Sean's bar where she found her booth and drank herself into oblivion.

Ian had found her and slid in across from her, talking some sense into her. He'd waited with her until she'd sobered up and then they'd driven to his house. She'd fallen onto his couch and slept, only to awaken from a nightmare at three a.m. She'd tossed the blanket off and driven home. Gail was asleep in her bed, and Johnnie had been too tired to fight it. She climbed in next to her, and Gail snuggled close, her nude body soft and warm. She'd kissed her, wiped her tears, and undressed her. Then she'd made love to her, making her come, which had made her cry. Gail had held her then, and Johnnie had finally fallen asleep.

"Gail is not good for you," Jolene said. "You need to sweat her away."

Johnnie didn't argue. She knew how to get rid of Gail for good, but for some reason she was keeping her around. Why was that?

"I don't know what I'm doing," she confessed. "I know I want Elaine, but she's—I'm—I don't think either one of us is really ready for what it would mean."

"Don't settle for second best," Jolene said. "You need to be happy alone before you can be happy with someone else."

Johnnie considered her words. "I am happy alone," she said.

"Are you? You got depressed when you were alone and you couldn't work."

"I—" But Johnnie stopped. She wanted to say it was just a fluke, a freak thing. But she wasn't sure what had caused it exactly. She sighed. "Fuck."

Jolene laughed a little.

"Stop worrying now and take in the red rocks."

Johnnie turned left and headed for Sedona. The red rocks loomed, carved especially for beauty, God's artistic gift to those who sought them. Johnnie eased down the windows and breathed in the cool air. Henry lived just beyond the town limits. Johnnie followed the dirt road that lead to his house and wound through the scarlet landscape, breeze blowing through the brush and rare tree. When they pulled in at the house, they waited for Henry to come around. Jolene commented on how good the house looked. Henry had been doing some work, and several of his metal sculptures decorated the front desert landscape. Johnnie took them in in sheer wonder and she considered again taking up welding. Henry sure was doing well with it.

"I hope he has some chili beer," Johnnie said, craving the beer with green chilies in the bottle.

"He knows you're coming," Jolene said.

As if he'd heard them, Henry came around the side of the house with a smile. He gave the hood of the truck a firm pat and then embraced Jolene as she climbed from the vehicle. They mumbled greetings and affections as they always did, and then Henry came to Johnnie. "White girl is skin and bones," he said, grabbing her shoulders. Johnnie rolled her eyes.

"Good thing I can cook."

"She needs medicine," Jolene said. "For her head and heart."

Johnnie gave her a look, but Jolene was already heading inside. Henry and Johnnie carried in their things.

"Is she right?" he asked, carrying Jolene's bag. She never packed much. Once you were homeless, you learned real quick what was vital and what could be left behind.

Johnnie slung her bag over her shoulder and carried a few art supplies. She loved to paint the rocks against the sky. And if a storm rolled in, she was in artistic heaven.

"Aren't you supposed to be able to tell?" she asked, grinning.

He laughed. "I'm a medicine man, not a mind reader."

Johnnie sighed as they stood at the door. "I guess she's right."

He nodded with thought. Then he touched her shoulder. "We'll get you straightened out."

They walked inside and Johnnie inhaled something that smelled delicious. She noted the Native American art, rugs, and paintings decorating the house. Henry had done well for himself and he knew many other Native American artists, so his home was vastly adorned with expensive art and handmade goods. Johnnie was always amazed and moved by it all.

"I do love your place," Johnnie said, relaxing.

She and Henry made their way down the hallway to the room she and Jolene would share. She dropped her bag on the far twin bed as Henry did the same with Jolene's things. Then they crossed back down the hall to the living room where Jolene sat, stroking Sugar, Henry's longhaired white cat.

Johnnie sat next to her, and Henry took up in his chair across from them. He didn't have a television or a cell phone. Instead he had shelves full of books and a room and a workshop in his backyard for his art. He reached down to a coffee table and grabbed his decorated bandana. He tied it on.

"Are we starting now?" Johnnie was a little surprised. She looked to Jolene and then realized she'd already told Henry what he needed to know well before their arrival.

"I figured you would want to sweat before dinner," he said.

Johnnie sat for a moment and then nodded. The sun was soon to set. She stood.

"Fine."

Henry stood as well, followed by Jolene. They went through the back door and into the vast Sedona landscape. Henry's workshop was off to the left, and unfinished pieces marked the property with promise of amazing things to come. Henry led the way quickly, not really giving Johnnie a chance to take in some of his new work. He crossed to the end of his property where large boulders and a dirt

hill sat. Johnnie knew the hill was really a hut. A small sweathouse. Smoke was already sneaking out the hanging flap of the entrance.

Johnnie knew what was expected so she began to undress. Henry entered the hut and created more steam by pouring water on the hot rocks. When he emerged, his face was glistening with sweat. He paid no mind to Johnnie's nude form. They were more like brother and sister and had seen one another nude on occasion when he went in as well. Today, though, he held her shoulders and looked her in the eye.

"You ready?"

She closed her eyes and cleared her mind as best she could. She nodded.

Jolene lifted the flap, and Johnnie knelt and crawled inside. Immediately, she felt the weight of the steam and the close quarters. But she forced it from her mind and sat, legs crossed, hands in her lap. She stared at the slats of sunlight coming through and then closed her eyes. Her thoughts went to the winter when she'd sat alone in there, sweated a good long sweat, and then emerged and rolled in the snow and dirt, cleaning herself with large handfuls of both. That had been a good day, a good sweat. She'd worked out quite a bit and then she'd gone back in with Henry and he'd sand painted and given her instruction.

Would he do it today?

She doubted it. Today it was about love. Henry claimed he didn't have much to offer yet on love. Especially love between two women. He didn't understand it, but he didn't judge her on it either. Neither did Jolene. That was what she loved most about them. Their strong quiet ways, letting her be her. They gave advice when she opened up to it; otherwise, they were just there for her. Always.

CHAPTER FORTY-NINE

The steam seeped into Johnnie's skin and she breathed it deep into her lungs. Sweat began to trickle down her back and ribs. She wiped her brow, wishing she'd asked for a bandana. She shifted, growing uncomfortable. But that was part of the process. You had to accept it and push through it. Her mind began to jump, first with the sweat and the steam, then to Elaine, then to Gail, a brief guilt laden flash of Monica, and then to her own image.

She jerked. She wasn't expecting that. The women in her life, yes. But facing herself, no. She didn't want to. She didn't know what to do.

She wiped sweat from her eyes, ignoring the sting of it. She looked to the exit, to the flap of hide gently swaying in the desert breeze. She could crawl out and take deep gulps of fresh air. But nothing would be solved. The negativity would still be deep inside her. Not yet having come up to her skin to be sweated out or wiped away.

"I don't like this," she called out.

There was silence for a moment and then Jolene poked her head in. "Too bad."

Johnnie panicked. "I'm seeing myself, Jolene. I don't know what to do with that."

"Ask it," she said.

"Ask it?"

Jolene disappeared.

Johnnie held her head in her hands, then placed her hands in the red orange dirt. She pulled them back and then studied her handprints. Henry needed to paint for her. That was it. That was what was needed. He needed to come in and let the colorful sand pour delicately from his hand, making images. Giving her medicine. Helping her know what to do.

"I need Henry to paint," she said, calling out to Jolene.

Henry poked his head in. "I can't," he said. "Only you can face yourself."

"But, Henry, I don't know how to do this."

"You must figure it out. No one knows you better than you."

"I want out," she said.

"No, you don't. You will only be mad at yourself if you come out now."

She stilled. "Goddamn it, Henry."

He disappeared and she heard him say, "Talk to yourself."

She closed her eyes and balled her fists. She sat very still and eventually felt her body relax and turn to hot lead. She was pliable now; she could be moved and bent and curled. Henry could create a masterpiece with her if he so chose. But Henry wasn't with her.

She saw Elaine again. Elaine touched her, felt her strength and examined her. Then she lightly stroked her, which aroused her. Johnnie's knees went weak. Elaine could read her mind. She knew Johnnie would do anything for her. But Elaine stepped back. It wasn't what she wanted. She reached out and raised Johnnie's chin with her fingers. She wanted Johnnie's best. Her strongest self. Her happiest self. She took another step back. Johnnie reached for her, but she spoke with her mind and said, "Not yet." She turned and vanished into the steam.

Johnnie clutched the darkness and pulled back a handful of steam. Sweat coated her body, but she had moved past the uncomfortableness.

"Elaine," she said. "Come back."

"I'm here for you, baby."

Johnnie sat back. Gail's voice tickled her ear. "You don't need anyone but me."

Johnnie felt gooseflesh erupt along her skin. Gail could always turn her on, calm her down. "Remember, I'm the only one who can love you. No one else can accept you and your past and your issues. Only I can. And let's face it, baby, there's no one like me."

Johnnie fell to her side as she felt Gail stroke her face, arm, and back. "I know," she said in return. "I'm too far gone. Too fucked up."

"I love you just right don't I?" Gail was sitting next to her, stroking her hair.

Johnnie closed her eyes. More images came. Images of her pacing when Gail disappeared without calling. Images of her alone at restaurants when Gail stood her up. Images of Gail turning on the charm only when they were around other lesbians. Only to have them become infatuated with her, leaving Johnnie to be the bad guy to tell them to get lost.

"No." Johnnie sat up and felt the dirt clinging to her wet body, but she didn't care. "You don't love me just right."

"Come on, love. I do. I'm just absent-minded. I just forget sometimes, that's all. And you know I'm busy."

Johnnie shoved her away. "I don't believe you anymore."

Gail reached for her, but Johnnie shoved her away again, and she vanished in the mist.

"I'm sick of you," Johnnie said, hugging her knees and rocking. "Sick of your shit. Stay away from me," she shouted.

"Good for you," Monica said, appearing across the rocks. "'Bout time."

Johnnie shook her head. "I have nothing to offer you, Monica," Johnnie said, blinking against the sting in her eyes.

"I only want a date."

"I can't."

"You mean you won't."

"I mean I don't want to."

Monica let down her long brown mane. "Ouch. I'm offended. You'll date Gail but not me?"

"It wouldn't be fair to you. I want someone else."

"Who?"

Johnnie rocked again. "Someone I can't have."

"Then what's the problem?"

"I just can't. Leave it at that."

"What about that day at your studio?"

Johnnie clutched dirt, growing agitated. "It was a mistake. I'm sorry."

"Kiss me again and we'll see."

Johnnie watched as she unbuttoned her blouse. "I'll love you, Johnnie. Protect you, treat you right."

"I can't," Johnnie shouted, throwing dirt across the stones.

Monica disappeared.

Johnnie pounded the earth. Why wouldn't people listen to her?

"Because you don't mean what you say."

Johnnie looked up. Her own image sat across from her with dirt smeared along the side of her face and right side of her body.

Johnnie scrambled backward. "Go away."

"Why? If you can't handle seeing me, how do you expect anyone else to?"

Johnnie had never liked her reflection. Not even as a child. Her mother had always told her she looked too masculine, too much like her father.

"You do look like your father," her reflection said. "But he's a handsome guy isn't he?"

"I guess."

"No, you know he is. He didn't have any trouble with the ladies, and really neither do you. You're androgynous. Women love that."

Johnnie looked at herself cautiously. She was right.

"Admit it, you coward. You're a good-looking cat."

Johnnie looked away.

"My God, you've been browbeat for so long you feel guilty liking yourself."

"I'm not supposed to like myself. It's vain. And I look like him."

"Fuck that. Fuck it. No more."

Her reflection wiped the dirt from her body. "I can't stand being trapped inside you anymore, letting you think this way. Your parents...they put you on the street. Not a penny to your name... your father ran you out of your business first, then put you on the street. That's not love and that's not someone who has the right to make you feel like shit about yourself. So fuck him. Fuck them. You've learned to live without them, so learn to live without them in your mind."

Johnnie watched as her reflection stood as best she could and reached across the rocks for her hand. She took it and stood in a crouched position. She wiped herself free of dirt.

"Now, say what you feel. Speak. No regrets. No guilt. You're not a bad person so you don't have to worry about what you say. We are one now. We are good, kind, caring, and strong."

Johnnie nodded.

Her reflection motioned toward the flap.

Johnnie nodded and took a deep breath, and stepped through. Darkness enveloped her. In a distant fog of sorts, Jolene rose from a chair and watched as Johnnie wiped herself down in dirt. Johnnie didn't speak and neither did Jolene. She simply wrapped her in a blanket and led her to the chair. Johnnie sat and sipped tepid water. The breeze chilled her.

When Jolene placed a caring hand on her shoulder, Johnnie looked up at her and said, "It's okay now. I'm ready."

Jolene nodded. "Good."

CHAPTER FIFTY

Downtown Sedona was madness on a Saturday afternoon. Jeeps from 4x4 tours rolled through the street, back bench seats full of eager tourists, cameras fixed to their faces. Cars trolled for street parking, then turned off for any parking they could possibly find. Sidewalks crawled with moving people, like scattered ants with no direction. Shop after shop lured them in, promising art, crafts, enticing scents, new age promise, and good old-fashioned Western motif. Elaine loved it, and she crossed the street to her favorite Mexican restaurant. In the background, the red rocks loomed against a darkening sky. Soon the lightning would start and the real show would begin.

She entered the busy restaurant and weaved between tables. In the far corner, she saw Michael who threw up a hand and a smile.

"Thank God you got here early," she said, sliding into her seat.

"Sedona on a Saturday in the spring. You know it."

"I should've known better." She pushed aside her menu, already knowing what she wanted.

"Aren't you glad you didn't come alone?" he asked, raising a knowing eyebrow.

"Yes, I suppose. But there are still some things I need to do on my own."

He kept the eyebrow up. "Such as?"

She shrugged. "Just stuff."

"You're not thinking about hiking are you?"

She sipped the iced tea he'd ordered for her.

"El, it's too soon. At least let me come with you."

"I want to go on my own."

He sighed and tossed his menu aside. "Fine. But you're telling me where you're going."

"To one of the vortexes."

"The one we've been to before?"

"Yes."

He seemed to relax. "Okay then."

She needed to stand in the center of the vortex and feel the energy. She needed it to pull her own energy out and spin it, making her dizzy. She needed it to feel alive. To know that she still had energy in her. That she hadn't become, somehow soulless.

The waiter came and they placed their order. Elaine relaxed and took in the view through the large windows. She rested her chin on her fist and took in her long-time friend. Michael was handsome by any standard. Thick brown hair, dark eyes, breathtaking smile. If men did it for her, she'd swoon. She especially liked his lips. They curled on the end, as if he were always up to something. His husband called it his joker smile. And he'd even bought him a shirt with "Why so serious?" on it.

"You're good-looking you know," Elaine said, hoping he would blush. It always amused her.

He looked at her and set down his beer. "You are too," he said. Then he leaned forward and whispered. "Wanna get outta here? Go get a room?"

She laughed. "Sure."

He sat back and gave her a half grin. "You can butter me up all you want, but you still aren't hiking alone."

She fought off a whine. He was so ridiculous sometimes. "Don't you have a wife to worry about?"

He batted his lashes. "My wife doesn't do irrational things. I don't have to worry about her."

"God, Michael. I'm fine."

"Fine, you want me to change the subject? I will. How's Johnnie?"

She clenched her jaw.

"That's what I thought," he said. "I know you still think about her. I know you care."

"Yeah, how do you know?"

"Because you ask Julia daily if she's called."

"Damn her."

"Mm hmm. And suddenly you're into collecting art."

"Hey, I've always admired art. That's just a new hobby."

"Have you bought one of her pieces yet?"

She looked away.

"How many?"

"I don't have to answer your questions."

"Jesus. Two, three? Five?"

"None."

He reared back. "None?"

"No. Happy now?"

"Whose art is in your office?"

"An abstract artist. He's amazing. A client recommended him. He's blind."

Michael seemed to be thinking about her words as he drank his beer. "Johnnie's not an abstract artist," he said.

"No."

He nodded to himself.

"How did you know that?" Elaine asked.

He shrugged. "I checked into her."

She stabbed her lemon with her fork and fished it from her glass. There was too much of it, making her tea sour. "I should be pissed. I know I should be pissed. But I'm too far gone to be pissed. So I'm gonna let this go, Michael. I'm going to let this go and try to enjoy a meal with you."

He bit his lower lip and nodded. "Okay. So, yeah I looked into her. Forgive me for caring. But you were, or were about to, or did, cross the line with her. I got concerned. And when she showed up at the hospital looking as though she'd been gutted with a dull knife, I did some checking. Turns out, she's okay. She's a good person. And she's one hell of an artist. She's got a little bit of a past...an anxiety disorder she deals with…but you know what? She fights on. She took her talent and she made it work. She didn't give up, and frankly, I think you could use someone like that in your life. Johnnie is hope. And you need hope."

He crossed his arms and watched her, waiting for her reaction.

She spoke slowly, carefully. "I know exactly what Johnnie is, and she is way more than just hope. She is possibly everything. But if you really care about me or her, you'll help me stay away from her. I just seem to do nothing but cause her hurt and vice versa. And it wouldn't be fair to her to let her in now. I still dream about Barb. Ache for Barb. Christ, I still spray her cologne on my sheets just so I can fall asleep. I still have her toothbrush. It still stands right next to mine. Tell me I'm ready, Michael. Knowing all that, tell me I'm ready."

He sat in silence and she saw his eyes fill with tears, but he blinked them away.

"I can't."

She sat back, justified. "Thank you."

"But I can help you," he said. "If you'll let me. We need to clean out her closet. Clean away her things."

"I tried when I redid the house. I don't think I can."

"Keep a few things, but the majority of it, I think for your sake you need to give it away to people who could use it."

"Michael, we are too close for you to counsel me."

He held up a hand. "Not me."

"The shrink? I see her twice a month. What more do you want?"

"That's a start."

"What then?"

The waiter brought their food, and they paused their conversation to bite into smothered chicken enchiladas. Elaine groaned and then felt her throat tighten as the realization came that she'd last eaten there with Barb. They'd come up for their anniversary, eaten there, and then gone off to their time-share and made love in a candlelit bathroom in the Jacuzzi tub. Then they'd sat on the patio as a storm rolled in and smoked cigars and drank wine until they couldn't stand. It had been one of the greatest weekends of her life.

"What?" Michael asked.

"Nothing." She took another bite. "Just memories."

He ate slowly as if unsure as to what to say. "Memories are okay."

She chewed and looked out the vast front window. The sky was darkening. If she wanted to get to the vortex, it would need to be soon.

Michael finished another bite and chased it with some beer. "So what I was saying...I think I know a way to help. It's right up your alley. Nothing religious, no shrinks. But very spiritual."

"Okay."

"I think you should go to a sweat lodge."

She stared at him in disbelief. "Are you kidding me?"

He blinked. "No, I'm not."

"I'm not going into one of those tents with a dozen other people where some guru tells me to let everything go. Besides, I've heard they aren't safe."

Michael looked defeated for a moment. But then he seemed to get the nerve to speak.

"I knew you'd say all those things. And you may not be wrong. So I asked for a real medicine man. One-on-one type deal."

"What? Where?"

"At the visitor center. I asked the old man there if he knew of any serious practicing medicine men. Turns out, he knows one."

Elaine pushed her food around, already feeling full. Michael had her intrigued, and a part of her didn't like it. A part of her liked the wallowing in misery. She felt comfortable there and alone. No one could reach her and she could be with Barb. She didn't want his clean hand offering to pull her up and out of the swamp of misery.

"Is he white?" she said, wanting to discredit Michael's man.

"No, he's Navajo."

"And he's here? In Sedona?"

"Yes."

"How much does he charge?"

"That's just it. The guy says he doesn't do it for profit. He may take a donation, but he doesn't do this for just anybody."

Elaine took another bite and then eased her plate away for good. "You've already arranged for me to meet him haven't you?"

Michael shifted. "Elaine, I love you. You know that."

"Damn it, Michael."

"Just try. For me."

But she really wasn't all that upset. She found herself a little curious. She sighed and waved the waiter down for a box to go. "I'll do it as long as you let me go to the vortex alone." She took a piece of ice into her mouth and chewed. Michael finished eating, taking his time. She drilled her fingers along the table.

"It's going to storm," he said.

"It's not too bad yet."

"I hate you," he said.

She smiled. "I hate you too."

She blew him a kiss. "Take my food back to the condo, will ya? I'll be hungry when I get back. She smiled at his grimace and left, weaving her way between tables.

CHAPTER FIFTY-ONE

The outside air had cooled considerably, and a bit of a wind had kicked up. Elaine crossed the street to her car and pulled onto the main road. Then she headed back toward the entrance of town and turned toward a lower creek area. By the time she parked, the lightning was growing closer and the dark sky loomed overhead. The wind blew against her as she exited the car and stretched, tugging on her hiking boots, stretching her quads. Her blood began to pump in anticipation as the earthy elements awakened her senses and the beautiful environment lured her forward. She pulled on a light backpack containing water and a few snacks, a plastic bag full of matches, and an emergency blanket.

People crawled up the parking lot toward her, faces pink with sun, hair windblown. They looked pleasantly spent and happy, breathless but beautiful. Some greeted her; some warned her of the storm. She assured them she'd be okay and made it to the bottom of the parking lot where she climbed over a wooden fence. She could've taken the well-known path, but she didn't feel she had time. So she cleared the fence and walked along the dry creek bed, creekside homes to her right, small creek to her left. As she walked, she took in the elements and held out her hands as if to thank whatever higher being there was for creating such a beautiful place. She closed her eyes briefly, thought of Barb, and whispered a prayer to her.

"I'm here," she said and she imagined, no felt, that Barb said it in return. She opened her eyes and focused on the red rocks in the distance. The lightning cracked around them, and soon she knew it would break the shell of a dark sky and leak out rain. But she didn't have far to go now. She found the path up to her right, left the homes behind and entered wilderness. The shade was cool and still, the breeze having gone, the calm before the storm. She hiked farther in, bypassed two more hikers with a smile, and then came to a stop at the area she was after.

"Barb." She could feel her and her hair stood up on her arms. She smiled and a tear fell. Carefully, she removed her backpack and stepped into the center of the vortex. She was surrounded by trees and foliage, as if they were protecting it. With a deep breath, she closed her eyes and held out her arms. The dizziness came at once, and she laughed nervously. "I'm here, Barb," she said. Then she closed her mouth and spoke with her mind. She offered her energy up and out, wanting the vortex to take it. The dizziness intensified, and she knelt, placing her hands in the grass and leaves. She angled her head to the sky, felt a stirring deep within her chest. Her heart careened but in an excited way. Like it did at night when she was so damned tired but couldn't settle to sleep. It pumped hot blood throughout her, and she settled down to sit as she felt it begin to pull up out of her skin. It tingled and toyed with her as if she were a puppet and someone above were pulling her strings. She knew if she opened her eyes she'd grow sick with dizziness and motion sickness and the feeling would be lost. So she kept her eyes closed and whispered, "Take me, just take me. Take me and make me feel. Put me back together again."

She sat and swayed, and soon a drop of cold smacked her forehead. It startled her, but she laughed. Another fell, then another. She held out her hands and opened her eyes. White streaks fell from the heavy blue-black sky.

She was laughing when someone stepped into the clearing. Elaine couldn't see very clearly.

"Sorry," she said, trying to stand. "I'll leave you to it." But the person came closer and took her gently by the arm. Elaine at once looked at her. "Johnnie," she breathed.

"We have to get you out of here," Johnnie said.

Elaine tried to pull away. Her energy was still mixed up, swirling, alive with no destination. "No, I'm okay."

It began to pour. Johnnie looked up; lightning splintering the sky.

"We need to make a run for it. Before that lightning is on us."

"But I feel so good," Elaine said. She held out her hands. "I need this. I can feel her."

Johnnie stepped back. "Elaine, please."

"Why are you here?" Elaine asked.

Johnnie looked to her left, hesitated. "Come on." She held out her hand.

Elaine stood in the pouring rain. Johnnie looked serious, anxious. Lightning cracked and thunder boomed, scaring her. Johnnie found her backpack, picked it up, and again held out her hand. "We have to go now."

Elaine moved, took her hand, and they hiked farther up. The trail was muddy, the tree roots slick. They lost footing a few times but kept on. Then Johnnie made a turn and they went off-trail. Thunder clacked again, directly overhead. Elaine winced.

"Up here," Johnnie said. She spread through branches and brush, held them open for Elaine. They walked through and came to an opening in the rock face. Johnnie took Elaine by the waist and pushed her up. Then she jumped up and climbed inside. Johnnie took her to the back of the cave and tossed rocks into the darkness.

"Why are you doing that?" Elaine asked, heart still racing.

"Rattlers," Johnnie said, before giving up and settling down. "They hibernate in dark places like caves. Just wanted to know if we were safe out here." She offered a seat to Elaine. They were in the middle of the small cave, away from the lightning but away from the dark entrails where snakes or who knew what else might be hibernating.

Elaine was trembling and so was Johnnie. The rain was steady and heavy.

"It's going to last an hour or so," Johnnie said. She unzipped her jacket, took it off, and pulled off her long sleeve shirt.

"Here." She handed both to Elaine.

Elaine waved her off.

"Elaine, take off your wet shirt and bra and put this on. It's not a request, it's not a nice gesture, it's a demand."

Elaine studied her a moment and then took them off. Johnnie was serious. She'd never seen her so serious. Slowly, she turned around and undressed. Her hands shook so badly she thought she might need help. But somehow she managed. When she finished, Johnnie stood, took her wet clothes, wrung them out, and laid them flat on the rock surface.

"Now your shorts," Johnnie said.

Elaine stared at her.

"Again, not a request." Johnnie looked away, arms crossed, and waited. Elaine peeled off her shorts. "I'm not taking off my underwear," she said.

"You can cover up with my blanket."

Elaine hesitated and then took those too off.

"Hand me your blanket, please."

Johnnie unzipped her bag and pulled a soft blanket out of a waterproof bag. She handed it to her.

Elaine wrapped her waist and sat.

But something wasn't right. Johnnie stood in a bra and wet shorts.

"Let's share the blanket," Elaine said. Johnnie sat and removed her shoes and wet socks. She ran both hands through her short hair.

"I'm good."

Elaine laughed. "Bullshit. You're shaking."

She stood, opened the blanket, and eyed her. "Come on. It's not a request."

Johnnie blushed despite her cold state. She was careful not to look at Elaine below the waist. She crossed to her and they sat, blanket warming them both.

Elaine busied herself removing her shoes and socks as Johnnie had done. She laid them out to dry.

"What are you doing here?" Elaine asked. "Did Michael send you?"

Johnnie appeared confused. "I came with a friend."

"And to the vortex?"

"I was coming here, to the cave."

Elaine glanced around. "Are those..."

"Native American drawings? Most likely."

"Are we supposed to be in here?"

"Probably not. But I'm not sure people know it exists. I only know because of Henry and Jolene."

"Your friends."

"Right."

Elaine was amazed. "Imagine who they were, how they lived. How long ago they lived."

"Henry knows. He can tell you. You should meet him," Johnnie said softly.

The rain continued to fall, and the lightning and thunder shook their surroundings.

"Why are you out here alone?" Johnnie asked.

Elaine sighed. "I wanted to go to the vortex. I needed..."

"Barb," Johnnie said.

Elaine got choked up and nodded.

Johnnie did something surprising. She pulled her close. "You'll find your way," she said. "Have faith."

CHAPTER FIFTY-TWO

Elaine felt tears run down her face, but she brushed them away. She was tired of crying. But Johnnie held her close and looked out at the rain with her.

"You can cry, you know," Johnnie said. "Even strong people cry."

Elaine laughed a little. "I just feel like I've done enough of that for one lifetime."

Johnnie was quiet and seemed thoughtful. "I can only imagine," she said. "I don't know if I'd survive if I lost someone I loved so deeply. Someone like..." But she turned her head, and the breeze chilled them, blowing her short hair.

"Someone like...who?" Elaine asked, unable not to.

Johnnie wouldn't look at her. "You already know," she said.

"No, I don't."

Johnnie scoffed. "I think you do." She turned and looked into her eyes. "I think you know I'm in love with you."

Elaine felt herself gasp, but it wasn't consciously done. Johnnie was staring into her, falling into her eyes. Elaine's heart began to pump so hard she could feel it. It even clouded her hearing.

"I—Johnnie," she breathed.

"You don't have to say anything," Johnnie said softly. "I know you still love Barb. And I understand why. If I lost someone like you, I'm not sure I'd ever recover." She stared off again into the rain.

Elaine leaned into her, gripping her arm. "You know I love you too, Johnnie."

She felt Johnnie tense. "No, I didn't know."

"I do. Somehow, someway, you have snuck under or over my wall. You reached my heart and infiltrated. I think I knew it the first day I met you. You standing there so nervous, yet refusing to leave. Paint on your jeans, your hands, showing the passion you have for your craft. You were so incredible, so real, so raw. I could *feel* who you were. Just like you can with people."

"But you can't be with me," Johnnie whispered.

Elaine again felt tears come. "I love Barb."

"You're confused," Johnnie said. "You feel guilty." Johnnie turned and gently wiped her tears. She softly, delicately kissed her cheeks, her trail of tears. "You don't have to worry. I understand. I'm not going to pressure you."

Elaine snuggled closer, and Johnnie held her as she softly cried. Elaine breathed in her skin, felt the strength of her upper body, clung to her like a tower of love and strength. Around them, the rain streamed down, and Elaine felt like the earth was crying with her. Mourning.

Johnnie soothed her, melted against her, and they rested their heads upon each other.

Eventually, when Elaine could cry no more, and the rain slowed and the birds sung once again, Elaine broke the silence.

"I hear you've seen a colleague of mine." Hearing so had stung a bit at the time, but she didn't blame Johnnie for trying out a new practitioner.

Johnnie laughed a little. "Yeah, she's not for me."

"Why not?"

"She's cocky. I don't do cocky."

Elaine smiled and nodded knowingly. "Most of our gay women love her."

"I'm not most gay women," Johnnie said.

"No. No, you're not."

They sat in silence for a moment and Elaine took Johnnie's hand, tracing her palm.

"Have you been painting?"

Johnnie groaned. "I suppose. Mostly abstract. Which is new for me. But my friend really turned me on to it. And of course, I still paint—"

"Me?"

Johnnie smiled, but she looked embarrassed. "I sold some," she said. "To a Brazilian collector."

"Really? I think I'm flattered."

"You should be. He's very picky about his portraits."

"Is he?"

"Yes, and now he wants nudes of you."

Elaine laughed, unable not to.

"I turned him down."

"Why?"

Johnnie looked at her incredulously. "Because you don't want me near you, much less painting you nude."

Elaine shrugged. "I don't know. I might."

Johnnie released her. "Please stop mind-fucking me. I get enough from Gail."

Elaine patted her leg and Johnnie jumped. "I'm sorry. I'm not trying to."

Johnnie looked at her, then covered her hand with her own. "You have a way of...moving me."

Elaine stared back. "So do you."

"But we can't."

"No."

They inched closer. Elaine closed her eyes to kiss her. Johnnie did the same. Lightning flashed and thunder boomed, startling them. They backed away.

Johnnie stood and paced the cave. Elaine couldn't help but notice the planes of her pale abdomen, the freckle near her belly button, the fullness of her ample breasts held by the tight sports bra.

"I think you should paint me."

"I think you don't know what you want," Johnnie said.

Elaine nodded. "I do actually. I just have to accept I can no longer have it."

Johnnie continued to stare out at the storm. "I'm kind of in the same boat. I can't have what I want."

Elaine snuggled closer in the blanket. The earth smelled fresh and clean around them. The cave dark and dank. She felt safe there, especially with Johnnie. She hadn't noticed, but her body had slowed with the thrumming and settled into a peace, a heavy peace, as if she'd need to be carried back to her car. When she called for Barb, she could feel her, but it wasn't a panicked need to feel her. It was a presence. A slowly fading presence, letting her know it was okay. As for her own soul, it had been stirred, awakened, and shoved back inside, and she felt a little strange, as if it weren't all fitting the parts it should.

"I feel like I need to see Barb," Elaine said.

Johnnie turned. "I needed to see myself."

"You've done such a great job," Elaine said, thinking about all she'd been through in the past and how well she had recovered from it.

Johnnie came to sit next to her once again. "I came up here to heal, to explore, to find."

Elaine saw the determination in her eyes. "I did too."

"Yet, here we are. The universe throws us together again."

"Maybe it knows what it's doing."

"Maybe."

"Johnnie, I want to kiss you. I could kiss you. We could make love right here in this cave in the rain in the red rocks. It would be magnificent."

Johnnie closed her eyes as if imagining. "Yes."

"Do you want that?"

Johnnie opened her eyes. "No. I want all of you. Not a piece."

Elaine felt her eyes flutter. "I think that's the best answer I've ever heard."

"Yeah, well, it sucks to have to say it."

"God, you are so romantic yet you know how to kill it in an instant."

Johnnie laughed. "Give me a chance," she said. "I'll give you more romance than you could ever handle."

"I hope to do just that."

They sat in silence for a while. A slab of sunlight angled into the cave.

"So we've agreed we cannot act on our feelings of attraction," Elaine said.

Johnnie stood and took her hand. "For now, let's get you dressed and get back to your car. You need a hot shower."

Elaine smiled. "Ever the worrier."

"Some things die hard," Johnnie said.

CHAPTER FIFTY-THREE

Johnnie walked into Henry's, opened the fridge, and sucked down a Smartwater. Jolene was humming at the table, making a craft. She didn't look up.

"You smell like rain."

"Yeah, well, I got caught in it."

"On purpose?"

"Not exactly."

Jolene looked up. "You've been to the cave." Johnnie wiped the chalkiness from the cave floor off her shorts.

"Aren't you going to ask about my shirt and jacket?"

Jolene continued to work on her project. "If you wanted me to know you'd tell me."

Johnnie shook her head. "Sometimes, Jolene, you are maddening."

Jolene didn't look back up. "Go shower, or go sit outside and take in more wet earth. You're bothering me."

"Where's Henry?"

"He went to meet with a white girl."

Johnnie shoved off to the bedroom where she unpacked clean clothes and turned on the shower in the bathroom. The warm water felt good and she lathered the storm away, but she couldn't wash Elaine from her mind. Once again, she was first and foremost, and Johnnie had tried not to think about her nude from the waist down. But now she thought about it. Wondered what it would've been like to touch her beneath the blanket. To take her mouth into hers, taste the rain on her cool skin. To hear her sigh, possibly moan as she kissed her back.

And then she thought about how Elaine would've pushed her away. Said no, they couldn't. Johnnie knew how hard it would have been to stop. How it would've stabbed her gut to hear those words. No, it was better this way. They had done the right thing.

She killed the water and stepped from the tub. She dried quickly, dressed, and walked back to the kitchen. Jolene was out back; Johnnie could see her lit up by the fire pit. She was no doubt roasting corn. She might even be making fry bread. Johnnie pushed out the door, inhaled the energy of the fresh stars, and joined her. She sank into a chair, watched the far off lightning and recalled how beautiful and yet how vulnerable Elaine had looked when all wet. She'd been talking in the vortex, moving in circles, eyes to the sky. She'd been feeling something. And as badly as Johnnie hated interrupting her, she was about two seconds away from getting struck by lightning.

"You're different," Jolene said, poking at foil covered corn with a stick.

"I had a good sweat," she said, referring to day before yesterday. She planned on having two more before she left.

"No, from today. Your energy. You've found it and controlled it." Johnnie stared into the fire. "I wish it felt that simple."

"It never will. Words can never do what we feel justice."

They sat in silence and Johnnie eased into the blanket of Jolene's silent embrace. She snuggled up there and pulled up her hood on her ASU sweatshirt.

When the corn and potatoes were done, they ate. When Henry returned, he joined them, bringing out the chili beer. They sat under the bright clean sky, and watched the fire dance and sparkle with personality. Johnnie didn't tell them about Elaine. She didn't need to. It was her moment. Hers and Elaine's. She knew she'd never forget it. And if she told, it might dissipate somehow.

"I'm off to bed," she finally said. Henry nodded and finished his beer.

"I have a white woman coming tomorrow," he said.

Johnnie gave a wave and headed off. Henry helping people wasn't new. But he was very picky about his clients. The woman must need help and be very special. She decided to wake early and try to leave before she arrived, leaving Henry and Jolene to do their thing.

CHAPTER FIFTY-FOUR

The day was bright, scrubbed clean from more late showers the night before. Elaine could still smell the moist earth, and she climbed from Michael's Mercedes and stretched. She was in a good but anxious mood. Henry's house looked safe enough, but she wasn't really worried about her safety. She was worried about what lay harbored inside her.

"Check out that metal sculpture," Michael said, pointing, then removing his designer shades. "That is incredible."

"Mm." She glanced up and down the street and found it quiet. Two other trucks sat in the driveway. One older, maybe seventies. The other she couldn't quite make out. "He's expecting us, right?"

Michael rounded the car and took her hand. "Yes."

They walked to the front door, but a voice called from around the back of the house.

"Hello," Henry called, greeting them with a smile. He wore old jeans, a turquoise squash belt buckle, a button-down shirt, and a turquoise bolo tie. He smelled of coffee. Elaine liked how his hair was smoothed back from his forehead and then tied into a long silver braid. She had liked him at once the day before when they'd met for coffee.

He was soft-spoken, sincere, had kind brown eyes hidden by webs of wrinkles. He hadn't promised anything, hadn't spoken of money. He'd only cared about her story. At one point, he'd even covered her hand with his own.

"You're nervous," he said, leading them into the back. "It's normal."

She exhaled and laughed nervously. Michael once again ripped off his shades to take in the art. He walked to each statue and touched it. He was sold. Elaine had never seen him so excited about art before. She wondered if he'd brought his checkbook.

"I have one in the work shed that's for you," Henry said. "Started it two weeks ago for a white man. Didn't know who, but I knew he'd be coming here."

"No shit?" Michael said. He shook his head. "Sorry. I just got excited."

Henry laughed. "We will look at it later. Right now we need to take care of Elaine."

They walked to the fire pit, and Elaine noted the small hut. Her heart fluttered. She didn't like tight spaces, but Henry said the flap would be left open for the first ceremony. She stood next to him at the fire pit and he tied on a bandana with an elaborate design on it. He held out his hand. He led her to the hut.

"I've painted for you," he said. "With the sand."

She nodded.

"You must strip and sit on it. It is the only way it can pull the negative from you. Then when you're finished, I mix the sand together with the earth and return it all to the earth and away from you."

She swallowed. It didn't sound so bad. "I'll leave you now, to remove your clothes."

He walked away and Michael went with him. Elaine slowly undressed and entered the hut. She found it cool and the sun angled in on her sand painting. It was so beautiful and precise she hated thinking about destroying it. But she did as instructed and sat on it.

Henry then peaked inside. "You ready?"

He entered and began to chant. She knew from his earlier instruction that she was to sit quietly. The sand painting was for healing he'd said, and he only did it for those in dire need. He'd asked her to tell no one about it. For it was still considered sacred.

She closed her eyes as he continued, and then when he finished, he left her alone with her thoughts. He told her to think of Barb, the accident, anything that caused her pain. She focused and brought up the pain, which seemed on the brim after the long chant. She fought the tears, wiped them away, but then let them fall into the dirt. The earth could have them.

When she was ready, he came in, did another chant, and then had her stand as best she could. He chanted as he destroyed the painting, returning it to the earth.

Then he led her from the hut where a woman who looked like him waited with a robe. When the woman saw her, she looked away quickly and excused herself. Michael came to her side. "How was it?"

"Different," she said.

"How do you feel?"

She breathed deeply. "Lighter."

He smiled. "Good."

She looked around, and when she saw Henry, she asked to use the restroom. He told her where to go in the house and then said his sister, Jolene, should be able to show her. Elaine set off, walking barefoot through the dirt to the back patio. She entered the sliding glass door and turned right down the hall. She heard hurried voices and she paused, recognizing one and then hearing her name. And then she remembered Johnnie talking about a Jolene. And yesterday she had mentioned a Henry. Her stomach flipped.

Suddenly, Johnnie stepped into the hallway, completely nude, wet from an apparent shower.

CHAPTER FIFTY-FIVE

Elaine blinked, completely confused. She turned away once she realized she was staring.

"Elaine, I know this looks bad. Strange. Whatever."

Elaine turned to look at Jolene, all of it sinking in. "So you're Jolene." She held out her hand, trying to control her racing emotions. "Elaine."

Jolene took it, too stunned to speak. Johnnie, however, was speed talking, completely panicked. "See, I didn't know it was you. We didn't know it was you. If I had known, I would've left and—"

"Johnnie please put on some clothes," Elaine whispered, heat kissing her skin from the sight. She looked better than she could've ever imagined. Curved and carved with muscle and full round pale breasts. She had the urge to walk up to her, run her hands up her arms, and skim her nipples with the backs of her fingers causing them to awaken, harden.

When their eyes met, Elaine knew Johnnie could sense her thoughts, for she blushed, clenched her jaw as if trying to fight her own feelings, and excused herself into a bedroom. Jolene pushed open the bathroom door and smiled politely.

"You can shower between ceremonies," she said. "Most people like to."

Elaine smiled. "Thanks."

She took a quick shower, her mind reeling with having run into Johnnie yet again. And as she washed away the remnants of her ceremony, she was surprised at how little her mind returned to Barb and what she'd just done to purify herself and her mind. Maybe it had helped. But now she had to deal with Johnnie. How could she conquer those thoughts?

She finished drying with a thick white towel and then re-emerged to find all of them outside, awaiting her return. Michael looked upset, and the rest looked worried.

"What's wrong?" she asked.

Henry spoke. "Given the circumstances, we weren't sure if you wanted to continue."

Elaine hugged herself and then fingered wet hair. It smelled like Johnnie's must smell. The realization excited her a little.

"You mean quit?"

"Because of me," Johnnie said. "I've interfered."

"No." Elaine shook her head. "Absolutely not. I need this. And you haven't interfered. We just ran into one another again. That's not anyone's fault."

Michael pushed out a sigh of relief.

Henry spoke. "Johnnie, you should go."

Johnnie nodded in agreement.

"Yes," Jolene said. "She will go."

Johnnie started to walk away, but Elaine asked her to wait up. They stopped on the patio while the others remained behind.

"You don't have to run off," Elaine said. She felt terrible; these were Johnnie's friends, her territory.

"I should, yes," Johnnie said. Her wet hair came down to tickle her brow, and she brushed it back and sank a casual hand in her pocket. The sight took Elaine's breath away. She stood studying her in a black tee and faded jeans. "It's best for you," she added.

Elaine saw the look in her eyes. The kind concern. The empathy. She knew there was no use in arguing. Johnnie wanted what was best for her and she'd do whatever necessary. But there was something she could do.

"Michael," she called out.

He trotted up to her. "Yes?"

"Give Johnnie your key to the condo. She can go hang out there."

He didn't hesitate. "Good idea." He fished in the pocket of his pressed jeans and handed over the key. He gave her the address and Johnnie nodded.

"I know that place," she said. "We've had friends stay there."

She took the key, eyes locked back on Elaine. "If I go and hang there, will you promise to stay here and let Henry help you?"

Michael smiled. "I like this woman." He shoved Elaine playfully.

She sighed. "Yes."

"Okay. Call me when you're finished." She looked at Elaine for a long moment before turning to leave.

"I like her a lot," Michael said, wrapping an arm around her shoulders and turning her back toward Jolene and Henry. "Tell me again what your deal is…why you haven't asked her to marry you yet?"

She shoved him back. Henry held out a hand for her and helped settle her into a chair. He handed her a bottle of tepid water.

"Did you eat a light breakfast?" he asked.

"I did."

He nodded. She'd followed his instructions exactly.

"You're going to go into the hut. There will be steam as I add water to the hot rocks. It will be pressing, uncomfortable. It may feel hard to breathe. Since you've got medical issues, I will be going in with you."

She agreed. It was a good idea and it helped her anxiety. "We will stay inside until I feel you are ready to emerge. When you emerge, we will rub dirt on ourselves to clean away the bad, the unhealthy. We will rehydrate you. And if we feel it necessary, we will go again after a while."

"Okay."

She drank the water, tried to relax, but it was impossible. Henry busied himself moving hot rocks from a low burning fire into the hut. When he finished he brought in a bucket of water, and she saw steam rise from the cupfuls he poured on. He came back out of the flap without the water. Then he approached her.

"Are you ready?"

She nodded and looked to Jolene for support. Jolene encouraged her quietly, helping her stand. She walked her to the flap where steam was still escaping. She helped her out of her robe. Beside her, Henry undressed as well. He entered the hut first and stuck out a hand for her. She took it and pushed through the flap. The small hut was full of steam and it was difficult to see Henry.

"Sit across the rocks from me," he instructed her.

She sat and crossed her legs, lotus style. Henry did the same. He began to chant, to sing. Elaine closed her eyes, doing her best to take steady breaths. Her head spun a bit and then she felt sweat bead her body. Soon she was slick with it and she was wiping her face and brow. It was so hot, humid, heavy.

Henry stopped singing and encouraged her to breathe deeply, allow the thoughts to come and go. To feel whatever came.

She again closed her eyes and breathed deeply. Her body felt heavy yet light. She felt one with the ground beneath her. As if she could ooze down into the dirt and disappear. She grew sleepy and relaxed. She was about to drift away when she heard a voice calling her.

"Barb?" She clenched her eyes, afraid if she opened them, she'd lose the voice.

"Lainey, I'm here. I'm always here."

Elaine began to cry. "Where? I miss you so much."

"I'm still with you. Every day. Every moment."

"I can feel you," she said, reaching out for her.

"Because I'm in here, right inside your heart."

"But I want to touch you, hold you."

"All you have to do is close your eyes and think of me and you can."

"But it's not good enough, I want more."

"You can have more, Lainey. With the other who's meant to love you."

Elaine cried again, opened her eyes, searching desperately. All she could see was Henry adding more water to the rocks. "I hear her," she said.

He nodded, chanted something again, and reached out to touch the scar on her chest. Then he sat back and closed his eyes.

Elaine closed her eyes, desperate to hear her again. "Barb? Where are you?"

"I'm going now, Lainey," she said softly.

"No, don't go."

"I need to. So you can grow and love and move on. I will always be in your heart. But you have to let the other in now."

Elaine wanted to cry, but no further tears would come. She felt a gentle pressure on her chest and then it released. She relaxed, felt so light. It was easier to breathe, to exist. She felt like she was floating off the dirt. Suddenly, she saw everything. Every grain of sand on the ground, every bead of sweat on her arms and faces of those she loved in the gathering of steam.

"I see now," she said. "I see it all."

Her eyes grew heavy with blissful peace. She smiled and was about to fall over on her side to sleep when she felt strong arms encase and lift her. More arms pulled her through the flap and she was seeing sky, darkening sky. She felt dirt being rubbed into her skin. Michael was talking to her, but all she could do was smile.

A soft robe was wrapped around her, and she was helped into a lounge chair. Jolene helped her sip water. Henry, also in a robe, came to her, said something in Navajo, and touched her scar again. Jolene chanted with him, and they placed their hands on her arms and shoulders. Then he held her face and said, "Let it go, child. Let it all go."

She exhaled and felt herself shudder. Henry backed away. Jolene held her hand.

"Breathe," she said. She helped her sip more water.

Elaine took the water and drank heartily. Her heart had suddenly awakened along with her mind. She blinked and took in her surroundings, saw the pop of colors everywhere. And she had a yearning like she never had before.

She tried to stand. "Johnnie," she said. "I need to go to her."

Jolene held her tightly. "Easy," she said. "Let's go rinse you down."

Carefully, she led her into the house and turned on the shower.

Elaine stepped into cool water and allowed it to further awaken her. After a few moments of letting it slosh over her, she lathered herself up and rinsed, then washed and conditioned her hair. When she finished, Jolene had clean clothes for her folded on the counter.

She helped her dry off.

"Are you sure you are strong enough to go to Johnnie?"

Elaine held her wrist and looked into her deep brown eyes. "I've never felt stronger in my life."

Jolene nodded. "You must go then."

She left the bathroom and Elaine dressed and combed her hair. When she walked down the hall, she found them all in the kitchen. Michael looked at her with worry etched on his handsome face.

"I'm well," she said with a smile. "I'm well, Michael."

He sighed and let the worry go. "Oh, thank God." He embraced her tightly.

"I need to go to Johnnie," she said.

He pulled away. "That's fine. Henry said he would show me all of his work."

Henry removed his bandanna and tightened his robe.

"If he brought his checkbook, you're in for a treat," Elaine said to him.

He only smiled.

"How can I ever thank you?" she asked.

She crossed to him and took his hands. "Walk every morning at sunrise and give thanks for all that is around you."

She nodded. "Okay."

He hugged her. "Now," he said. "You have a mission. You must go."

She backed away, smiled at them all, and headed out the front door.

She had a mission.

Johnnie.

CHAPTER FIFTY-SIX

Johnnie settled down on a lounge chair out on the patio with a glass of ice water. Eddie had convinced her to let go of the soda, and the transition had been somewhat difficult at first, but now she wanted nothing but water. She sipped the cool water as she watched the big storm roll in over the red mountains. The sky was a blue purple, and lightning zigzagged and played tag. She smiled at the streaking rain, smelling the fresh earth it kicked up. She stood and held out her hand, caught the cold drops. Thunder boomed then cracked. She jerked but didn't move. She'd always been stirred by storms, and she never failed to thoroughly enjoy one.

She was still holding her hand out to catch the rain when she turned slightly and caught sight of someone standing at the Arcadian door.

"Elaine," she said softly. She pulled her hand in. "You're all wet."

Elaine didn't move; she just stood there in her wet clothes. Johnnie crossed to her and stepped inside.

"Hey, how did it go?" Elaine looked different, calm yet stirred. She moved with purpose, but heat marked her cheekbones, and her eyes flashed with what could only be determination and desire. Johnnie felt her own skin heat at the sight. "Everything okay?" she couldn't help but ask.

Elaine didn't speak. She opened her mouth to speak, but she couldn't seem to find the words. Then, when she did speak, she was serious, confident, and not to be argued with.

"Stand still," she said. She took a step and ran her hands up under Johnnie's shirt, causing her breath to shake. When she grabbed the fabric, she tugged it up and off and tossed it aside. Johnnie tried to say something, to touch her, but Elaine wanted none of it.

"Don't speak." She studied her body carefully and then wrapped her arms around her to unfasten her bra. She sighed with what could only be pleasure as she took in her breasts. Johnnie's nipples tensed with excitement, and the sensation seemed to go straight to her clit.

Elaine came close, breathed upon her breasts, teased them. "I want to breathe you in and excite you as I breathe out." Johnnie sucked in a breath and clenched her fists.

"Elaine," she whispered.

Elaine lifted a hand, then covered her mouth with her fingers. "Shut up." She lowered her hands and allowed them to drift to Johnnie's waist. She unbuttoned her jeans and tugged them down and off. Then she peeled off Johnnie's socks and rose to hook her fingers in her G-string. She hesitated then, looked up at her, and ran her hands around to her ass where she found bare flesh. She smiled wickedly and yanked off the G-string.

Johnnie watched as Elaine straightened and took her by the hand. She led her outside to the private patio that backed up to the mountains. She pushed her gently into the lounge chair. Johnnie eased back and rested against the cushioned chair. Elaine climbed on with her knees and pushed Johnnie's legs apart.

Johnnie almost spoke, but thunder clamored over them, and Elaine lowered her head.

"Do you know how long I've waited for this moment? To feel you in my mouth, to taste your heavenly nectar? It feels like ages, so, so long. And I've ached and ached for you, for this."

Johnnie held her face with one hand, her whole body pulsing with anticipation.

"I can only imagine how you taste, how you feel, how you're going to sound when I bathe your beautiful body in pleasure."

Johnnie shifted, the feel of Elaine's breath on her causing her to yearn for more of her.

"I want your mouth on me," she said.

"Do you?"

"Yes."

"Have you dreamt about it, Johnnie? Like I have?"

Johnnie tensed, gripping the armrests. "Yes. I've dreamt of you from the moment I first heard your voice."

"I remember. I remember you wanted this." She knelt closer and lightly kissed her thighs. "You wanted me so badly. Wanted my touch. The heat of my breath."

"Yes."

She kissed her again and moved upward. She rubbed her cheek against her leg, encouraging her to open them farther. Johnnie moaned and struggled for breath. Elaine snuck out her tongue and licked the length of her, teasing the inside of her folds. Her eyes flashed as she groaned and looked up at Johnnie.

"Oh God, Johnnie, you're so good. So unbelievably good." She parted her with her thumbs and licked her again and again. And then as Johnnie shook and trembled from the sensation, she lowered her head completely and fed.

Her eager mouth was hot and seeking, and it found Johnnie's hungry flesh in an instant, kissing, licking, sucking. Johnnie threw her head back and nearly screamed with pleasure. Thunder answered and lightning flashed. Mist from the careening rain fell upon her bare flesh, but she didn't care. She was too caught up in Elaine and her mouth and what she was doing to her.

Elaine moaned and pressed in harder. Johnnie knotted her hands in her hair and hissed, feeling her head bob as she fed. Johnnie clenched her eyes and then forced them open. She didn't want to miss a second. Elaine locked eyes with her and eased fingers up inside her. Johnnie leaned forward at the burning, full feeling and called out.

"Elaine, God, Elaine, fucking yes!"

Elaine gave a wicked laugh and fucked her long and slow, played with her G-spot. Johnnie couldn't breathe, couldn't speak. She just made small noises and loud cries matched by the thunder and lightning. The patio shook and the rain turned to hail. Some of it hit Elaine, but she didn't stop. She kept herself attached to Johnnie, feeding and fucking.

Johnnie stared into the great storm as the pleasure turned to thick waves. She felt them building, coming closer. She closed her eyes, squeezed Elaine's hair in her hands, and cried out as the first heavy wave hit her. It crashed into her, forcing her back in the chair. She rocked with it, lifting her hips to Elaine in an offering. Again and again, she rocked as wave after beautiful hot wave came, crashing into her, melting her, destroying her with pleasure. Thunder shook them again, lightning cracked close by. Elaine groaned and kept on. She didn't stop until Johnnie stilled and spasmed from aftershock.

Eventually, they both stilled, and Elaine turned her head and collapsed atop her, panting. Hail pelted her feet and lower legs. Thunder growled, growing distant. When the hail stopped, Elaine lifted, met Johnnie's eyes, and grinned. She crawled up to her.

"Say it," she said. "Before I die from contentment."

Johnnie reach out and touched her face. She opened her mouth, but the words were difficult to find.

"It's okay to be scared," she said. "I am too."

Johnnie inhaled deeply. Then stared into her flashing eyes. "I love you," she said.

Elaine pressed into her and kissed her deeply. Johnnie kissed her back, and they sat like that for what felt like an eternity, kissing, tasting, exploring. Languid in love.

Then Elaine pulled back.

She smiled.

"I love you too."

Johnnie kissed her, deeper, harder. She flipped her so she was on the bottom.

Elaine laughed. "I just want to enjoy what it felt like in having you…finally."

Johnnie moved lower, kissed her neck. Bit. It caused her to jerk and sigh.

"Are you sure?" Johnnie asked, nibbling her ear.

"Mm, I don't know."

Johnnie laughed, pressed into her, between her legs. "I bet you're so wet right now."

Elaine's breath shook as Johnnie kissed her collarbone. "I am."

"Are you sure I can't change your mind?" Johnnie teased her.

Elaine laughed, held onto her, and ran her nails down her back. Johnnie cried out and laughed and then attacked her fully.

Elaine laughed again and then stopped her and held her face. "Don't ever leave," Elaine whispered.

Johnnie kissed her softly. "I'm not going anywhere."

CHAPTER FIFTY-SEVEN

Johnnie entered the large art gallery with her nerves on edge. People milled about everywhere, walking, talking, looking, and seeking. The show was a success; she could tell by the number of pieces with orange stickers stuck to the description plate. Most were already sold. And the number of people, it was overwhelming.

Johnnie looked behind her and found Jolene hesitating at the door. She grabbed her hand and then tucked her hand into her arm. They walked side by side, weaving between people.

"Johnnie!" She turned and Eddie hurried up to her, two glasses of champagne in hand. "You little shit, this place is hopping." He handed over the glasses and leaned in to kiss Jolene on the cheek.

Johnnie wanted to smile, to be happy, but she was disappointed. Elaine had said she couldn't make it. That she needed to meet a client out of town. Johnnie hadn't argued even though it was so unusual for Elaine to say anything of the sort. She never mentioned meeting clients out of town before. But Johnnie tried not to worry. All things being said, their relationship was going really well. Johnnie spent most nights at her place even though she'd run Gail out of her place weeks ago and changed the locks. She'd heard Gail was back in Costa Rica so she didn't really worry about it anymore. And as for Monica, she never spoke to her again once Eddie had made it clear that Johnnie was in love with Elaine. That and he had threatened her with her life to leave Johnnie alone to be happy.

Johnnie looked around and smiled, trying to enjoy it. Her paintings hung everywhere.

"Your big one sold," Eddie said.

"You're kidding."

They followed him through a maze.

"And so did the nude of Elaine."

Johnnie couldn't believe it. She'd worked so hard, and tonight was the fruit of all that work. And it seemed to be a great success.

"Who bought it?" Johnnie asked.

Eddie shrugged. "Who cares? I want to know who bought your tree."

They came to a stop at the head of an aisle.

Eddie stepped aside, and Elaine came into view. She was standing next to the large canvas of the tree. The one Johnnie had painted during the bottoms. She looked to Eddie who shrugged and grinned. She looked to Jolene who grinned as well.

Her cell phone rang. Johnnie answered, looking at Elaine who was holding her phone to her ear.

"Hello."

"Just walk to me," she said. "Pretend no one else is here. Just me."

"I don't know if I can," Johnnie said.

"You can. I know you can. Come to me," Elaine said. She was wearing a little black dress and matching heels. She looked drop-dead gorgeous with her shining black hair falling to her shoulders, contrasting with her red lips.

Johnnie pushed out a breath. She took a step. Jolene released her.

"Go to her," she said.

Johnnie kept the phone to her ear. She walked slowly. People crossed in front of her. The DJ's music played. Her name was lit up in neon. She ignored it all and kept stepping.

"Come to me, Johnnie," Elaine said.

Johnnie sped up. The tree was lit up in lights, and Elaine was directly in front of it, spotlighted. Johnnie approached and let out a long-held breath.

"I made it," she said into the phone.

Elaine smiled and lowered hers. "Yes, you did."

She leaned in and kissed her delicately. Johnnie heated.

"You look so damn good," Elaine said. "I can't wait to get you home." Her voice was deep, throaty. Just like it had been that very first meeting in her office. She ran fingers up and down Johnnie's black fitted blazer. Touched the turquoise necklace Jolene had given her. It was hanging against the bare flesh of her chest She took her hands.

"You're here," Johnnie breathed. "And in that," she said, looking her up and down. "Oh my God, I can't breathe, Elaine."

Elaine leaned in. "Are you okay?"

"No," Johnnie said. "This is the best fucking moment of my life."

Elaine laughed.

"Allow me to inhale all of this and have an anxiety attack, okay?" Johnnie pulled her close. "Thank you so much for coming."

"I wouldn't miss it for the world."

"So the client..."

"Bullshit."

"All of it?"

"All of it."

"And Eddie and Jolene knew?"

"Mm. And Ian."

"Ian?" Johnnie looked around for him.

"He's my friend," Elaine said. "The one I've been buying art from."

Johnnie shook her head. "You guys were all—you all knew— you all—" She couldn't speak.

Elaine looked toward the painting. "Aren't you going to ask who bought your tree?"

Johnnie looked at her, watched her smile mischievously. "You?"

Elaine nodded. "Guilty."

"Oh my God, why?"

Elaine wrapped a hand around her waist. "Because this tree represents our beginning."

Johnnie stood and stared at it for a long moment. The tree was coming out of the darkness and into the light. Elaine was right. It was them.

"Did you buy your nude?" Johnnie asked.

Elaine laughed. "No, we don't need that one."

Johnnie tugged her closer. "Why not?"

Elaine touched her lips. "Because you've got the real thing now."

Johnnie laughed and leaned in and kissed her. They kissed in front of the tree, not caring who saw or who was watching.

Michael appeared with two glasses full of wine. "It's about time you two shared this," he said.

Elaine toasted Johnnie. "To my love, here and now."

Johnnie clinked her glass. "And always."

They drank and kissed.

It was their new beginning.

A new life.

And Johnnie, for the first time, walked toward it without fear.

THE END

About the Author

Ronica Black lives in the desert southwest with her menagerie of animals and her menagerie of art. When she's not writing, she's still creating, whether that be drawing, painting, or woodworking. She loves long walks into the sunset, rescuing animals, anything pertaining to art, and spending time with those she loves. When she can, she enjoys returning to her roots in North Carolina, where she can sit on the front porch with her family, catch up on all the gossip, and enjoy a nice cold Cheerwine.

Ronica is a two-time Golden Literary Society winner and a three-time finalist for the Lambda Literary Awards.

Books Available from Bold Strokes Books

Complications by MJ Williamz. Two women battle for the heart of one. (978-1-62639-769-9)

Crossing the Wide Forever by Missouri Vaun. As Cody Walsh and Lillie Ellis face the perils of the untamed West, they discover that love's uncharted frontier isn't for the weak in spirit or the faint of heart. (978-1-62639-851-1)

Fake It Till You Make It by M. Ullrich. Lies will lead to trouble, but can they lead to love? (978-1-62639-923-5)

Girls Next Door by Sandy Lowe and Stacia Seaman eds. Bestselling romance authors tell it from the heart—sexy, romantic stories of falling for the girls next door. (978-1-62639-916-7)

Pursuit by Jackie D. The pursuit of the most dangerous terrorist in America will crack the lines of friendship and love, and not everyone will make it out under the weight of duty and service. (978-1-62639-903-7)

Shameless by Brit Ryder. Confident Emery Pearson knows exactly what she's looking for in a no-strings-attached hookup, but can a spontaneous interlude open her heart to more? (978-1-63555-006-1)

The Practitioner by Ronica Black. Sometimes love comes calling whether you're ready for it or not. (978-1-62639-948-8)

Unlikely Match by Fiona Riley. When an ambitious PR exec and her super-rich coding geek-girl client fall in love, they learn that giving something up may be the only way to have everything. (978-1-62639-891-7)

Where Love Leads by Erin McKenzie. A high school counselor and the mom of her new student bond in support of the troubled girl, never expecting deeper feelings to emerge, testing the boundaries of their relationship. (978-1-62639-991-4)

Forsaken Trust by Meredith Doench. When four women are murdered, Agent Luce Hansen must regain trust in her most valuable investigative tool—herself—to catch the killer. (978-1-62639-737-8)

Her Best Friend's Sister by Meghan O'Brien. For fifteen years, Claire Barker has nursed a massive crush on her best friend's older sister. What happens when all her wildest fantasies come true? (978-1-62639-861-0)

Letter of the Law by Carsen Taite. Will federal prosecutor Bianca Cruz take a chance at love with horse breeder Jade Vargas, whose dark family ties threaten everything Bianca has worked to protect—including her child? (978-1-62639-750-7)

New Life by Jan Gayle. Trigena and Karrie are having a baby, but the stress of becoming a mother and the impact on their relationship might be too much for Trigena. (978-1-62639-878-8)

Royal Rebel by Jenny Frame. Charity director Lennox King sees through the party girl image Princess Roza has cultivated, but will Lennox's past indiscretions and Roza's responsibilities make their love impossible? (978-1-62639-893-1)

Unbroken by Donna K. Ford. When Kayla and Jackie, two women with every reason to reject Happy Ever After, fall in love, will they have the courage to overcome their pasts and rewrite their stories? (978-1-62639-921-1)

Where the Light Glows by Dena Blake. Mel Thomas doesn't realize just how unhappy she is in her marriage until she meets Izzy Calabrese. Will she have the courage to overcome her insecurities and follow her heart? (978-1-62639-958-7)

Escape in Time by Robyn Nyx. Working in the past is hell on your future. (978-1-62639-855-9)

Forget-Me-Not by Kris Bryant. Is love worth walking away from the only life you've ever dreamed of? (978-1-62639-865-8)

Highland Fling by Anna Larner. On vacation in the Scottish Highlands, Eve Eddison falls for the enigmatic forestry officer Moira Burns, despite Eve's best friend's campaign to convince her that Moira will break her heart. (978-1-62639-853-5)

Phoenix Rising by Rebecca Harwell. As Storm's Quarry faces invasion from a powerful neighbor, a mysterious newcomer with powers equal to Nadya's challenges everything she believes about herself and her future. (978-1-62639-913-6)

Soul Survivor by I. Beacham. Sam and Joey have given up on hope, but when fate brings them together it gives them a chance to change each other's life and make dreams come true. (978-1-62639-882-5)

Strawberry Summer by Melissa Brayden. When Margaret Beringer's first love Courtney Carrington returns to their small town, she must grapple with their troubled past and fight the temptation for a very delicious future. (978-1-62639-867-2)

The Girl on the Edge of Summer by J.M. Redmann. Micky Knight accepts two cases, but neither is the easy investigation it appears. The past is never past—and young girls lead complicated, even dangerous lives. (978-1-62639-687-6)

Unknown Horizons by CJ Birch. The moment Lieutenant Alison Ash steps aboard the Persephone, she knows her life will never be the same. (978-1-62639-938-9)

Divided Nation, United Hearts by Yolanda Wallace. In a nation torn in two by a most uncivil war, can love conquer the divide? (978-1-62639-847-4)

Fury's Bridge by Brey Willows. What if your life depended on someone who didn't believe in your existence? (978-1-62639-841-2)

Lightning Strikes by Cass Sellars. When Parker Duncan and Sydney Hyatt's one-night stand turns to more, both women must fight demons past and present to cling to the relationship neither of them thought she wanted. (978-1-62639-956-3)

Love in Disaster by Charlotte Greene. A professor and a celebrity chef are drawn together by chance, but can their attraction survive a natural disaster? (978-1-62639-885-6)

Secret Hearts by Radclyffe. Can two women from different worlds find common ground while fighting their secret desires? (978-1-62639-932-7)

Sins of Our Fathers by A. Rose Mathieu. Solving gruesome murder cases is only one of Elizabeth Campbell's challenges; another is her growing attraction to the female detective who is hell-bent on keeping her client in prison. (978-1-62639-873-3)

The Sniper's Kiss by Justine Saracen. The power of a kiss: it can swell your heart with splendor, declare abject submission, and sometimes blow your brains out. (978-1-62639-839-9)

Troop 18 by Jessica L. Webb. Charged with uncovering the destructive secret that a troop of RCMP cadets has been hiding, Andy must put aside her worries about Kate and uncover the conspiracy before it's too late. (978-1-62639-934-1)

Worthy of Trust and Confidence by Kara A. McLeod. Agent Ryan O'Connor is about to discover the hard way that when you can only handle one type of answer to a question, it really is better not to ask. (978-1-62639-889-4)